PENGUIN PLAYS

HOME
THE CHANGING ROOM
AND
MOTHER'S DAY

David Storey was born in 1933 and is the third son of a mine-worker. He was educated at the Queen Elizabeth School at Wakefield and the Slade School of Fine Art. He has had various jobs ranging from professional footballer to schoolteaching and showground tent-erecting. He is now both a novelist and a dramatist.

His novels include *This Sporting Life*, which won the Macmillan Fiction Award in 1960 and was also filmed; *Flight into Camden*, which won the John Llewelyn Rhys Memorial Prize and also the Somerset Maugham Award in 1963; *Radcliffe*; *Pasmore*, which won the Faber Memorial Prize in 1973; *A Temporary Life*; *Saville*, which won the Booker Prize in 1976; and *A Prodigal Child*. He has received numerous drama awards including the New York Critics' Best Play of the Year Award in three years out of four. His plays include *The Restoration of Arnold Middleton*; *In Celebration*, which has been filmed; *The Contractor*; *The Farm*; *Life Class*; *Sisters*; and *Early Days*. Several of David Storey's novels are published by Penguin as are two other volumes of his plays.

David Storey lives in London. He was married in 1956 and has four children.

HOME
THE CHANGING ROOM
AND
MOTHER'S DAY

DAVID STOREY

PENGUIN BOOKS

Penguin Books Ltd, Harmondsworth, Middlesex, England
Penguin Books, 40 West 23rd Street, New York, New York 10010, U.S.A.
Penguin Books Australia Ltd, Ringwood, Victoria, Australia
Penguin Books Canada Ltd, 2801 John Street, Markham, Ontario, Canada L3R 1B4
Penguin Books (N.Z.) Ltd, 182–190 Wairau Road, Auckland 10, New Zealand

Home
First published in Great Britain by Jonathan Cape 1970
First published in the United States of America by Random House, Inc., 1971
Published in Penguin Books in Great Britain 1972
Copyright © David Storey, 1970
The Changing Room
First published in Great Britain by Jonathan Cape 1972
First published in the United States of America by Random House, Inc., 1972
Published in Penguin Books in Great Britain 1973
Copyright © David Storey, 1972
Mother's Day
First published in Great Britain by Penguin Books 1978
First published in the United States of America by Penguin Books 1984
Copyright © David Storey, 1978
All rights reserved

This edition published in Penguin Books in Great Britain 1978
Reprinted 1984
This edition published in Penguin Books in the United States of America 1984

Made and printed in Singapore by
Richard Clay (S.E. Asia) Pte Ltd
Set in Monotype Bembo

CONTENTS

Home   7

The Changing Room   83

Mother's Day   171

HOME

TO KAREL REISZ

WHO FIRST BROUGHT THESE

ENDS TOGETHER

This play was first presented at the Royal Court Theatre, London, on 17 June 1970, under the direction of Lindsay Anderson.
The cast was as follows:

Harry	JOHN GIELGUD
Jack	RALPH RICHARDSON
Marjorie	DANDY NICHOLS
Kathleen	MONA WASHBOURNE
Alfred	WARREN CLARKE

CHARACTERS

HARRY

JACK

MARJORIE

KATHLEEN

ALFRED

ACT ONE

Scene 1

*The stage is bare but for a round metalwork table, set slightly off-centre, stage left, and two metalwork chairs.**

    HARRY *comes on, stage right, a middle-aged man in his forties. He wears a casual suit, perhaps tweed, with a suitable hat which, after glancing pleasurably around, he takes off and puts on the table beside him, along with a pair of well-used leather gloves and a folded newspaper.*

    Presses his shoulders back, eases neck, etc., making himself comfortable. Settles down. Glances at his watch, shakes it, makes sure it's going; winds it slowly, looking round.

    Stretches neck again. Leans down, wafts cotton from his turn-ups. Examines shoes, without stooping.

    Clears his throat. Clasps his hands in his lap, gazes out, abstracted, head nodding slightly, half-smiling.

JACK. Harry!

    (JACK *has come on from the other side, stage left. He's dressed in a similar fashion, but with a slightly more dandyish flavour: handkerchief hanging from top pocket, a rakish trilby. Also has a simple though rather elegant cane.*)

HARRY. Jack.

JACK. Been here long?

HARRY. No. No.

JACK. Mind?

HARRY. Not at all.

    (JACK *sits down.*

    He stretches, shows great relief at being off his feet, etc.)

* In the Royal Court production the indications of a setting were provided: a white flag-pole, stage right, and upstage a low terrace with a single step down, centre, and balustrade, stage left.

JACK. Nice to see the sun again.

HARRY. Very.

JACK. Been laid up for a few days.

HARRY. Oh dear.

JACK. Chill. In bed.

HARRY. Oh dear. Still ... Appreciate the comforts.

JACK. What? ... You're right. Still ... Nice to be out.

HARRY. 'Tis.

JACK. Mind?

HARRY. All yours.

     (JACK *picks up the paper; gazes at it without unfolding it.*)

JACK. Damn bad news.

HARRY. Yes.

JACK. Not surprising.

HARRY. Gets worse before it gets better.

JACK. 'S right ... Still ... Not to grumble.

HARRY. No. No.

JACK. Put on a bold front. (*Turns paper over.*)

HARRY. That's right.

JACK. Pretty. (*Indicates paper.*)

HARRY. Very.

JACK. By jove ... (*Reads intently a moment.*) Oh, well.

HARRY. That the one? (*Glances over.*)

JACK (*nods*). Yes ... (*Clicks his tongue.*)

HARRY (*shakes his head*). Ah, well.

JACK. Yes ... Still ...

HARRY. Clouds ... Watch their different shapes.

JACK. Yes? (*Looks up at the sky at which* HARRY *is gazing.*)

HARRY. See how they drift over?

JACK. By jove.

HARRY. First sight ... nothing. Then ... just watch the edges
... See.

JACK. Amazing.

HARRY. Never notice when you're just walking.

JACK. No ... Still ... Best time of the year.

HARRY. What?

JACK. Always think this is the best time.

HARRY. Oh, yes.

JACK. Not too hot. Not too cold.

HARRY. Seen that? (*Points at the paper.*)

JACK (*reads. Then*). By jove ... (*Reads again briefly.*) Well ...
you get some surprises ... Hello ... (*Reads farther down,
turning edge of paper over.*) Good God.

HARRY. What I felt.

JACK. The human mind. (*Shakes his head.*)

HARRY. Oh dear, yes.

JACK. One of these days ...

HARRY. Ah, yes.

JACK. Then where will they be?

HARRY. Oh, yes.

JACK. Never give it a thought.

HARRY. No ... Never.

JACK (*reads again*). By jove ... (*Shakes his head.*)
      (HARRY *leans over; removes something casually from* JACK'*s
      sleeve.*)
   Oh ...

HARRY. Cotton.

JACK. Oh ... Picked it up ... (*Glances round at his other sleeve,
then down at his trousers.*)

HARRY. See you've come prepared.

JACK. What ... ? Oh.
      (HARRY *indicates* JACK'*s coat pocket.*
      JACK *takes out a folded plastic mac, no larger, folded, than
      his hand.*)
   Best to make sure.

HARRY. Took a risk. Myself.

JACK. Oh, yes ... What's life worth ...

HARRY. Oh, yes.

JACK. I say. That was a shock.

HARRY. Yesterday ...?

JACK. Bolt from the blue, and no mistake.

HARRY. I'd been half-prepared ... even then.

JACK. Still a shock.

HARRY. Absolutely.

JACK. My wife ... you've met? ... Was that last week?

HARRY. Ah, yes ...

JACK. Well. A very delicate woman.

HARRY. Still. Very sturdy.

JACK. Oh, well. Physically, nothing to complain of.

HARRY. Oh, no.

JACK. Temperament, however ... inclined to the sensitive side.

HARRY. Really.

JACK. Two years ago ... (*Glances off.*) By jove. Isn't that Saxton?

HARRY. Believe it is.

JACK. He's a sharp dresser, and no mistake.

HARRY. Very.

JACK. They tell me ... Well, I never.

HARRY. Didn't see that, did he?

    (*They laugh, looking off.*)

Eyes in the back of your head these days.

JACK. You have. That's right.

HARRY. Won't do that again in a hurry. What? (*Laughs.*)

JACK. I had an uncle once who bred horses.

HARRY. Really.

JACK. Used to go down there when I was a boy.

HARRY. The country.

JACK. Nothing like it. What? Fresh air.

HARRY. Clouds. (*Gestures up.*)

JACK. I'd say so.

HARRY. *My* wife was coming up this morning.

JACK. Really?

HARRY. Slight headache. Thought might be better ...

JACK. Indoors. Well. Best make sure.

HARRY. When I was in the army ...

JACK. Really? What regiment?

HARRY. Fusiliers.

JACK. Really? How extraordinary.

HARRY. You?

JACK. No. No. A cousin.

HARRY. Well ...

JACK. Different time, of course.

HARRY. Ah.

JACK. Used to bring his rifle ... No. That was Arthur. Got them muddled. (*Laughs.*)

HARRY. Still.

JACK. Never leaves you.

HARRY. No. No.

JACK. In good stead.

HARRY. Oh, yes.

JACK. All your life.

HARRY. Oh, yes.

JACK. I was – for a very short while – in the Royal Air Force.

HARRY. Really?

JACK. Nothing to boast about.

HARRY. Oh, now. Flying?

JACK. On the ground.

HARRY. Chrysanthemums is my wife's hobby.

JACK. Really.

HARRY. Thirty-seven species round the house.

JACK. Beautiful flower.

HARRY. Do you know there are over a hundred?

JACK. Really?

HARRY. Different species.

JACK. Suppose you can mix them up.

HARRY. Oh. Very.

JACK. He's coming back ...

HARRY. ...?

JACK. Swanson.

HARRY. Saxton.

JACK. Saxton! Always did get those two mixed up. Two boys at school: one called Saxton, the other Swanson. Curious thing was, they both looked alike.

HARRY. Really?

JACK. Both had a curious skin disease. Here. Just at the side of the nose.

HARRY. Eczema.

JACK. Really?

HARRY. Could have been.

JACK. Never thought of that ... When I was young I had an ambition to be a priest, you know.

HARRY. Really?

JACK. Thought about it a great deal.

HARRY. Ah, yes. A great decision.

JACK. Oh, yes.

HARRY. Catholic or Anglican?

JACK. Well ... Couldn't really make up my mind.

HARRY. Both got a great deal to offer.

JACK. Great deal? My word.

HARRY. Advantages one way. And then ... in another.

JACK. Oh, yes.

HARRY. One of my first ambitions ...

JACK. Yes.

HARRY. Oh, now. You'll laugh.

JACK. No. No ... No. Really.

HARRY. Well ... I would have liked to have been a dancer.

JACK. Dancer ... Tap or 'balley'?

HARRY. Oh, well. Probably a bit of both.

JACK. A fine thing. Grace.

HARRY. Ah, yes.

JACK. Physical momentum.

HARRY. Yes.

JACK. Swanson might have appreciated that! (*Laughs.*)

HARRY. Saxton.

JACK. Saxton! By jove ... At school we had a boy called Ramsbottom.

HARRY. Really.

JACK. Now I wouldn't have envied that boy's life.

HARRY. No.

JACK. The euphemisms to which a name ... well. One doesn't have to think very far.

HARRY. No.

JACK. A name can be a great embarrassment in life.

HARRY. It can ... We had – let me think – a boy called Fish.

JACK. Fish!

HARRY. And another called Parsons!

JACK. Parsons!

HARRY. Nicknamed 'Nosey'.

JACK. By jove! (*Laughs; rises.*) Some of these nicknames are very clever.

HARRY. Yes.

JACK (*moves away stage right*). I remember, when I was young, I had a very tall friend ... extremely tall as a matter of fact. He was called 'Lolly'.

HARRY. Lolly!

JACK. It fitted him very well. He ... (*Abstracted. Pause.*) Yes. Had very large teeth as well.

HARRY. The past. It conjures up some images.

JACK. It does. You're right.

HARRY. You wonder how there was ever time for it all.

JACK. Time ... Oh ... Don't mention it.

HARRY. A fine cane.

JACK. What? Oh, that.

17

HARRY. Father had a cane. Walked for miles.

JACK. A habit that's fast dying out.

HARRY. Oh, yes.

JACK. Knew a man, related to a friend of mine, who used to walk twenty miles a day.

HARRY. Twenty!

JACK. Each morning.

HARRY. That really shows some spirit.

JACK. If you keep up a steady pace, you can manage four miles in the hour.

HARRY. Goodness.

JACK. Five hours. Set off at eight each morning. Back for lunch at one.

HARRY. Must have had a great appetite.

JACK. Oh. Absolutely. Ate like a horse.

HARRY. Stand him in good stead later on.

JACK. Ah, yes ... Killed, you know. In the war.

HARRY. Oh dear.

JACK. Funny thing to work out.

HARRY. Oh, yes.

    (*Pause.*)

JACK (*sits*). You do any fighting?

HARRY. What?

JACK. Army.

HARRY. Oh, well, then ... modest amount.

JACK. Nasty business.

HARRY. Oh! Doesn't bear thinking about.

JACK. Two relatives of mine killed in the war.

HARRY. Oh dear.

JACK. You have to give thanks, I must say.

HARRY. Oh, yes.

JACK. Mother's father ... a military man.

HARRY. Yes.

JACK. All his life.

HARRY. He must have seen some sights.

JACK. Oh, yes.

HARRY. Must have all had meaning then.

JACK. Oh, yes. India. Africa. He's buried as a matter of fact in Hong Kong.

HARRY. Really?

JACK. So they tell me. Never been there myself.

HARRY. No.

JACK. Hot climates, I think, can be the very devil if you haven't the temperament.

HARRY. Huh! You don't have to tell me.

JACK. Been there?

HARRY. No, no. Just what one reads.

JACK. Dysentery.

HARRY. Beriberi.

JACK. Yellow fever.

HARRY. Oh dear.

JACK. As well, of course, as all the other contingencies.

HARRY. Oh yes.

JACK. At times one's glad simply to live on an island.

HARRY. Yes.

JACK. Strange that.

HARRY. Yes.

JACK. Without the sea – all around – civilization would never have been the same.

HARRY. Oh, no.

JACK. The ideals of life, liberty, freedom, could never have been the same – democracy – well, if we'd been living on the Continent, for example.

HARRY: Absolutely.

JACK. Those your gloves?

HARRY. Yes.

JACK. Got a pair like that at home.

HARRY. Yes?

JACK. Very nearly. The seam goes the other way, I think. (*Picks one up to look.*) Yes. It does.

HARRY. A present.

JACK. Really?

HARRY. My wife. At Christmas.

JACK. Season of good cheer.

HARRY. Less and less, of course, these days.

JACK. Oh, my dear man. The whole thing has been ruined. The moment money intrudes ... all feeling goes straight out of the window.

HARRY. Oh, yes.

JACK. I had an aunt once who owned a little shop.

HARRY. Yes?

JACK. Made almost her entire income during the few weeks before Christmas.

HARRY. Really.

JACK. Never seemed to occur to her that there might be some ethical consideration.

HARRY. Oh dear.

JACK. Ah, well.

HARRY. Still ...

JACK. Apart from that, she was a very wonderful person.

HARRY. It's very hard to judge.

JACK. It is.

HARRY. I have a car, for instance.

JACK. Yes?

HARRY. One day, in December, I happened to knock a pedestrian over in the street.

JACK. Oh dear.

HARRY. It was extremely crowded.

JACK. You don't have to tell me. I've seen them.

HARRY. Happened to see something they wanted the other side. Dashed across. Before you know where you are ...

JACK. Not serious, I hope?

HARRY. No. No. No. Fractured arm.

JACK. From that, you know, they might learn a certain lesson.

HARRY. Oh, yes.

JACK. Experience is a stern master.

HARRY. Ah, yes. But then ...

JACK. Perhaps the only one.

HARRY. It is.

JACK. I had a cousin, on my mother's side, who once fell off a cliff.

HARRY. Really.

JACK. Quite a considerable height.

HARRY. Ah, yes.

JACK. Fell into the sea, fortunately. Dazed. Apart from that, quite quickly recovered.

HARRY. Very fortunate.

JACK. Did it for a dare. Only twelve years old at the time.

HARRY. I remember I fell off a cliff, one time.

JACK. Oh dear.

HARRY. Not very high. And there was someone there to catch me. (*Laughs.*)

JACK. They can be very exciting places.

HARRY. Oh, very.

JACK. I remember I once owned a little boat.

HARRY. Really.

JACK. For fishing. Nothing very grand.

HARRY. A fishing man.

JACK. Not really. More an occasional pursuit.

HARRY. I've always been curious about that.

JACK. Yes?

HARRY. 'A solitary figure crouched upon a bank.'

JACK. Never stirring.

HARRY. No. No.

JACK. Can be very tedious, I know.

HARRY. Still. A boat is more interesting.

JACK. Oh, yes. A sort of tradition, really.

HARRY. In the family.

JACK. No. No. More in the ... island, you know.

HARRY. Ah, yes.

JACK. Drake.

HARRY. Yes!

JACK. Nelson.

HARRY. Beatty.

JACK. Sir Walter Raleigh.

HARRY. There was a very fine man ... poet.

JACK. Lost his head, you know.

HARRY. It's surprising the amount of dust that collects in so short a space of time. (*Runs hand lightly over table.*)

JACK. It is. (*Looks round.*) Spot like this, perhaps, attracts it.

HARRY. Yes ... (*Pause*). You never became a priest, then?

JACK. No ... No.

HARRY. Splendid to have a vocation.

JACK. 'Tis ... Something you believe in.

HARRY. Oh, yes.

JACK. I could never ... resolve certain difficulties, myself.

HARRY. Yes?

JACK. The hows and the wherefores I could understand. How we came to be, and His presence, lurking everywhere, you know. But as to the 'why' ... I could never understand. Seemed a terrible waste of time to me.

HARRY. Oh, yes.

JACK. Thought it better to leave it to those who didn't mind.

HARRY. Ah, yes.

JACK. I suppose the same was true about dancing.

HARRY. Oh, yes. I remember turning up for instance, to my first class, only to discover that all the rest of them were girls.

JACK. Really?

HARRY. Well ... there are men dancers, I know. Still ...
Took up football after that.

JACK. To professional standard, I imagine.

HARRY. Oh, no. Just the odd kick around. Joined a team that
played in the park on Sunday mornings.

JACK. The athletic life has many attractions.

HARRY. It has. It has.

(*Pause.*)

JACK. How long have you been here, then?

HARRY. Oh, a couple of er.

JACK. Strange – meeting the other day.

HARRY. Yes.

JACK. On the way back, thought to myself, 'What a chance
encounter.'

HARRY. Yes.

JACK. So rare, these days, to meet someone to whom one can
actually talk.

HARRY. I know what you mean.

JACK. One works. One looks around. One meets people. But
very little communication actually takes place.

HARRY. Very.

JACK. None at all in most cases! (*Laughs.*)

HARRY. Oh, absolutely.

JACK. The agonies and frustrations. I can assure you. In the
end one gives up in absolute despair.

HARRY. Oh, yes. (*Laughs, rising, looking off.*)

JACK. Isn't that Parker? (*Looking off.*)

HARRY. No ... N-no ... Believe his name is Fielding.

JACK. Could have sworn it was Parker.

HARRY. No. Don't think so ... Parker walks with a limp.
Very slight.

JACK. That's Marshall.

HARRY. Really. Then I've got Parker mixed up again.
(*Laughs.*)

23

JACK. Did you see the one who came in yesterday?

HARRY. Hendricks.

JACK. Is that his name?

HARRY. I believe that's what I heard.

JACK. He looked a very suspicious character to me. And his wife ...

HARRY. I would have thought his girl-friend.

JACK. Really? Then that makes far more sense ... I mean, I have great faith in the institution of marriage as such.

HARRY. Oh, yes.

JACK. But one thing I've always noticed. When you find a married couple who display their affection in public, then that's an infallible sign that their marriage is breaking up.

HARRY. Really?

JACK. It's a very curious thing. I'm sure there must be some psychological explanation for it.

HARRY. Insecurity.

JACK. Oh, yes.

HARRY. Quite frequently one can judge people entirely by their behaviour.

JACK. You can. I believe you're right.

HARRY. Take my father, for instance.

JACK. Oh, yes.

HARRY. An extraordinary man by any standard. And yet, throughout his life, he could never put out a light.

JACK. Really.

HARRY. Superstition. If he had to turn off a switch, he'd ask someone else to do it.

JACK. How extraordinary.

HARRY. Quite casually. One never noticed. Over the years one got quite used to it, of course. As a man he was extremely polite.

JACK. Ah, yes.

HARRY (*sits*). Mother, now. She was quite the reverse.

JACK. Oh, yes.

HARRY. Great appetite for life.

JACK. Really?

HARRY. Three.

JACK. Three?

HARRY. Children.

JACK. Ah, yes.

HARRY. Youngest.

JACK. You were?

HARRY. Oh, yes.

JACK. One of seven.

HARRY. Seven!

JACK. Large families in those days.

HARRY. Oh, yes.

JACK. Family life.

HARRY. Oh, yes.

JACK. Society, well, without it, wouldn't be what it's like today.

HARRY. Oh, no.

JACK. Still.

HARRY. Ah, yes.

JACK. We have a wonderful example.

HARRY. Oh. My word.

JACK. At times I don't know where some of us would be without it.

HARRY. No. Not at all.

JACK. A friend of mine – actually, more of an acquaintance, really – was introduced to George VI at Waterloo.

HARRY. Waterloo?

JACK. The station.

HARRY. By jove.

JACK. He was an assistant to the station-master at the time, in a lowly capacity, of course. His Majesty was making a week-end trip into the country.

HARRY. Probably to Windsor.

(*Pause.*)

JACK. Can you get to Windsor from Waterloo?

HARRY. I'm ... No. I'm not sure.

JACK. Sandringham, of course, is in the country.

HARRY. The other way.

JACK. The other way.

HARRY. Balmoral in the Highlands.

JACK. I had an aunt once who, for a short while, lived near Gloucester.

HARRY. That's a remarkable stretch of the country.

JACK. Vale of Evesham.

HARRY. Vale of Evesham.

JACK. Local legend has it that Adam and Eve originated there.

HARRY. Really?

JACK. Has very wide currency, I believe, in the district. For instance. You may have read that portion in the Bible ...

HARRY. I have.

JACK. The profusion of vegetation, for example, would indicate that it couldn't, for instance, be anywhere in the Middle East.

HARRY. No. No.

JACK. On the other hand, the profusion of animals ... snakes, for example ... would indicate that it might easily be a more tropical environment, as opposed, that is, to one which is merely temperate.

HARRY. Yes ... I see.

JACK. Then again, there is ample evidence to suggest that during the period in question equatorial conditions prevailed in the very region in which we are now sitting.

HARRY. Really? (*Looks around.*)

JACK. Discoveries have been made that would indicate that lions and tigers, elephants, wolves, rhinoceros, and so forth, actually inhabited these parts.

HARRY. My word.

JACK. In those circumstances, it wouldn't be unreasonable to suppose that the Vale of Evesham was such a place itself. The very cradle, as it were, of ...

HARRY. Close to where your aunt lived.

JACK. That's right.

HARRY. Mind if I have a look?

JACK. Not at all.

(HARRY *takes the cane.*)

HARRY. You seldom see canes of this quality these days.

JACK. No. No. That's right.

HARRY. I believe they've gone out of fashion.

JACK. They have.

HARRY. Like beards.

JACK. Beards!

HARRY. My father had a small moustache.

JACK. A moustache I've always thought became a man.

HARRY. Chamberlain.

JACK. Roosevelt.

HARRY. Schweitzer.

JACK. Chaplin.

HARRY. Hitler ...

JACK. Travel, I've always felt, was a great broadener of the mind.

HARRY. My word.

JACK. Travelled a great deal – when I was young.

HARRY. Far?

JACK. Oh. All over.

HARRY. A great thing.

JACK. Sets its mark upon a man.

HARRY. Like the army.

JACK. Like the army. I suppose the fighting you do has very much the same effect.

HARRY. Oh, yes.

JACK. Bayonet?

HARRY. What?

JACK. The er.

HARRY. Oh bayonet ... ball and flame. The old three, as we used to call them.

JACK. Ah, yes.

HARRY. A great welder of character.

JACK. By jove.

HARRY. The youth of today: might have done some good.

JACK. Oh. My word, yes.

HARRY. In the Royal Air Force, of course ...

JACK. Bombs.

HARRY. Really.

JACK. Cannon.

HARRY. Ah, yes ... Couldn't have got far, in our job, I can tell you, without the Royal Air Force.

JACK. No. No.

HARRY. Britannia rules the waves ... and rules the skies, too. I shouldn't wonder.

JACK. Oh, yes.

HARRY. Nowadays, of course ...

JACK. Rockets.

HARRY. Ah, yes.

JACK. They say ...

HARRY. Yes?

JACK. When the next catastrophe occurs ...

HARRY. Oh, yes.

JACK. That the island itself might very well be flooded.

HARRY. Really.

JACK. Except for the more prominent peaks, of course.

HARRY. Oh, yes.

JACK. While we're sitting here waiting to be buried ...

HARRY. Oh, yes.

JACK (*laughing*). We'll end up being drowned.

HARRY. Extraordinary! (*Laughs.*) No Vale of Evesham then.

JACK. Oh, no.

HARRY. Nor your aunt at Gloucester!

JACK. She died a little while ago, you know.

HARRY. Oh. I am sorry.

JACK. We weren't very attached.

HARRY. Oh, no.

JACK. Still. She was a very remarkable woman.

HARRY. Ah, yes.

JACK. In her own particular way. So few characters around these days. So few interesting people.

HARRY. Oh, yes.

JACK. Uniformity.

HARRY. Mrs Washington. (*Looking off.*)

JACK. Really? I've been keeping an eye open for her. (*Stands.*)

HARRY. Striking woman.

JACK. Her husband was related to a distant cousin of mine, on my father's side. (*Straightening tie, etc.*)

HARRY. My word.

JACK. I shouldn't be surprised if she recognizes me ... No ...

HARRY. Scarcely glanced. Her mind on other things.

JACK. Oh, yes. (*Sits.*)

HARRY. Parker. (*Looking off.*)

JACK. Oh, yes.

HARRY. You're right. He's not the man with the limp.

JACK. That's Marshall.

HARRY. That's right. Parker is the one who has something the matter with his arm. I knew it was something like that.

JACK. Polio.

HARRY. Yes?

JACK. I had a sister who contracted polio. Younger than me. Died within a matter of hours.

HARRY. Oh. Goodness.

JACK. Only a few months old at the time. Scarcely learnt to speak.

HARRY. What a terrible experience.

JACK. I had another sister die. She was how old? Eleven.

HARRY. Oh dear.

JACK. Large families do have their catastrophes.

HARRY. They do.

JACK. I remember a neighbour of ours, when we lived in the country, died one morning by falling down the stairs.

HARRY. Goodness.

JACK. The extraordinary thing was, the following day they were due to move into a bungalow.

HARRY. Goodness. (*Shakes his head.*)

JACK. One of the great things, of course, about my aunt's house.

HARRY. Yes?

JACK. In Gloucester. Was that it had an orchard.

HARRY. Now they *are* lovely things.

JACK. Particularly in the spring.

HARRY. In the spring especially.

JACK. And the autumn, of course.

HARRY. 'Boughs laden.'

JACK. Apple a day.

HARRY. Oh, yes.

JACK. I had a niece once who was a vegetarian.

HARRY. Really.

JACK. Ate nut rissoles.

HARRY. I tried once to give up meat.

JACK. Goes back, you know.

HARRY. Oh, yes.

JACK. Proctor. The young woman with him is Mrs Jefferies.

HARRY. Really.

JACK. Interesting people to talk to. He's been a missionary, you know.

HARRY. Yes?

JACK. Spent most of his time, he said, taking out people's teeth.

HARRY. Goodness.

JACK. Trained for it, of course. Mrs Jefferies, on the other hand.

HARRY. Yes.

JACK. Was a lady gymnast. Apparently very famous in her day.

HARRY. My word.

JACK. Developed arthritis in two of her er.

HARRY. Oh dear.

JACK. Did you know it was caused by a virus?

HARRY. No.

JACK. Apparently. I had a maiden aunt who suffered from it a great deal. She was a flautist. Played in an orchestra of some distinction. Never married. I thought that very strange.

HARRY. Yes.

JACK. Musicians, of course, are a strange breed altogether.

HARRY. Oh, yes.

JACK. Have you noticed how the best of them have very curly hair?

HARRY. Really.

JACK. My maiden aunt, of course, has died now.

HARRY. Ah, yes.

JACK. Spot of cloud there.

HARRY. Soon passes.

JACK. Ever seen this? (*Takes out a coin.*) There. Nothing up my sleeve. Ready? One, two, three ... Gone.

HARRY. My word.

JACK. Here ... (*Takes out three cards.*) Pick out the Queen of Hearts.

HARRY. This one.

JACK. No!

HARRY. Oh!

(*They laugh.*)

JACK. Try again ... There she is. (*Shuffles them round on the table.*) Where is she?

HARRY. Er ...

JACK. Take your time.

HARRY. This one ... Oh!

(*They laugh.*)

JACK. That one!

HARRY. Well. I'll have to study those.

JACK. Easy when you know how. I have some more back there. One of my favourite tricks is to take the Ace of Spades out of someone's top pocket.

HARRY. Oh ... (*Looks.*)

JACK. No. No. No. (*Laughs.*) It needs some preparation ... Sometimes in a lady's handbag. That goes down very well.

HARRY. Goodness.

JACK. I knew a man at one time – a friend of the family, on my father's side – who could put a lighted cigarette into his mouth, take one half from one ear, and the other half from the other.

HARRY. Goodness.

JACK. Still lighted.

HARRY. How did he do that?

JACK. I don't know.

HARRY. I suppose – physiologically – it's possible, then.

JACK. Shouldn't think so.

HARRY. No.

JACK. One of the advantages, of course, of sitting here.

HARRY. Oh, yes.

JACK. You can see everyone walking past.

HARRY. Oh, yes.

JACK. Jennings isn't a man I'm awfully fond of.

HARRY. No.

JACK. You've probably noticed yourself.

HARRY. I have. In the army, I met a man ... Private ... er.

JACK. The equivalent rank, of course, in the air force, is air-craftsman.

HARRY. Or able seaman. In the navy.

JACK. Able seaman.

   (*They laugh.*)

HARRY. Goodness.

JACK. Funny name. (*Laughs.*) Able seaman. I don't think I'd like to be called that.

HARRY. Yes! (*Laughs.*)

JACK. Able seaman! (*Snorts.*)

HARRY. Fraser. Have you noticed him?

JACK. Don't think I have.

HARRY. A thin moustache.

JACK. Black.

HARRY. That's right.

JACK. My word.

HARRY. Steer clear, probably, might be better.

JACK. Some people you can sum up at glance.

HARRY. Oh, yes.

JACK. My mother was like that. Delicate. Not unlike my wife.

HARRY. Nevertheless, very sturdy.

JACK. Oh, yes. Physically, nothing to complain about. My mother, on the other hand, was actually as delicate as she looked. Whereas my wife looks ...

HARRY. Robust.

JACK. Robust. My mother actually looked extremely delicate.

HARRY. Still. Seven children.

JACK. Oh, yes.

HARRY. My father was a very ... emotional man. Of great feeling.

JACK. Like mine.

HARRY. Oh, very much like yours.

JACK. But dominated somewhat.

HARRY. Yes?

JACK. By your mother.

HARRY. Oh. I suppose he was. Passionate but ...

JACK. Dominated. One of the great things, of course, about the war was its feeling of camaraderie.

HARRY. Friendship.

JACK. You found that too? On the airfield where I was stationed it was really like one great big happy family. My word. The things one did for one another.

HARRY. Oh, yes.

JACK. The way one worked.

HARRY. Soon passed.

JACK. Oh, yes. It did. It did.

HARRY. Ah, yes.

JACK. No sooner was the fighting over than back it came. Back-biting. Complaints. Getting what you can. I sometimes think if the war had been prolonged another thirty years we'd have all felt the benefit.

HARRY. Oh, yes.

JACK. One's children would have grown up far different. That's for sure.

HARRY. Really? How many have you got?

JACK. Two.

HARRY. Oh, that's very nice.

JACK. Boy married. Girl likewise. They seem to rush into things so early these days.

HARRY. Oh, yes.

JACK. And you?

HARRY. Oh. No. No. Never had the privilege.

JACK. Ah, yes. Responsibility. At times you wonder if it's worth it. I had a cousin, on my father's side, who threw herself from a railway carriage.

HARRY. Oh dear. How awful.

JACK. Yes.

HARRY. Killed outright.

JACK. Well, fortunately, it had just pulled into a station.

HARRY. I see.

JACK. Daughter's married to a salesman. Refrigerators: he sells appliances of that nature.

HARRY. Oh. Opposite to me.

JACK. Yes?

HARRY. Heating engineer.

JACK. Really. I'd never have guessed. How extraordinary.

HARRY. And yourself.

JACK. Oh, I've tinkered with one or two things.

HARRY. Ah, yes.

JACK. What I like about my present job is the scope that it leaves you for initiative.

HARRY. Rather. Same with mine.

JACK. Distribution of food-stuffs in a wholesale store.

HARRY. Really.

JACK. Thinking out new ideas. Constant speculation.

HARRY. Oh, yes.

JACK. Did you know if you put jam into small cardboard containers it will sell far better than if you put it into large glass jars?

HARRY. Really?

JACK. Psychological. When you buy it in a jar you're wondering what on earth – subconsciously – you're going to do with the glass bottle. But with a cardboard box that anxiety is instantly removed. Result: improved sales; improved production; lower prices; improved distribution.

HARRY. That's a fascinating job.

JACK. Oh, yes. If you use your brains there's absolutely nothing there to stop you.

HARRY. I can see.

JACK. Heating must be a very similar problem.

HARRY. Oh, yes.

JACK. The different ways of warming up a house.

HARRY. Yes.

JACK. Or not warming it up, as the case may be.

HARRY. Yes!

(*They laugh.*)

JACK. I don't think I've met your wife.

HARRY. No. No ... As a matter of fact. We've been separated for a little while.

JACK. Oh dear.

HARRY. One of those misfortunes.

JACK. Happens a great deal.

HARRY. Oh, yes.

JACK. Each have our cross.

HARRY. Oh, yes.

JACK. Well. Soon be time for lunch.

HARRY. Will. And I haven't had my walk.

JACK. No. Still.

HARRY. Probably do as much good.

JACK. Oh, yes.

HARRY. Well, then ... (*Stretches. Gets up.*)

JACK. Yours or mine?

HARRY. Mine ... I believe. (*Picks up the newspaper.*)

JACK. Ah, yes.

HARRY. Very fine gloves.

JACK. Yes.

HARRY. Pacamac.

JACK. All correct.

HARRY. Cane.

JACK. Cane.

HARRY. Well, then. Off we go.

JACK. Off we go.

(HARRY *breathes in deeply; breathes out.*)

HARRY. Beautiful corner.

JACK. 'Tis.

> (*Pause; last look round.*)

HARRY. Work up an appetite.

JACK. Right, then. Best foot forward.

HARRY. Best foot forward.

JACK. Best foot forward, and off we go.

> (*They stroll off, taking the air, stage left.*)

Scene 2

KATHLEEN *and* MAJORIE *come on, stage right.*

KATHLEEN *is a stout middle-aged lady; she wears a coat, which is unbuttoned, a headscarf and strap shoes. She is limping, her arm supported by* MARJORIE.

MARJORIE *is also middle-aged. She is dressed in a skirt and cardigan. She carries an umbrella and a large, well-used bag.*

KATHLEEN. Cor ... *blimey!*

MARJORIE. Going to rain, ask me.

KATHLEEN. Rain all it wants, ask me. Cor ... *blimey!* Going to kill me is this. (*Limps to a chair, sits down and holds her foot.*)

MARJORIE. Going to rain and catch us out here. That's what it's going to do. (*Puts umbrella up; worn, but not excessively so.*)

KATHLEEN. Going to rain all right, i'n't it? Going to rain all right ... Put your umbrella up – sun's still shining. Cor blimey. Invite rain that will. Commonsense, girl ... Cor *blimey* ... My bleedin' feet ... (*Rubs one foot without removing shoe.*)

MARJORIE. Out here and no shelter. Be all right if it starts. (*Moves umbrella one way then another, looking up.*)

KATHLEEN. Cor *blimey* ... 'Surprise me they don't drop off ... Cut clean through, these will.

MARJORIE (*looking skywards, however*). Clouds all over. Told you we shouldn't have come out.

KATHLEEN. Get nothing if you don't try, girl ... Cor *blimey!* (*Winces.*)

MARJORIE. I don't know.

KATHLEEN. Here. You'll be all right, won't you?

MARJORIE. ...?

KATHLEEN. Holes there is. See right through, you can.

MARJORIE. What?

KATHLEEN. Here. Rain comes straight through that. Won't get much shelter under that. What d'I tell you? Might as well sit under a shower. (*Laughs.*) Cor blimey. You'll be all right, won't you?

MARJORIE. Be all right with you in any case. Walk no faster than a snail.

KATHLEEN. Not surprised. Don't want me to escape. That's my trouble, girl.

MARJORIE. Here ... (*Sits.*)

(JACK *and* HARRY *slowly pass upstage, taking the air, chatting.* MARJORIE *and* KATHLEEN *wait for them to pass.*)

KATHLEEN. What've we got for lunch?

MARJORIE. Sprouts.

KATHLEEN (*massaging foot*). Seen them, have you?

MARJORIE. Smelled 'em!

KATHLEEN. What's today, then?

MARJORIE. Friday.

KATHLEEN. End of week.

MARJORIE. Corn' beef hash.

KATHLEEN. That's Wednesday.

MARJORIE. Sausage roll.

KATHLEEN. Think you're right ... Cor blimey. (*Groans, holding her foot.*)

MARJORIE. Know what you ought to do, don't you?

(KATHLEEN *groans, holding her foot.*)

Ask for another pair of shoes, girl, you ask me.

KATHLEEN. Took me laced ones, haven't they? Only ones that fitted. Thought I'd hang myself, didn't they? Only five inches long.

MARJORIE. What they think you are?

KATHLEEN. Bleedin' mouse, more likely.

MARJORIE. Here. Not like the last one I was in.

KATHLEEN. No?

MARJORIE. Let you paint on the walls, they did. Do anyfing. Just muck around ... Here ... I won't tell you what some of them did.

KATHLEEN. What?

(MARJORIE *leans over, whispers.*)

Never.

MARJORIE. Cross me heart.

KATHLEEN. Glad I wasn't there. This place is bad enough. You seen Henderson, have you?

MARJORIE. Ought to lock him up, you ask me.

KATHLEEN. What d'you do, then?

MARJORIE. Here?

KATHLEEN. At this other place.

MARJORIE. Noffing. Mucked around ...

KATHLEEN. Here ...

(JACK *and* HARRY *stroll back again, slowly, upstage, in conversation; head back, deep breathing, bracing arms ...* MARJORIE *and* KATHLEEN *wait till they pass.*)

MARJORIE. My dentist comes from Pakistan.

KATHLEEN. Yours?

MARJORIE. Took out all me teeth.

KATHLEEN. Those not your own, then?

MARJORIE. All went rotten when I had my little girl. There she is, waitress at the seaside.

KATHLEEN. And you stuck here ...

MARJORIE. No teeth ...

KATHLEEN. Don't appreciate it.

MARJORIE. They don't.

KATHLEEN. Never.

MARJORIE. Might take this down if it doesn't rain.

KATHLEEN. Cor blimey ... take these off if I thought I could get 'em on again ... (*Groans.*) Tried catching a serious disease.

MARJORIE. When was that?

KATHLEEN. Only had me in two days. Said, nothing the matter with you, my girl.

MARJORIE. Don't believe you.

KATHLEEN. Next thing: got home; smashed everything in sight.

MARJORIE. No?

KATHLEEN. Winders. Cooker ... Nearly broke me back ... Thought I'd save the telly. Still owed eighteen months. Thought: 'Everything or nothing, girl.'

MARJORIE. Rotten programmes. (*Takes down umbrella.*)

KATHLEEN. Didn't half give it a good old conk.

MARJORIE (*looking round*). There's one thing. You get a good night's sleep.

KATHLEEN. Like being with a steam engine, where I come from. Cor blimey, that much whistling and groaning; think you're going to take off.

MARJORIE. More like a boa constrictor, ask me. Here ...
(JACK *and* HARRY *stroll back, still taking the air, upstage; bracing, head back ...*)
Started crying everywhere I went ... Started off on Christmas Eve.

KATHLEEN. S'happy time, Christmas.

MARJORIE. Didn't stop till Boxing Day.

KATHLEEN. If He ever comes again I hope He comes on Whit Tuesday. For me that's the best time of the year.

MARJORIE. Why's that?

KATHLEEN. Dunno. Whit Tuesday's always been a lucky day for me. First party I ever went to was on a Whit Tuesday. First feller I went with. Can't be the date. Different every year.

MARJORIE. My lucky day's the last Friday in any month with an 'r' in it when the next month doesn't begin later than the following Monday.

KATHLEEN. How do you make that out?

MARJORIE. Dunno. I was telling the doctor that the other day ... There's that man with the binoculars watching you.

KATHLEEN. Where?

MARJORIE. Lift your dress up.

KATHLEEN. No.

MARJORIE. Go on ... (*Leans over; does it for her.*) Told you ...

KATHLEEN. Looks like he's got diarrhoea!

(*They laugh.*)

See that chap the other day? Showed his slides of a trip up the Amazon River.

MARJORIE. See that one with no clothes on? Supposed to be cooking his dinner.

KATHLEEN. Won't have him here again ...

MARJORIE. Showing all his ps and qs.

KATHLEEN. Oooooh! (*Laughs, covering her mouth.*)

MARJORIE. Here ...

(JACK *and* HARRY *stroll back across, a little farther down stage, glancing over now at* MARJORIE *and* KATHLEEN.)

KATHLEEN. Lord and Lady used to live here at one time.

MARJORIE. Who's that?

KATHLEEN. Dunno.

MARJORIE. Probably still inside, ask me ... (*Glances after* JACK *and* HARRY *as they stroll off.*) See that woman with dyed hair? Told me she'd been in films. 'What films?' I said. 'Blue films?'

KATHLEEN. What she say?

MARJORIE. 'The ones I was in was not in colour.'

(*They laugh.*)

I s'll lose me teeth one of these days ... oooh!

KATHLEEN. Better'n losing something else ...

MARJORIE. Oooooh!

(*They laugh again.*)

42

KATHLEEN. Here ...

    (JACK *and* HARRY *have strolled back on.*)

JACK (*removing hat*). Good day, ladies.

KATHLEEN. Good day yourself, your lordships.

JACK. Oh, now. I wouldn't go as far as that. (*Laughs politely and looks at* HARRY.)

HARRY. No. No. Still a bit of the common touch.

JACK. Least, so I'd hope.

HARRY. Oh, yes.

MARJORIE. And how have you been keeping, professor?

JACK. Professor? I can see we're a little elevated today.

MARJORIE. Don't know about elevated. But *we*'re sitting down.

    (KATHLEEN *and* MARJORIE *laugh.*)

KATHLEEN. Been standing up, we have, for hours.

HARRY. Hours?

MARJORIE. When you were sitting down.

JACK. Oh dear ... I wasn't aware ...

KATHLEEN. 'Course you were. My bleedin' feet. Just look at them. (*Holds them again.*)

MARJORIE. Pull your skirt down, girl.

KATHLEEN. Oh Gawd ...

JACK. My friend here, Harry, is a specialist in house-warming, and I myself am a retailer in preserves.

MARJORIE. Oooooh! (*Screeches; laughs – covering her mouth – to* KATHLEEN.) What did I tell you?

KATHLEEN. No atomic bombs today?

JACK (*looks up at the sky behind him. Then*) No, no. Shouldn't think so.

MARJORIE. And how's your mongol sister?

HARRY. Mongol ...? I'm afraid you must have the wrong person, Ma'm.

KATHLEEN. Ooooh! (*Screeches; laughs.*)

JACK. My friend, I'm afraid, is separated from his wife.

As a consequence, I can assure you, of many hardships ...

MARJORIE. Of course ...

JACK. And I myself, though happily married in some respects, would not pretend that my situation is all it should be ...

KATHLEEN. Ooooh!

JACK. One endeavours ... but it is in the nature of things, I believe, that, on the whole, one fails.

KATHLEEN. Ooooh!

HARRY. My friend ... Jack ... has invented several new methods of retailing jam.

KATHLEEN. Ooooh!

MARJORIE. Jam. I like that.

JACK. Really?

MARJORIE (to KATHLEEN). Strawberry. My favourite.

KATHLEEN. Raspberry, mine.

MARJORIE. Ooooh!

(KATHLEEN and MARJORIE laugh.)

JACK. A friend of mine, on my father's side, once owned a small factory which was given over, exclusively, to its manufacture.

KATHLEEN. Ooooh!

JACK. In very large vats.

KATHLEEN. Ooooh!

MARJORIE. I like treacle myself.

JACK. Treacle, now, is a very different matter.

MARJORIE. Comes from Malaya.

HARRY. That's rubber, I believe.

MARJORIE. In tins.

HARRY. The rubber comes from Ma laya, I believe.

MARJORIE. I eat it, don't I? I ought to know.

KATHLEEN. She has treacle on her bread.

JACK. I believe it comes, as a matter of fact, from the West Indies.

44

KATHLEEN. West Indies? Where's that?

MARJORIE. Near Hong Kong.

HARRY. That's the East Indies, I believe.

MARJORIE. You ever been to the North Indies?

HARRY. I don't believe ...

MARJORIE. Well, that's where treacle comes from.

HARRY. I see ...

(*Pause. The tone has suddenly become serious.*)

JACK. We were just remarking, as a matter of fact, that Mrs
Glover isn't looking her usual self.

KATHLEEN. Who's she?

HARRY. She's ...

JACK. The lady with the rather embarrassing disfigurement ...

MARJORIE. Her with one ear?

KATHLEEN. The one who's only half a nose.

MARJORIE. She snores.

KATHLEEN. You'd snore as well, wouldn't you, if you only
had half a nose.

MARJORIE. Eaten away.

KATHLEEN. What?

MARJORIE. Her husband ate it one night when she was sleeping.

KATHLEEN. Silly to fall asleep with any man, I say. These
days they get up to anything. Read it in the papers an' next
thing they want to try it themselves.

HARRY. The weather's been particularly mild today.

KATHLEEN. Not like my flaming feet. Oooh ...

JACK. As one grows older these little things are sent to try us.

KATHLEEN. Little? Cor blimey; I take size seven.

HARRY. My word.

JACK. My friend, of course, in the heating business, has a wide
knowledge of the ways and means whereby we may, as we
go along, acquire these little additional comforts.

MARJORIE. He wishes he was sitting in this chair, doesn't he?

HARRY. What ...

JACK. It's extraordinary that more facilities of this nature aren't supplied, in my view.

KATHLEEN. Only bit of garden with any flowers. Half a dozen daisies ...

HARRY. Tulips ...

JACK. Roses ...

KATHLEEN. I know daisies, don't I? Those are daisies. Grow three feet tall.

HARRY. Really?

MARJORIE. Rest of it's all covered in muck.

JACK. Oh, now. Not as bad as that.

MARJORIE. What? I call that muck. What's it supposed to be?

HARRY. A rockery, I believe.

KATHLEEN. Rockery? More like a rubbish tip, ask me.

JACK. Probably the flowers haven't grown yet.

MARJORIE. Flowers? How do you grow flowers on old bricks and bits of plaster?

HARRY. Certain categories, of course ...

JACK. Oh, yes.

HARRY. Can be trained to grow in these conditions.

KATHLEEN. You're round the bend, you are. Ought to have you up there, they did.

HARRY (to JACK). They tell me the flowers are just as bad at that end, too.

(HARRY and JACK laugh at their private joke.)

MARJORIE. If you ask me, all this is just typical.

JACK. Typical?

MARJORIE. One table. Two chairs ... Between one thousand people.

KATHLEEN. Two, they tell me.

MARJORIE. Two thousand. One thousand for this chair, and one thousand for that.

HARRY. There are, of course, the various benches.

KATHLEEN. Benches? Seen better sold for firewood.

MARJORIE. Make red marks they do across your bum.

KATHLEEN. Ooooh! (*Screeches, covering her mouth.*)

HARRY. Clouding slightly.

JACK. Slightly. (*Looking up.*)

MARJORIE. Pull your skirt down, girl.

KATHLEEN. Ooooh!

HARRY. Of course, one alternative would be to bring, say, a couple of more chairs out with us.

JACK. Oh, yes. Now that would be a solution.

HARRY. Four chairs. One each. I don't believe, say, for an afternoon they'd be missed from the lecture hall.

MARJORIE. Here, you see *Up the Amazon* last night?

JACK. Tuesday ...

HARRY. Tuesday.

JACK. Believe I did, now you mention it.

MARJORIE. See that feller with a loincloth?

KATHLEEN. Oooh! (*Laughs, covering her mouth.*)

JACK. I must admit, there are certain attractions in the primitive life.

KATHLEEN. Ooooh!

JACK. Air, space ...

MARJORIE. Seen all he's got, that's all you seen.

JACK. I believe there was a moment when the eye ...

KATHLEEN. Moment ... Ooooh!

HARRY. I thought his pancakes looked rather nice.

KATHLEEN. Ooooh!

HARRY. On the little log ...

KATHLEEN. Ooooh!

MARJORIE. Not his pancakes he's seen, my girl.

KATHLEEN. Ooooh!

JACK. The canoe, now, was not unlike my own little boat.

KATHLEEN. Ooooh!

HARRY. Fishing there somewhat more than a mere pastime.

JACK. Oh, yes.

HARRY. Life and death.

JACK. Oh, yes.

MARJORIE. Were you the feller they caught climbing out of a window here last week?

JACK. Me?

MARJORIE. Him.

HARRY. Don't think so ... Don't recollect that.

JACK. Where, if you don't mind me asking, did you acquire that information?

MARJORIE. Where? (*To* KATHLEEN) Here, I thought you told me it was him.

KATHLEEN. Not me. Mrs Heller.

MARJORIE. You sure?

KATHLEEN. Not me, anyway.

JACK. I had a relative – nephew, as a matter of fact – who started a window-cleaning business ... let me see. Three years ago now.

HARRY. Really?

JACK. Great scope there for an adventurous man.

MARJORIE. In bathroom windows 'specially.

KATHLEEN. Ooooh!

JACK. Heights ... distances ...

HARRY. On very tall buildings, of course, they lower them from the roof.

JACK. Oh, yes.

HARRY. Don't have the ladders long enough, you know.

KATHLEEN. Ooooh!

JACK. Your friend seems in a very jovial frame of mind.

HARRY. Like to see that.

JACK. Oh, yes. Gloom: one sees it far too much in this place. Mr Metcalf, now: I don't think he's spoken to anyone since the day that he arrived.

48

MARJORIE. What's he, then?

HARRY. He's the gentleman who's constantly pacing up and down.

JACK. One says hello, of course. He scarcely seems to notice.

KATHLEEN. Hear you were asking if they'd let you out.

JACK. Who?

MARJORIE. Your friend.

HARRY. Oh. Nothing as dramatic ... Made certain inquiries ... temporary visit ... Domestic problems, you know. Without a man very little, I'm afraid, gets done.

MARJORIE. It gets too much done, if you ask me. That's half the trouble.

KATHLEEN. Oooooh!

HARRY. However ... It seems that certain aspects of it can be cleared up by correspondence. One doesn't wish, after all, to impose unduly ...

JACK. Oh, no.

HARRY. Events have their own momentum. Take their time.

MARJORIE. You married to me, they would. I can tell you.

KATHLEEN. Oooooh!

HARRY. Oh, now ... Missis ... er ...

MARJORIE. Madam.

KATHLEEN. Oooooh!

HARRY. Well ... er ... that might be a situation that could well be beneficial to us both, in different circumstances, in different places ...

JACK. Quite ...

MARJORIE. Listen to him!

HARRY. We all have our little foibles, our little failings.

JACK. Oh, indeed.

HARRY. Hardly be human without.

JACK. Oh, no.

HARRY. The essence of true friendship, in my view, is to make allowances for one another's little lapses.

MARJORIE. Heard all about your little lapses, haven't we?

KATHLEEN. Ooooooh!

JACK. All have our little falls from grace.

MARJORIE. Pull your skirt down, girl!

KATHLEEN. Ooooooh!

MARJORIE. Burn down the whole bleedin' building, he will. Given up smoking because they won't let him have any matches.

KATHLEEN. Oooh!

JACK. The rumours that drift around a place like this ... hardly worth the trouble ...

HARRY. Absolutely.

JACK. If one believed everything one heard ...

HARRY. Oh, yes.

JACK. I was remarking to my friend earlier this morning: if one can't enjoy life as it takes one, what's the point of living it at all? One can't, after all, spend the whole of one's life inside a shell.

HARRY. Oh, no.

MARJORIE. Know what he'd spend it inside if he had half a chance.

KATHLEEN. Ooooooh!

MARJORIE. Tell my husband of you, I shall.

KATHLEEN. Bus-driver.

JACK. Really? I've taken a lifelong interest in public transport.

KATHLEEN. Oooh!

MARJORIE. Taken a lifelong interest in something else more 'n likely.

KATHLEEN. Ooooooh!

MARJORIE. Pull your skirt down, girl!

KATHLEEN. Ooooooh!

MARJORIE. Know his kind.

KATHLEEN. Ooooooh!

JACK. Respect for the gentler sex, I must say, is a fast-diminishing concept in the modern world.

HARRY. Oh, yes.

JACK. I recollect the time when one stood for a lady as a matter of course.

HARRY. Oh yes.

MARJORIE. Know the kind of standing he's on about.

KATHLEEN. Oooooh!

JACK. Each becomes hardened to his ways.

KATHLEEN. Ooooooh!

JACK. No regard for anyone else's.

MARJORIE. Be missing your dinner, you will.

JACK. Yes. So it seems.

HARRY. Late ...

JACK. Nevertheless, one breaks occasionally one's usual ... Normally it's of benefit to all concerned ...

MARJORIE. Here. Are you all right?

JACK. Slight moment of discomposure ...

(JACK *has begun to cry, vaguely. Takes out a handkerchief to wipe his eyes.*)

HARRY. My friend is a man – he won't mind me saying this ...

JACK. No ... No ...

HARRY. Of great sensibility and feeling.

KATHLEEN. Here. You having us on?

JACK. I assure you, madam ... I regret any anxiety or concern which I may, unwittingly, have caused. In fact – I'm sure my friend will concur – perhaps you'll allow us to accompany you to the dining-hall. I have noticed, in the past, that though one has to queue, to leave it any later is to run the risk of being served with a cold plate; the food cold, and the manners of the cook – at times, I must confess ... appalling.

KATHLEEN (*to* MARJORIE). We'll have to go. There'll be nothing left.

MARJORIE. It's this seat he's after.

HARRY. I assure you, madam ... we are on our way.

KATHLEEN. Here: you mind if I lean on your arm?

MARJORIE. Kathleen!

HARRY. Oh, now. That's a very pretty name.

KATHLEEN. Got straps: make your ankles swell. (*Rising.*)

HARRY. Allow me.

KATHLEEN. Oh. Thank you.

HARRY. Harry.

KATHLEEN. Harry.

HARRY. And this is my friend – Jack.

KATHLEEN. Jack ... And this is my friend Marjorie.

JACK. Marjorie ... Delightful.

MARJORIE (*to* KATHLEEN). Here. You all right?

KATHLEEN. You carrying it with you, or are you coming?

JACK. Allow me ... Marjorie. (*Holds her seat.*)

MARJORIE. Here ... (*Gets up, suspicious.*)

HARRY. Perhaps after lunch we might meet here again.

JACK. A little chat ... Time passes very slowly.

MARJORIE. Here, where's my bag?

KATHLEEN. Need carrying out, I will.

> (HARRY has taken KATHLEEN's *arm.*)

HARRY. Now then. All right?

KATHLEEN. Have you all the time, I shall.

HARRY. Ready? ... All aboard then, are we?

MARJORIE. Well, then. All right ... (*Takes* JACK's *arm.*)

JACK. Right, then ... Dining-hall: here we come!

> (*They start off,* HARRY *and* KATHLEEN *in front; slowly.*)

HARRY. Sausages today, if I'm not mistaken.

KATHLEEN. Oooh!

MARJORIE. Corned beef hash.

KATHLEEN. Oooh!

JACK. One as good as another, I always say.

KATHLEEN. Ooooooh!

HARRY. Turned out better.
JACK. Turned out better.
HARRY. Altogether.
JACK. Altogether.
HARRY. Well, then. Here we go.

(*They go.*)

FADE

ACT TWO

ALFRED *comes in: a well-made young man, about thirty. His jacket's unbuttoned; he has no tie.*

He sees the table; walks past it, slowly, eyeing it. Pauses. Glances back at it.

Comes back, watching the table rather furtively, sideways.

He pauses, hands behind his back, regarding it.

Suddenly he moves it, grasps it; struggles with it as if it had a life of its own.

Groans. Struggles. Lifts the table finally above his head.

Struggles with it ...

MARJORIE *comes on, as before, her umbrella furled.*

MARJORIE. Here. You all right?

ALFRED. What?

MARJORIE. Alfred i'n'it?

ALFRED. Yeh. (*Still holds the table above his head.*)

MARJORIE. You'll break that, you will.

ALFRED. Yeh ... (*Looks up at it.*)

>   (MARJORIE, *however, isn't much interested; she's already looking round.*)

MARJORIE. You seen my mate?

ALFRED. ...?

MARJORIE. Woman that limps.

ALFRED. No.

>   (ALFRED *pauses before all his answers.*)

MARJORIE. One day you get seconds and they go off without you. You like treacle pud?

ALFRED. Yeh.

MARJORIE. Get seconds?

ALFRED. No.

MARJORIE. Shoulda waited.

ALFRED. Yeh.

MARJORIE. Said they'd be out here after 'Remedials'.

ALFRED. ...?

MARJORIE. You do remedials?

ALFRED. Yeh.

MARJORIE. What 'you do?

ALFRED. Baskets.

MARJORIE. Baskets. Shoulda known.

ALFRED. You got sixpence?

MARJORIE. No.

(ALFRED *lifts the table up and down ceremoniously above his head.*)

Better go find her. Let anybody turn them round her hand, she will.

ALFRED. Yeh.

(*She goes.*

ALFRED *lowers the table slowly, almost like a ritual.*

Crouches; picks up one chair by the foot of one leg and lifts it, slowly, exaggerating the effort, etc.

Stands, slowly, as he gets it up.

Bends arm slowly; lifts the chair above his head.

Puts it down.

Stands a moment, gazing down at the two chairs and the table, sideways.

Walks round them.

Walks round a little farther. Then:

Grabs the second chair and lifts it, one-handed, like the first chair, but more quickly.

Lifts it above his head; begins to wrestle with it as if it too possessed a life of its own, his grip, however, still one-handed.

MARJORIE *crosses upstage, pauses, looks, walks on.*

She goes off; ALFRED *doesn't see her.*

ALFRED *struggles; overcomes the chair.*

Almost absent-mindedly lowers it, looks left, looks right, casually; puts the chair beneath his arm and goes.)

KATHLEEN (*off*). Oh Gawd ... Oh ... Nah, this side's better ... Oh.

(Comes on limping, her arm in HARRY'S.

HARRY *carries a wicker chair under his other arm.)*

HARRY. Oh. Look at that.

KATHLEEN. Where's the other one gone, then?

HARRY. Well, that's a damned nuisance.

KATHLEEN. Still only two. Don't know what they'll say.

HARRY. Oh dear.

KATHLEEN. Pinch anything round here. Can't turn your back. Gawd ...!

(Sinks down in the metal chair as HARRY *holds it for her.)*

HARRY. There, now.

KATHLEEN (*sighs*). Good to get off your feet ...

HARRY. Yes, well ...

(Sets his own chair to get the sun, fussing.)

KATHLEEN. Better sit on it. No good standing about. Don't know where she's got to. Where's your friend looking?

HARRY. Went to 'Remedials', I believe.

KATHLEEN. Get you in there won't let you out again. Here ...

*(*HARRY *looks across.)*

He really what he says he is?

HARRY. How do you mean?

KATHLEEN. Told us he was a doctor. Another time he said he'd been a sanitary inspector.

HARRY. Really? Hadn't heard of that.

KATHLEEN. Go on. Know what inspecting he'll do. You the same.

HARRY. Oh, now. Certain discriminations can be ...

KATHLEEN. I've heard about you.

HARRY. Oh, well, you er.

KATHLEEN. Making up things.

HARRY. Oh, well. One ... embodies ... of course.

KATHLEEN. What's that, then?

HARRY. Fancies ... What's life for if you can't ... (*Flutters his fingers.*)

KATHLEEN. We've heard about that an' all. (*Imitates his action.*)

HARRY. Well. I'm sure you and I have, in reality, a great deal in common. After all, one looks around; what does one see?

KATHLEEN. Gawd ... (*Groans, feeling her feet.*)

HARRY. A little this. A little that.

KATHLEEN. Here. Everything you know is little.

HARRY. Well ... I er ... Yes ... No great role for this actor, I'm afraid. A little stage, a tiny part.

KATHLEEN. You an actor, then?

HARRY. Well, I did, as a matter of fact, at one time ... actually, a little ...

KATHLEEN. Here, little again. You notice?

HARRY. Oh ... You're right.

KATHLEEN. What parts you play, then?

HARRY. Well, as a matter of fact ... not your Hamlets, of course, your Ophelias; more the little bystander who passes by the ...

KATHLEEN. Here. Little.

HARRY. Oh ... yes! (*Laughs.*)

KATHLEEN. Play anything romantic?

HARRY. Oh, romance, now, was ... never very far away.

KATHLEEN. Here ...

HARRY. One was cast, of course ...

KATHLEEN. Think I could have been romantic.

HARRY. Oh, yes.

KATHLEEN. Had the chance ... Got it here.

HARRY. Oh, yes ...

KATHLEEN. Had different shoes than this ...

HARRY. Oh, yes ... everything, of course, provided ...

KATHLEEN. Going to be a commotion, you ask me ...

HARRY. Commotion ...?

KATHLEEN. When they get here.

(*Indicates chairs.*)

Three chairs – if he brings one as well ... He'll have to stand. (*Laughs.*)

HARRY. Could have been confiscated, you know.

KATHLEEN. Confiscated?

HARRY. Often happens. See a little pleasure and down they come.

KATHLEEN. Here ... little.

HARRY. Goodness ... Yes.

(*Pause.*)

One of the advantages of this spot, you know, is that it catches the sun so nicely.

KATHLEEN. What bit there is of it.

HARRY. Bit?

KATHLEEN. All that soot. Cuts it down. 'Stead of browning you turns you black.

HARRY. Black?

KATHLEEN. All over.

HARRY. An industrial nation ...

KATHLEEN. Gawd ... (*Eases her feet.*)

HARRY. Can't have the benefit of both. Nature as well as er ... The one is incurred at the expense of the other.

KATHLEEN. Your friend come in for following little girls?

HARRY. What ...

KATHLEEN. Go on. You can tell me. Cross my heart and hope to die.

HARRY. Well ... that's ...

KATHLEEN. Well, then.

HARRY. I believe there were ... er ... certain proclivities, shall we say?

KATHLEEN. Proclivities? What's them?

HARRY. Nothing criminal, of course.

KATHLEEN. Oh, no ...

HARRY. No prosecution ...

KATHLEEN. Oh, no ...

HARRY. Certain pressures, in the er ... Revealed themselves.

KATHLEEN. In public?

HARRY. No. No ... I ... Not what I meant.

KATHLEEN. I don't know what you're saying half the time. You realize that?

HARRY. Communication is a difficult factor.

KATHLEEN. Say that again.

HARRY. I believe he was encouraged to come here for a little er.

KATHLEEN. Here. Little.

HARRY. Oh, yes ... As it is, very few places left now where one can be at ease.

KATHLEEN. Could go on his holidays. Seaside.

HARRY. Beaches? ... Crowded all the while.

KATHLEEN. Could go to the country.

HARRY. Spaces ...

KATHLEEN. Sent me to the country once. All them trees. Worse'n people ... Gawd. Take them off if I thought I could get them on again. Can't understand why they don't let me have me laces. Took me belt as well. Who they think I'm going to strangle? Improved my figure, it did, the belt. Drew it in a bit.

HARRY. Oh, now, I would say, myself, the proportions were in reasonable condition.

KATHLEEN. Oh, now ...

HARRY. Without, of course, wishing to seem immodest ...

KATHLEEN. Get little enough encouragement in my life. Gawd ... My friend, you know, was always crying.

HARRY. Oh, now.

KATHLEEN. Everywhere she went ... cigarettes ... No sooner in the shop, opens her mouth, and out it comes. Same on buses.

HARRY. Oh dear, now.

KATHLEEN. Doesn't like sympathy.

HARRY. Ah, yes.

KATHLEEN. Get all I can, myself.

HARRY. Husband a bus-driver, I believe.

KATHLEEN. Hers. Not mine.

HARRY. Ah, yes.

KATHLEEN. Mine's a corporation employee.

HARRY. Ah, yes. One of the ...

KATHLEEN. Cleans up muck. Whenever there's a pile of muck they send him to clean it up.

HARRY. I see.

KATHLEEN. You worked in a bank, then?

HARRY. Well, in a er.

KATHLEEN. Clean job. Don't know why he doesn't get a clean job. Doorman ... Smells awful, he does. Gets bathed one night and the next day just the same.

HARRY. Ah, yes.

KATHLEEN. Puts you off your food.

HARRY. Yes.

KATHLEEN. 'They ought to fumigate you,' I said.

HARRY. Yes?

KATHLEEN. Know what he says?

HARRY. Yes?

KATHLEEN. 'Ought to fumigate you, my girl, and forget to switch it orf.'

HARRY. Goodness.

KATHLEEN. Going to be tea-time before they get here.

HARRY (examines watch). No, no. Still a little time.

KATHLEEN. Your wife alive?

HARRY. Er.

KATHLEEN. Separated?

HARRY. Well, I ...

KATHLEEN. Unsympathetic.

HARRY. Yes?

KATHLEEN. Your wife.

HARRY. Well ... One can ask too much these days, I believe, of er.

KATHLEEN. Met once a fortnight wouldn't be any divorce. Ridiculous, living together. 'S not human.

HARRY. No ...

KATHLEEN. Like animals ... Even they run off when they're not feeling like it.

HARRY. Oh, yes.

KATHLEEN. Not natural ... One man. One woman. Who's He think He is?

(HARRY *looks round*.)

No ... Him. (*Points up.*)

HARRY. Oh, yes ...

KATHLEEN. Made Him a bachelor. Cor blimey: no wife for Him.

HARRY. No.

KATHLEEN. Saved somebody the trouble.

HARRY. Yes.

KATHLEEN. Does it all by telepathy.

HARRY. Yes.

KATHLEEN. Kids?

HARRY. What? ... Oh ... No.

KATHLEEN. Got married how old?

HARRY. Twenty er.

KATHLEEN. Man shouldn't marry till he's forty. Ridiculous. Don't know what they want till then. After that, too old to bother.

HARRY. Oh, yes.

KATHLEEN. Here ...

(ALFRED *comes in carrying the chair. Sees them, nods; then goes back the way he's come.*)

Here! (*Calls after.*) That's where it's gone.

HARRY. Don't believe …

KATHLEEN. That's Alfred.

HARRY. Yes?

KATHLEEN. Wrestler.

HARRY. Yes.

KATHLEEN. Up here. (*Taps her head.*)

HARRY. Oh.

KATHLEEN. Where you going when you leave here?

HARRY. Well … I … er.

KATHLEEN. Lost your job?

HARRY. Well, I …

KATHLEEN. Wife not have you?

HARRY. Well, I …

KATHLEEN. Another man.

HARRY. Oh, now …

KATHLEEN. Still … Could be worse.

HARRY. Oh, yes.

(*Pause.*)

KATHLEEN. What's he want with that, then? Here … you
were slow to ask.

HARRY. Yes …

KATHLEEN. You all right?

HARRY. Touch of the … (*Wipes his eyes, nose.*)

KATHLEEN. Here, couple of old cry-babies you are. Bad as
my friend.

HARRY. Yes … Well …

KATHLEEN. Shoot my brains out if I had a chance. Gawd! …
(*Feels her feet.*) Tried to kill myself with gas.

HARRY. Yes …?

KATHLEEN. Kiddies at my sister's. Head in oven. Knock on
door. Milkman. Two weeks behind, he said. Broke everything, I did.

HARRY. Yes?

KATHLEEN. Nearly killed him. Would, too, if I could have

62

IE. way from men.

d (after.)

IE.

h. ortable.)

IE. ially.

ave uch er.

IE. ts. Used to send the police in threes.

tru d one was never enough.

ly

IE.

an a leopard ...

IE. hould see her. Spots all over.

IE. washes.

ne dvantages of a late lunch, of course, is that

ves er space to tea.

IE s your friend's name?

arr

IE. s he do, then?

en er ... Thought a slight ...

IE ne with her all right. Have another.

h,

n 't know what we're coming to.

ystery ... (Gazes up.)

E watches him. Then:)

at you put away for, then?

hat?

ere.

ttle ...

l?

ls.

the street.

got hold. Won't tap on our door, I can tell you. Not again.

HARRY. Goodness.

KATHLEEN. You all right?

HARRY. Yes ... I ... er.

KATHLEEN. Here. Hold my hand if you like.

HARRY. Oh, now.

KATHLEEN. Go on.

(Puts her hand on the table.)

Not much to look at.

HARRY. Oh, now. I wouldn't say that.

KATHLEEN. Go on.

HARRY. Well, I ... (Takes her hand.)

KATHLEEN. Our age: know what it's all about.

HARRY. Oh, well ... A long road, you know.

KATHLEEN. Can't get to old age fast enough for me. Sooner they put me under ...

HARRY. Oh, now ...

KATHLEEN. Different for a man.

HARRY. Well, I ...

KATHLEEN. I know. Have your troubles. Still. Woman's different.

HARRY. Oh, I ...

KATHLEEN. Wouldn't be a woman. Not again ... Here!

(ALFRED has entered. He goes past, upstage, carrying the chair. Glances at them. Goes off.)

Been here years, you know. Do the work of ten men if they set him to it.

HARRY. I say ... (Looking off.)

KATHLEEN. Dunno where they've been ... (Calls.) Oi! ... Deaf as a post. Here, no need to let go ... Think you're shy.

HARRY. Oh, well ...

KATHLEEN. Never mind. Too old to be disappointed.

HARRY. Oh, now ...

(JACK *and* MARJORIE *enter, the former carrying a wicker chair.*)

MARJORIE. Here you are, then. Been looking for you all over.

KATHLEEN. Been here, haven't we, all the time.

(HARRY *stands.*)

JACK. Sun still strong.

HARRY. Oh, yes.

MARJORIE. Here. Where's the other chair?

KATHLEEN. He's taken it over there.

MARJORIE. What's he doing?

KATHLEEN. Dunno. Here, sit on his knee if you want to!

MARJORIE. Catch me. Who do you think I am? (*Sits.*)

KATHLEEN. Well, no good you both standing.

JACK (*to* HARRY). No, no. After you, old man.

HARRY. No. no. After you ...

KATHLEEN. Be here all day, you ask me. Here, I'll stand ... Gawd ...

JACK. Oh, no ...

HARRY. Ridiculous.

MARJORIE. Take it in turns.

JACK. Right, I'll er.

HARRY. Do. Do. Go ahead.

JACK. Very decent. Very. (*Sits; sighs.*)

MARJORIE. Been carrying that around, looking for you, he has.

KATHLEEN. Been here, we have, all the time.

MARJORIE. What you been up to, then?

KATHLEEN. Nothing you might mind.

MARJORIE (*to* HARRY). Want to watch her. Men all the time.

KATHLEEN. One who knows.

MARJORIE. Seen it with my own eyes.

KATHLEEN. Lot more besides.

JACK. Think it might look up. Clearing ... (*Gazing up.*)

HARRY. Oh. Very. (*Gazes up.*)

64

MARJORIE. Fallen

JACK. Damn nuis

HARRY. Oh. Very

MARJORIE. Has to

KATHLEEN. See the

MARJORIE. Can't le
Milkman, windo

KATHLEEN. Know y

MARJORIE. Nothing

KATHLEEN. Can't g
wetting.

JACK. Spot more su
wonder.

HARRY. Oh, yes.

JACK. By jove, Farrer, i

HARRY. Say he was a ch

JACK. Shouldn't be sur
shoulders.

HARRY. Deep chest.

JACK. Oh, yes.

KATHLEEN. You know wl
girl.

MARJORIE. You know w
else.

KATHLEEN (*to* HARRY).
mind ... Gawd strev
help.)

MARJORIE. Mind she d

KATHLEEN. Mind she d

MARJORIE. See the doc

KATHLEEN. See him al
the head.

(KATHLEEN has
They go off.)

JACK. Really? (*Looks around.*)

MARJORIE. Here ... What you in for?

JACK. A wholly voluntary basis, I assure you.

MARJORIE. Wife put you away?

JACK. Oh, no. No, no. Just a moment ... needed ... Thought I might ...

MARJORIE. Ever been in the padded whatsit?

JACK. Don't believe ... (*Looking around.*)

MARJORIE. Here ... Don't tell my friend.

JACK. Oh, well ...

MARJORIE. Lie there for hours, you can.

JACK. Oh, now.

MARJORIE. Been here twice before.

JACK. Really ...

MARJORIE. Don't tell my friend.

JACK. Oh, no.

MARJORIE. Thinks it's my first.

JACK. Goodness ...

MARJORIE. One of the regulars. Wouldn't know what to do without me.

JACK. Oh, yes. Familiar faces.

MARJORIE. Come for three months; out again. Back again at Christmas.

JACK. Oh, yes.

MARJORIE. Can't stand Christmas.

JACK. No. Well. Season of festivities ... good cheer.

MARJORIE. Most people don't talk to you in here. You noticed?

JACK. Very rare. Well ... find someone to communicate.

MARJORIE. 'Course. Privileged.

JACK. Yes?

MARJORIE. Being in the reception wing.

JACK. Oh, yes.

MARJORIE. Good as cured.

JACK. Oh, yes.

MARJORIE. Soon be out.

JACK. Oh, goodness ... Hardly worth the trouble.

MARJORIE. No.

JACK. Home tomorrow!

MARJORIE. You been married long?

JACK. Oh, yes ... What?

MARJORIE. You in love?

JACK. What?

MARJORIE. Your wife.

JACK. Clouds ... This morning, my friend was remarking on the edges.

MARJORIE. Hardly worth the trouble.

JACK. Oh, yes.

MARJORIE. Going home.

JACK. Oh, well ... one had one's ... thought I might plant some seeds. Soil not too good, I notice ...

MARJORIE. Tell you something?

JACK. Oh, yes.

MARJORIE. Set up here for good.

JACK. Oh, yes.

MARJORIE. Here, you listening? What you in for?

JACK. Oh ...

MARJORIE. Here; you always crying.

JACK. Light ... eye ... (*Wipes his eye with his handkerchief.*)

MARJORIE. Tell you something.

JACK. Yes.

MARJORIE. Not leave here again.

JACK. Oh, no.

> (*They are silent.*
>
> ALFRED *comes on. He stands at the back, leaning on the chair.*)

MARJORIE. You going to sit on that or something?

ALFRED. What?

MARJORIE. Sit.

ALFRED. Dunno.

MARJORIE. Give it to somebody who can, you do.

ALFRED. What? (*Comes down.*)

MARJORIE. Give it to somebody who can.

ALFRED. Yeh.

MARJORIE. You know my friend?

ALFRED. No.

MARJORIE. This is Alfred.

JACK. Oh ... Good ... day. (*Stands formally.*)

ALFRED. Where you get your cane?

JACK. Oh ... (*Looks down at it.*) Came with me.

ALFRED. I had a cane like that once.

JACK. Ah, yes.

ALFRED. Nicked it.

JACK. Oh, now.

MARJORIE. Had it when he came. Didn't you? Sit down.

JACK. Yes. (*Sits.*)

ALFRED. Wanna fight?

JACK. No ...

ALFRED. You?

MARJORIE. No, thanks.

ALFRED. Got sixpence?

JACK. No.

MARJORIE. Here. You seen my friend?

ALFRED. No.

MARJORIE. What you in for?

ALFRED. In what?

MARJORIE. Thinks he's at home, he does. Doesn't know his
own strength, do you?

ALFRED. No.

MARJORIE. Took a bit of his brain, haven't they?

ALFRED. Yeh.

MARJORIE. Feel better?

ALFRED. Yeh.

MARJORIE. His mother's eighty-four.

ALFRED. Seventy.

MARJORIE. Thought you said she was eighty-four.

ALFRED. Seventy.

MARJORIE. Won't know his own name soon.

ALFRED. You wanna fight?

MARJORIE. Knock you down one hand behind my back.

ALFRED. Garn.

MARJORIE. Half kill you, I will.

ALFRED. Go on.

MARJORIE. Wanna try? (*Stands.*)

    (ALFRED *backs off a couple of steps.* MARJORIE *sits.*)
Take that chair off you, you don't look out.

JACK. Slight breeze. Takes the heat off the sun.

MARJORIE. Wanna jump on him if he bullies you.

JACK. Oh, yes.

MARJORIE (*to* ALFRED). What you looking at then?

ALFRED. Sky. (*Looks up.*)

MARJORIE. They'll lock you up if you don't look out. How old's your father?

ALFRED. Twenty-two.

MARJORIE. Older than him, are you?

ALFRED. Yeh.

MARJORIE. Older than his dad he is. Don't know where that leaves him.

JACK. Hasn't been born, I shouldn't wonder.

MARJORIE. No! (*Laughs.*) Hasn't been born, he shouldn't wonder. (*Pause.*) Painted rude letters in the road.

ALFRED. Didn't.

MARJORIE. Did.

ALFRED. Didn't.

MARJORIE. Did. Right in the town centre. Took them three weeks to scrub it off.

got hold. Won't tap on our door, I can tell you. Not again.

HARRY. Goodness.

KATHLEEN. You all right?

HARRY. Yes ... I ... er.

KATHLEEN. Here. Hold my hand if you like.

HARRY. Oh, now.

KATHLEEN. Go on.

> (*Puts her hand on the table.*)

Not much to look at.

HARRY. Oh, now. I wouldn't say that.

KATHLEEN. Go on.

HARRY. Well, I ... (*Takes her hand.*)

KATHLEEN. Our age: know what it's all about. ·

HARRY. Oh, well ... A long road, you know.

KATHLEEN. Can't get to old age fast enough for me. Sooner they put me under ...

HARRY. Oh, now ...

KATHLEEN. Different for a man.

HARRY. Well, I ...

KATHLEEN. I know. Have your troubles. Still. Woman's different.

HARRY. Oh, I ...

KATHLEEN. Wouldn't be a woman. Not again ... Here!

> (ALFRED *has entered. He goes past, upstage, carrying the chair. Glances at them. Goes off.*)

Been here years, you know. Do the work of ten men if they set him to it.

HARRY. I say ... (*Looking off.*)

KATHLEEN. Dunno where they've been ... (*Calls.*) Oi! ... Deaf as a post. Here, no need to let go ... Think you're shy.

HARRY. Oh, well ...

KATHLEEN. Never mind. Too old to be disappointed.

HARRY. Oh, now ...

    (JACK *and* MARJORIE *enter, the former carrying a wicker
chair.*)

MARJORIE. Here you are, then. Been looking for you all over.

KATHLEEN. Been here, haven't we, all the time.

    (HARRY *stands.*)

JACK. Sun still strong.

HARRY. Oh, yes.

MARJORIE. Here. Where's the other chair?

KATHLEEN. He's taken it over there.

MARJORIE. What's he doing?

KATHLEEN. Dunno. Here, sit on his knee if you want to!

MARJORIE. Catch me. Who do you think I am? (*Sits.*)

KATHLEEN. Well, no good you both standing.

JACK (*to* HARRY). No, no. After you, old man.

HARRY. No. no. After you ...

KATHLEEN. Be here all day, you ask me. Here, I'll stand ...
Gawd ...

JACK. Oh, no ...

HARRY. Ridiculous.

MARJORIE. Take it in turns.

JACK. Right, I'll er.

HARRY. Do. Do. Go ahead.

JACK. Very decent. Very. (*Sits; sighs.*)

MARJORIE. Been carrying that around, looking for you, he has.

KATHLEEN. Been here, we have, all the time.

MARJORIE. What you been up to, then?

KATHLEEN. Nothing you might mind.

MARJORIE (*to* HARRY). Want to watch her. Men all the time.

KATHLEEN. One who knows.

MARJORIE. Seen it with my own eyes.

KATHLEEN. Lot more besides.

JACK. Think it might look up. Clearing ... (*Gazing up.*)

HARRY. Oh. Very. (*Gazes up.*)

MARJORIE. Fallen in love, she has.

JACK. Damn nuisance about the chair, what?

HARRY. Oh. Very.

MARJORIE. Has to see the doctor about it, she has.

KATHLEEN. See the doctor about you, girl.

MARJORIE. Can't let no tradesman near the house. Five kids. Milkman, window-cleaner ...

KATHLEEN. Know your trouble, don't you?

MARJORIE. Nothing's bad as yours.

KATHLEEN. Can't go down the street without her trousers wetting.

JACK. Spot more sun, see those flowers out. Shouldn't wonder.

HARRY. Oh, yes.

JACK. By jove, Farrer, isn't it? (*Rises.*)

HARRY. Say he was a champion quarter-miler.

JACK. Shouldn't be surprised. Build of an athlete. Square shoulders.

HARRY. Deep chest.

JACK. Oh, yes.

KATHLEEN. You know what you should do with your mouth, girl.

MARJORIE. You know what you should do with something else.

KATHLEEN (*to* HARRY). Take a little stroll if you don't mind ... Gawd strewth ... (*Gets up;* HARRY *hastens to help.*)

MARJORIE. Mind she doesn't stroll you to the bushes.

KATHLEEN. Mind she doesn't splash.

MARJORIE. See the doctor about you, my girl!

KATHLEEN. See him all the time: your trouble. Not right in the head.

(KATHLEEN *has taken* HARRY's *arm.*
They go off.)

MARJORIE. Can't keep away from men.

JACK. Oh dear. (*Gazing after.*)

MARJORIE. Gardens.

JACK. Oh. (*Sits, uncomfortable.*)

MARJORIE. Parks especially.

JACK. I have heard of such er.

MARJORIE. Complaints. Used to send the police in threes. Can't trust two and one was never enough.

JACK. My word.

MARJORIE. Oh, yes.

JACK. Can never tell a leopard ...

MARJORIE. What? Should see her. Spots all over.

JACK. Oh dear.

MARJORIE. Never washes.

JACK. One of the advantages of a late lunch, of course, is that it leaves a shorter space to tea.

MARJORIE. What's your friend's name?

JACK. Harry ...

MARJORIE. What's he do, then?

JACK. Temporary er ... Thought a slight ...

MARJORIE. Get one with her all right. Have another.

JACK. Oh, yes ...

MARJORIE. Don't know what we're coming to.

JACK. Life ... mystery ... (*Gazes up.*)

    (MARJORIE *watches him. Then:*)

MARJORIE. What you put away for, then?

JACK. Oh ... what?

MARJORIE. In here.

JACK. Oh ... Little ...

MARJORIE. Girl?

JACK. Girl?

MARJORIE. Girls.

JACK. Girls?

MARJORIE. In the street.

JACK. Really? (*Looks around.*)

MARJORIE. Here ... What you in for?

JACK. A wholly voluntary basis, I assure you.

MARJORIE. Wife put you away?

JACK. Oh, no. No, no. Just a moment ... needed ... Thought I might ...

MARJORIE. Ever been in the padded whatsit?

JACK. Don't believe ... (*Looking around.*)

MARJORIE. Here ... Don't tell my friend.

JACK. Oh, well ...

MARJORIE. Lie there for hours, you can.

JACK. Oh, now.

MARJORIE. Been here twice before.

JACK. Really ...

MARJORIE. Don't tell my friend.

JACK. Oh, no.

MARJORIE. Thinks it's my first.

JACK. Goodness ...

MARJORIE. One of the regulars. Wouldn't know what to do without me.

JACK. Oh, yes. Familiar faces.

MARJORIE. Come for three months; out again. Back again at Christmas.

JACK. Oh, yes.

MARJORIE. Can't stand Christmas.

JACK. No. Well. Season of festivities ... good cheer.

MARJORIE. Most people don't talk to you in here. You noticed?

JACK. Very rare. Well ... find someone to communicate.

MARJORIE. 'Course. Privileged.

JACK. Yes?

MARJORIE. Being in the reception wing.

JACK. Oh, yes.

MARJORIE. Good as cured.

JACK. Oh, yes.

MARJORIE. Soon be out.

JACK. Oh, goodness ... Hardly worth the trouble.

MARJORIE. No.

JACK. Home tomorrow!

MARJORIE. You been married long?

JACK. Oh, yes ... What?

MARJORIE. You in love?

JACK. What?

MARJORIE. Your wife.

JACK. Clouds ... This morning, my friend was remarking on the edges.

MARJORIE. Hardly worth the trouble.

JACK. Oh, yes.

MARJORIE. Going home.

JACK. Oh, well ... one had one's ... thought I might plant some seeds. Soil not too good, I notice ...

MARJORIE. Tell you something?

JACK. Oh, yes.

MARJORIE. Set up here for good.

JACK. Oh, yes.

MARJORIE. Here, you listening? What you in for?

JACK. Oh ...

MARJORIE. Here; you always crying.

JACK. Light ... eye ... (*Wipes his eye with his handkerchief.*)

MARJORIE. Tell you something.

JACK. Yes.

MARJORIE. Not leave here again.

JACK. Oh, no.

    (*They are silent.*

    ALFRED *comes on. He stands at the back, leaning on the chair.*)

MARJORIE. You going to sit on that or something?

ALFRED. What?

MARJORIE. Sit.

ALFRED. Dunno.

MARJORIE. Give it to somebody who can, you do.

ALFRED. What? (*Comes down.*)

MARJORIE. Give it to somebody who can.

ALFRED. Yeh.

MARJORIE. You know my friend?

ALFRED. No.

MARJORIE. This is Alfred.

JACK. Oh ... Good ... day. (*Stands formally.*)

ALFRED. Where you get your cane?

JACK. Oh ... (*Looks down at it.*) Came with me.

ALFRED. I had a cane like that once.

JACK. Ah, yes.

ALFRED. Nicked it.

JACK. Oh, now.

MARJORIE. Had it when he came. Didn't you? Sit down.

JACK. Yes. (*Sits.*)

ALFRED. Wanna fight?

JACK. No ...

ALFRED. You?

MARJORIE. No, thanks.

ALFRED. Got sixpence?

JACK. No.

MARJORIE. Here. You seen my friend?

ALFRED. No.

MARJORIE. What you in for?

ALFRED. In what?

MARJORIE. Thinks he's at home, he does. Doesn't know his own strength, do you?

ALFRED. No.

MARJORIE. Took a bit of his brain, haven't they?

ALFRED. Yeh.

MARJORIE. Feel better?

ALFRED. Yeh.

MARJORIE. His mother's eighty-four.

ALFRED. Seventy.

MARJORIE. Thought you said she was eighty-four.

ALFRED. Seventy.

MARJORIE. Won't know his own name soon.

ALFRED. You wanna fight?

MARJORIE. Knock you down one hand behind my back.

ALFRED. Garn.

MARJORIE. Half kill you, I will.

ALFRED. Go on.

MARJORIE. Wanna try? (*Stands.*)

    (ALFRED *backs off a couple of steps.* MARJORIE *sits.*)
Take that chair off you, you don't look out.

JACK. Slight breeze. Takes the heat off the sun.

MARJORIE. Wanna jump on him if he bullies you.

JACK. Oh, yes.

MARJORIE (*to* ALFRED). What you looking at then?

ALFRED. Sky. (*Looks up.*)

MARJORIE. They'll lock you up if you don't look out. How old's your father?

ALFRED. Twenty-two.

MARJORIE. Older than him, are you?

ALFRED. Yeh.

MARJORIE. Older than his dad he is. Don't know where that leaves him.

JACK. Hasn't been born, I shouldn't wonder.

MARJORIE. No! (*Laughs.*) Hasn't been born, he shouldn't wonder. (*Pause.*) Painted rude letters in the road.

ALFRED. Didn't.

MARJORIE. Did.

ALFRED. Didn't.

MARJORIE. Did. Right in the town centre. Took them three weeks to scrub it off.

ALFRED. Two.

MARJORIE. Three.

ALFRED. Two.

MARJORIE. Three. Apprentice painter and decorator. Didn't know what he was going to decorate. (*To* ALFRED) They'll apprentice you no more. (*To* JACK) Doesn't know his own strength, he doesn't.

JACK (*looking round*). Wonder where ...

MARJORIE. Send the police out for them, they will.

JACK. Clouds ... (*Looking up.*)

MARJORIE. Seen it all, I have. Rape, intercourse. Physical pleasure.

JACK. I had a cousin once ...

MARJORIE. Here, you got a big family, haven't you?

JACK. Seven brothers and sisters. Spreads around, you know.

MARJORIE. Here, you was an only child last week.

JACK. A niece of mine – I say niece ... she was only ...

MARJORIE. What you do it for?

JACK. Oh, now ...

MARJORIE (*to* ALFRED). Wanna watch him. Trained as a doctor he has.

JACK. Wonder where ... (*Gazing round.*)

MARJORIE (*to* ALFRED). What you paint in the road?

ALFRED. Nothing.

MARJORIE. Must have painted something. Can't paint nothing. Must have painted something or they couldn't have rubbed it off.

ALFRED. Paint you if you don't watch out.

MARJORIE. I'll knock your head off.

ALFRED. Won't.

MARJORIE. Will.

ALFRED. Won't.

MARJORIE. Will.

ALFRED. Won't.

MARJORIE. What you doing with that chair?

ALFRED. Nothing. (*Spins it beneath his hand.*)

MARJORIE. Faster than a rocket he is. Wanna watch him ... Where you going?

(JACK *has got up.*)

JACK. Thought I might ... Oh ...

(HARRY *and* KATHLEEN *have come on from the other side, the latter leaning on* HARRY'*s arm.*)

KATHLEEN. Gawd ... they're coming off. I'll have nothing left ... Oh ...

(HARRY *helps her to the chair.*)

MARJORIE. Here, where you been?

KATHLEEN. There and back.

MARJORIE. Know where you been, my girl.

KATHLEEN. Don't.

HARRY. Canteen. We've ...

KATHLEEN. Don't tell her. Nose ten miles long she has. Trip over it one day she will. What's he doing? (*Indicating* ALFRED.)

MARJORIE. Won't give up his chair, he won't.

HARRY. Still got three, what?

JACK. Yes ... what. Clouds ...

HARRY. Ah ... Rain.

JACK. Shouldn't wonder.

MARJORIE. Here. Put that chair down.

(ALFRED *still stands there.*

MARJORIE *stands.* ALFRED *releases the chair quickly.*)

(*To* JACK) You get it.

JACK. Er ... right.

(*Goes and gets the chair.* ALFRED *doesn't move.*)

MARJORIE. One each, then.

HARRY. Yes ...

MARJORIE. Well ... (*Indicates they sit.*)

KATHLEEN. Gawd ... (*Holds her feet.*)

72

MARJORIE. Had a job once.

KATHLEEN. Gawd.

MARJORIE. Packing tins of food.

KATHLEEN (*to* ALFRED). What you looking at?

ALFRED. Nothing.

MARJORIE. Pull your skirt down, girl.

KATHLEEN. Got nothing up mine ain't got up yours.

MARJORIE. Put them in cardboard boxes.

JACK. Really? I had a ...

MARJORIE. Done by machine now.

KATHLEEN. Nothing left for you to do, my girl. That's your
trouble.

MARJORIE. 'Tis.

KATHLEEN. Cries everywhere, she does.

HARRY. Oh. One has one's ...

KATHLEEN. 'Specially at Christmas. Cries at Christmas.
Boxing Day. Sometimes to New Year.

JACK. Oh, well, one ...

KATHLEEN (*indicating* ALFRED). What's he doing, then?

MARJORIE. Waiting to be born, he is.

KATHLEEN. What?

MARJORIE. Eight o'clock tomorrow morning. Better be
there. (*Laughs. To* ALFRED) You better be there.

ALFRED. Yeh.

MARJORIE. Late for his own birthday, he is. (*To* ALFRED)
Never catch up, you won't.

HARRY (*holding out hand; inspects it*). Thought I ... No.

JACK. Could be. (*Looks up.*)

HARRY. Lucky so far.

JACK. Oh, yes.

HARRY. Possibility ... (*Looking up.*)

JACK. By jove ...

MARJORIE. One thing you can say about this place ...

KATHLEEN. Yes.

MARJORIE. 'S not like home.

KATHLEEN. Thank Gawd.

MARJORIE (to ALFRED). What you want?

ALFRED. Nothing.

KATHLEEN. Give you nothing if you come here ... What you staring at?

ALFRED. Nothing.

MARJORIE. Taken off a bit of his brain they have.

KATHLEEN (to ALFRED). Where they put it then?

MARJORIE. Thrown it in the dustbin.

KATHLEEN. Could have done with that. (Laughs.) Didn't cut a bit of something else off, did they?

MARJORIE. You know what your trouble is, my girl.

JACK. Time for tea, I shouldn't wonder. (Stands.)

HARRY. Yes. Well ... let me see. Very nearly.

JACK. Stretch the old legs ...

HARRY. Oh, yes.

MARJORIE. Not your legs need stretching, ask me.

JACK. Ah, well ... Trim. (Bends arms; stretches.)

MARJORIE. Fancies himself he does.

KATHLEEN. Don't blame him.

MARJORIE. Watch yourself, my girl.

KATHLEEN. No harm come from trying.

MARJORIE. Good job your feet like they are, ask me.

KATHLEEN. Have them off in the morning. Not stand this much longer.

MARJORIE. Slow her down; know what they're doing.

KATHLEEN. Know what she is?

JACK. Well, I ...

KATHLEEN. P.O.

JACK. P.O.

KATHLEEN. Persistent Offender.

MARJORIE. Ain't no such thing.

KATHLEEN. Is.

74

MARJORIE. Isn't.

KATHLEEN. Heard it in the office. Off Doctor ... what's his name.

MARJORIE. Never heard of that doctor, I haven't. Must be a new one must that. Doctor what's his name is a new one on me.

KATHLEEN. I know what I heard.

MARJORIE. Here. What's he crying about?

(HARRY *is drying his eyes.*)

KATHLEEN. Always crying one of these two.

MARJORIE. Call them the water babies, you ask me. (*To* ALFRED) You seen this?

(ALFRED *gazes woodenly towards them.*)

KATHLEEN. He's another.

MARJORIE. Don't know what'll become of us, girl.

KATHLEEN. Thought you was the one to cry.

MARJORIE. So d'I.

KATHLEEN. My dad was always crying.

MARJORIE. Yeh?

KATHLEEN. Drank too much. Came out of his eyes.

MARJORIE. Ooh! (*Laughs, covering her mouth.*)

KATHLEEN. Here, what's the matter with you, Harry?

HARRY. Oh, just a er.

JACK. Could have sworn ... (*Holds out hand; looks up.*)

KATHLEEN. 'S not rain. 'S him. Splashing it all over, he is.

JACK. There, now ...

MARJORIE. Here. Look at him: thinks it's raining.

KATHLEEN (*to* JACK). Here. Your friend ...

(JACK *breathes deeply: fresh-air exercises.*)

JACK. Freshening.

MARJORIE. I don't know. What they come out for?

KATHLEEN. Crying all over, they are.

MARJORIE (*to* JACK). You going to help your friend, then, are you?

75

JACK. Oh. Comes and goes ...

KATHLEEN (*to* HARRY). Wanna hold my hand?

    (HARRY *doesn't answer.*)

MARJORIE. Not seen so many tears. Haven't.

KATHLEEN. Not since Christmas.

MARJORIE. Not since Christmas, girl.

KATHLEEN. Ooooh!

MARJORIE (*to* JACK). You all right?

    (JACK *doesn't answer. Stands stiffly turned away, looking off.*)

  Think you and I better be on our way, girl.

KATHLEEN. Think we had.

MARJORIE. Try and make something. What you get for it?

KATHLEEN. Get nothing if you don't try, girl.

MARJORIE. No.

KATHLEEN. Get nothing if you do, either.

MARJORIE. Ooooh! (*Laughs, covering her mouth; stands.*) Don't slow you down, do they? (*Indicates shoes.*)

KATHLEEN. Get my laces back or else, girl ... Oh! (*Winces, standing. To* ALFRED) What you staring at?

ALFRED. Nothing.

KATHLEEN. Be dead this time tomorrow.

MARJORIE. No complaints then, my girl.

KATHLEEN. Not too soon for me.

MARJORIE. Going to say goodbye to your boy-friend?

KATHLEEN. Dunno that he wants to know ...

MARJORIE. Give you a hand, girl?

KATHLEEN. Can't move without.

MARJORIE. There ... on our way.

KATHLEEN. Gawd.

MARJORIE. Not stop here again.

KATHLEEN. Better get out of here, girl ... Gawd! Go mad here you don't watch out.

(*Groaning,* KATHLEEN *is led off by* MARJORIE.
Pause.

ALFRED *comes up. Holds table, waits, then lifts it. Raises
it above his head. Turns. Walks off.*)

JACK. By jove.
(HARRY *stirs.*)
Freshening ... Surprised if it doesn't blow over by tomor-
row.

HARRY. Oh, yes ...

JACK. Saw Harrison yesterday.

HARRY. Yes?

JACK. Congestion.

HARRY. Soot.

JACK. Really?

HARRY. Oh, yes. (*Dries his eyes.*)

JACK. Shouldn't wonder if wind veers. North-west.

HARRY. East.

JACK. Really? Higher ground, of course, one notices.

HARRY. Found the er. (*Gestures after* MARJORIE *and* KATH-
LEEN.)

JACK. Oh, yes.

HARRY. Extraordinary.

JACK. 'Straordinary.

HARRY. Get used to it after a while.

JACK. Oh, yes ... I have a sister-in-law, for example, who
wears dark glasses.

HARRY. Really?

JACK. Each evening before she goes to bed.

HARRY. Really.

JACK. Following morning: takes them off.

HARRY. Extraordinary.

JACK. Sunshine – never wears them.

HARRY. Well ... I ... (*Finally wipes his eyes and puts his handkerchief away.*) Extraordinary.

JACK. The older one grows, of course ... the more one takes into account other people's foibles.

HARRY. Oh, yes.

JACK. If a person can't be what they are, what's the purpose of being anything at all?

HARRY. Oh, absolutely.

(ALFRED *has returned. He picks up one of the metalwork chairs; turns it one way then another, gazes at* JACK *and* HARRY, *then slowly carries it off.*)

JACK. I suppose in the army, of course, one becomes quite used to foibles.

HARRY. Oh, yes.

JACK. Navy, too, I shouldn't wonder.

HARRY. Oh, yes.

JACK. A relative of mine rose to lieutenant–commander in a seagoing corvette.

HARRY. My word.

JACK. In the blood.

HARRY. Bound to be.

JACK. Oh, yes. Without the sea; well, hate to think.

HARRY. Oh, yes.

JACK. At no point is one more than seventy-five miles from the sea.

HARRY. Really.

JACK. That is the nature of this little island.

HARRY. Extraordinary when you think.

JACK. When you think what came from it.

HARRY. Oh, yes.

JACK. Radar.

HARRY. Oh, yes.

JACK. Jet propulsion.

HARRY. My word.

JACK. Television.

HARRY. Oh ...

JACK. Steam-engine.

HARRY. Goodness.

JACK. Empire the like of which no one has ever seen.

HARRY. No. My word.

JACK. Light of the world.

HARRY. Oh, yes.

JACK. Penicillin.

HARRY. Penicillin.

JACK. Darwin.

HARRY. Darwin.

JACK. Newton.

HARRY. Newton.

JACK. Milton.

HARRY. My word.

JACK. Sir Walter Raleigh.

HARRY. Goodness. Sir ...

JACK. Lost his head.

HARRY. Oh, yes. (*Rises; comes downstage.*)

JACK. This little island.

HARRY. Shan't see its like.

JACK. Oh, no.

HARRY. The sun has set.

JACK. Couple of hours ...

HARRY. What?

JACK. One of the strange things, of course, about this place.

HARRY. Oh, yes.

JACK. Is its size.

HARRY. Yes.

JACK. Never meet the same people two days running.

HARRY. No.

JACK. Can't find room, of course.

HARRY. No.

JACK. See them at the gates.

HARRY. Oh, my word.

JACK. Of an evening, looking in. Unfortunately the money isn't there.

HARRY. No.

JACK. Exchequer. Diverting wealth to the proper ...

HARRY. Oh, yes.

JACK. Witness: one metalwork table, two metalwork chairs; two thousand people.

HARRY. My word, yes.

JACK. While overhead ...

HARRY. Oh, yes ...
> (*They both gaze up.*
> (ALFRED *comes in; he picks up the remaining white chair.*)

ALFRED. You finished?

JACK. What ...?

ALFRED. Take them back. (*Indicates their two wicker chairs.*)

HARRY. Oh, yes ...

ALFRED. Don't take them back: get into trouble.

JACK. Oh, my word.
> (ALFRED, *watching them, lifts the metal chair with one hand, holding its leg; demonstrates his strength.*
> *They watch in silence.*
> ALFRED *lifts the chair above his head; then, still watching them, turns and goes.*)

Shadows.

HARRY. Yes.

JACK. Another day.

HARRY. Ah, yes.

JACK. Brother-in-law I had was an artist.

HARRY. Really?

JACK. Would have appreciated those flowers. Light fading ... Clouds.

HARRY. Wonderful thing.

JACK. Oh, yes.

HARRY. Would have liked to have been an artist myself. Musician.

JACK. Really?

HARRY. Flute.

JACK. Beautiful instrument.

HARRY. Oh, yes.

(*They gaze at the view.*)

HARRY. Shadows.

JACK. Choose any card ... (*Holds pack out from his pocket.*)

HARRY. Any?

JACK. Any one ...

HARRY (*takes one*). ... Yes!

JACK. Eight of Diamonds.

HARRY. My word!

JACK. Right?

HARRY. Absolutely.

JACK. Intended to show the ladies.

HARRY. Another day.

JACK. Oh, yes.

(JACK *re-shuffles cards; holds them out.*)

HARRY. Again?

JACK. Any one.

HARRY. Er ...

JACK. Three of Spades.

HARRY. Two of Hearts.

JACK. What? (*Inspects the cards briefly; puts them away.*)

HARRY. Amazing thing, of course, is the er.

JACK. Oh, yes.

HARRY. Still prevails.

JACK. Oh, my goodness.

HARRY. Hendricks I find is a ...

JACK. Oh, yes.

HARRY. Moustache ... Eye-brows.

JACK. Divorced.

HARRY. Oh, yes.

JACK. Moral fibre. Set to a task, never complete it. Find some way to back out.

HARRY. Oh, yes.

JACK. The sea is an extraordinary ...

HARRY. Oh, yes.

JACK. Cousin of mine ...

HARRY. See the church.

(*They gaze off.*)

JACK. Shouldn't wonder He's disappointed. (*Looks up.*)

HARRY. Oh, yes.

JACK. Heart-break.

HARRY. Oh, yes.

JACK. Same mistake ... Won't make it twice.

HARRY. Oh, no.

JACK. Once over. Never again.

(ALFRED *has come on.*)

ALFRED. You finished?

JACK. Well, I ... er ...

ALFRED. Take 'em back.

JACK. Oh, well. That's very ...

(ALFRED *grasps the two wicker chairs. Glances at* JACK *and* HARRY; *picks up both the chairs.*

Glances at JACK *and* HARRY *again, holding the chairs. Takes them off.*)

What I ... er ... yes.

(HARRY *has begun to weep.*

JACK *gazes off.*

A moment later JACK *also wipes his eyes.*

After a while the light slowly fades.)

CURTAIN

THE
CHANGING ROOM

TO JAKE

This play was first presented at the Royal Court Theatre, London, on 9 November 1971, under the direction of Lindsay Anderson. The cast was as follows:

Harry	JOHN BARRETT
Patsy	JIM NORTON
Fielding	DAVID DAKER
Mic Morley	EDWARD PEEL
Kendal	WARREN CLARKE
Luke	DON MCKILLOP
Fenchurch	PETER CHILDS
Colin Jagger	MARK MCMANUS
Trevor	MICHAEL ELPHICK
Walsh	EDWARD JUDD
Sandford	BRIAN GLOVER
Barry Copley	GEOFFREY HINSLIFF
Jack Stringer	DAVID HILL
Bryan Atkinson	PETER SCHOFIELD
Billy Spencer	ALUN ARMSTRONG
John Clegg	MATTHEW GUINNESS
Frank Moore	JOHN PIRCE
Danny Crosby	BARRY KEEGAN
Cliff Owens	FRANK MILLS
Tallon	BRIAN LAWSON
Thornton	PAUL DAWKINS
Mackendrick	JOHN RAE

CHARACTERS

HARRY	Cleaner: 50–60
PATSY	Wing threequarter: 23–5
FIELDING	Forward: 35–6
Mic MORLEY	Forward: 28
KENDAL	Forward: 29
LUKE	Masseur: 40–50
FENCHURCH	Wing threequarter: 23–5
Colin JAGGER	Centre threequarter: 26
TREVOR	Full-back: 26
WALSH	Forward: 35–40
SANDFORD	Assistant trainer: 40
Barry COPLEY	Scrum-half: 27–8
Jack STRINGER	Centre threequarter: 30
Bryan ATKINSON	Forward: 32
Billy SPENCER	Reserve: 20
John CLEGG	Hooker: 30
Frank MOORE	Reserve: 21
Danny CROSBY	Trainer: 45–50
Cliff OWENS	Stand-off half: 30–32
TALLON	Referee
THORNTON	Chairman: 50
MACKENDRICK	Club Secretary: 60

ACT ONE

A changing room; afternoon. The light comes from glazed panels high in the wall and from an electric light.

Across the back of the stage is the main changing bench, set up against the wall and running its entire length. A set of hooks, one for each player, is fastened at head height to the wall, with the name of a player above each hook. Underneath the bench, below each hook, is a locker, also labelled. A jersey and a pair of shorts have been set out beneath one of the hooks. A rubbing-down table with an adjustable head-rest stands in front of the bench. Stage right, a glazed door opens to an entrance porch. Downstage left is a fireplace, with a bucket of coal, overhung by a mirror advertising ale. Upstage left is the open entry to the bath and showers: buckets, stool, hose and tap, etc. Downstage right is a wooden door, closed, leading to the offices. A second table stands against the wall. There's a pair of metal scales with individual metal weights on a metal arm. By the rubbing-down table stands a large wicker-work basket. A wooden chair with a rounded back is set against the wall, stage left.

Tannoy music is being played, light, militaristic.

HARRY *enters from the bath. He's a broken-down man, small, stooped, in shirt-sleeves, rolled, and a sleeveless pullover. He's smoking and carries a sweeping-brush, on the lookout for anything he might have missed. He sweeps, looks round the floor, sweeps; finally lifts corner of the boxed-in rubbing-down table and sweeps the debris underneath. Takes out his cigarette, looks round, finds nowhere to drop it, then crosses to the fire; drops it in, sets the brush against the wall, puts coal from the bucket on the fire, warms his hands, shivers.*

PATSY *enters from the porch. He's a smart, lightly built man,*

87

very well groomed, hair greased, collar of an expensive overcoat turned up. Brisk, businesslike, narcissistic, no evident sense of humour.

PATSY. Harry ...

HARRY. Patsy ...

PATSY. Cold.

HARRY. Bloody freezing, lad. (*Rubs his hands; reaches to the fire again.*)

> (PATSY, *evidently familiar with his routine, goes to his locker. Gets out his boots, unfolds his jersey and shorts already lying on the bench.*)

PATSY. No towel.

HARRY. No. No. Just fetching those ... (*Takes his brush and exits through bath entrance.*)

> (PATSY, *having checked his jersey, examined its number (2), collar, etc.—no marks—does the same with his boots: laces, studs, lining. He then crosses to the fire, takes out a comb from an inside pocket and smooths his hair down in the mirror. He's doing this as* HARRY *re-enters carrying several neatly folded towels. He puts one on the bench by* PATSY's *peg, then goes to the wickerwork basket, lifts the lid and gets out several more towels. Having checked them, counting soundlessly to himself, he puts them all in the basket, save three which he begins to arrange on the massage table.*
>
> PATSY, *having combed his hair and admired himself in the mirror, clears his nose and spits in the fire.*)

HARRY (*laying out towels*). Thought it'd be snowed off.

PATSY. Snow?

HARRY. Bloody forecast.

PATSY. Not cancel ought in this dump, I can tell you ... Shoulder ... I've no skin on from here to here. There's not a blade o' grass on that bloody pitch ... sithee ... **look** at that ...

(*Pulls up his sleeve.* HARRY *looks across with no evident interest.*)

HARRY. Aye.

PATSY. Watered t'bloody pitch we 'ad last week. Froze over ten minutes after. Took a run at t'bloody ball ... took off ... must have travelled twenty bloody yards without having lift a finger.

HARRY. Aye.

PATSY. Ice.

(HARRY *is laying out the rest of the jerseys now, and shorts.*)

PATSY. Be better off with a pair of skates. (*Glances behind him, into the mirror; smooths hair.*) If there's a young woman comes asking for me afterwards, will you tell her to wait up in the office? Be frozen to death out theer.

HARRY. Aye ...

PATSY. By Christ ... (*Rubs his hands, standing with his back to the fire.*)

HARRY. Comes from Russia.

PATSY. What?

HARRY. Cold ... Comes fro' Russia ...

PATSY. Oh ... (*Nods.*)

HARRY. Read a book ... they had a special machine ... blew these winds o'er, you see ... specially freezing ... mixed it with a chemical ... frozen ought ... Froze the entire country ... Then Ireland ... Then crossed over to America and froze it out ... Then, when everything wa' frozen, they came o'er in special boots and took over ... Here ... America ... Nobody twigged it. Nobody cottoned on, you see.

PATSY. Oh ... (*Glances at himself in mirror again.*) You think that's what's happening now, then?

HARRY. Cold enough ... Get no warning ... Afore you know what's happening ... Ruskies here.

PATSY. Couldn't be worse than this lot.

HARRY. What?

PATSY. Stopped ten quid i' bloody tax last week ... I tell you ... I'm paying t'government to keep me i' bloody work ... madhouse ... If I had my time o'er again I'd emigrate ... America ... Australia ...

HARRY. Wherever you go they'll find you out.

PATSY. What?

HARRY. Ruskies ... Keep your name down in a bloody book ... (*Looks across.*) Won't make any difference if you've voted socialist. Have you down theer ... up against a wall ...

PATSY. Thy wants to read one or two bloody facts, old lad.

HARRY. Facts? What facts? ... I read in one paper that in twenty-five years not one country on earth'll not be communist ...

> (PATSY *crosses back to his peg and starts taking off his overcoat.*)

Don't worry. There'll be no lakin' bloody football then.

PATSY. They lake football i' Russia as much as they lake it here.

HARRY. Aye ...

> (HARRY *waits, threatening;* PATSY *doesn't answer, pre-occupied with his overcoat.*)

You: football ... You: coalmine ... You: factory ... You: air-force ... You ... *Siberia.*

PATSY. Haven't you got a bloody coat-hanger? Damn well ask for one each week.

HARRY. Aye. Don't worry ... (*Starts to go.*) Not bloody listen until they find it's bloody well too late. (*Goes off to the bath entrance, disgruntled.*)

> (FIELDING *enters: large, well-built man, slow, easy-going, thirty-five to thirty-six. He's dressed in an overcoat and muffler; he has a strip of plaster above his left eye.*)

FIELDING. Patsy.

PATSY. Fieldy ...

FIELDING. Freeze your knuckles off today. (*Blows in hands, goes over to fire; stoops, warms hands.*) By Christ ...

> (PATSY *is holding up his coat in one hand, dusting it down lightly, paying no attention to* FIELDING's *entrance.*
> HARRY *comes back in with wooden coat-hanger.*)

HARRY. Have no bloody servants theer, you know.

PATSY (*examining coat*). What's that?

HARRY. No servants. Do your own bloody carrying theer.

> (*Gives* PATSY *the hanger and goes back to laying out the playing-kit.*)

FIELDING. What's that, Harry? (*Winks to* PATSY.)

PATSY. Bloody Russians. Going to be invaded.

HARRY. Don't you worry. It can happen any time, you know.

PATSY. Going to freeze us, with a special liquid ... Then come over ... (*To* HARRY) What wa're it? ... i' special boots.

HARRY. It all goes back, you know.

PATSY. Back?

HARRY. To bloody Moscow ... Ought you say here's reported back ... Keep all thy names in a special book.

FIELDING. Keep thy name in a special bloody book ... Riley ... First name: Harry ... Special qualifications: can talk out of the back of his bloody head.

HARRY. Don't you worry.

FIELDING. Nay, I'm not worried. They can come here any day of the bloody week for me. Sup of ale ...

PATSY. Ten fags ...

FIELDING. That's all I need. (*Sneezes hugely. Shakes his head, gets out his handkerchief, blows his nose, lengthily and noisily.*) Come on, then, Harry ... Switch it off.

> (*After gazing at* FIELDING, *threatening,* HARRY *turns off the Tannoy.*)

I thought o' ringing up this morning ... Looked out o'
the bloody winder. Frost ... (*Crosses over to* PATSY.)
Got this house, now, just outside the town ... wife's idea,
not mine ... bloody fields ... hardly a bloody sign of
human life ... cows ... half a dozen sheep ... goats ...

> (*Starts peeling the plaster from above his eye.* PATSY *pays
> no attention, arranging his coat on the hanger and picking off
> one or two bits.*)

Middle of bloody nowhere ... if I can't see a wall outside
on t'window I don't feel as though I'm living in a house ...
How's it look?

PATSY (*glances up, briefly*). All right.

FIELDING. Bloody fist. Loose forra'd ... Copped him one
afore the end. Had a leg like a bloody melon ... (*Feeling
the cut.*) Get Lukey to put on a bit of grease ... Should be
all right. How's your shoulder?

PATSY. All right. (*Eases it.*) Came in early. Get it strapped.
(*Indicates, however, that there's no one here.*)

FIELDING. Where we lived afore, you know, everything you
could bloody want: pit, boozer, bloody dogs. As for
now ... trees, hedges, miles o' bloody grass ... (*Inspecting
his kit which* HARRY *has now hung up.*) Weer's the jock-
straps, Harry? ... I thought of ringing up and backing
out. Flu ... some such like. (*Sneezes.*) By God ... He'll
have me lakin' here, will Harry, wi' me bloody cobblers
hanging out.

> (MORLEY *has now entered from the porch: thick-set, squat
> figure, dark-haired. Wears a jacket, unbuttoned, with a
> sweater underneath; hard, rough, uncomplicated figure.*)

Nah, Morley, lad, then: how's thy keeping?

MORLEY. Shan't be a second ... Just o'd on. (*Goes straight over
to the bath entrance, unbuttoning his flies.*)

> (*He's followed in by* KENDAL: *tall, rather well-built, late
> twenties, wearing an old overcoat with a scarf, and carrying*

a paper parcel. A worn, somewhat faded man.
HARRY *has gone to the basket and is now getting out a pile of jock-straps which he lays on the table.*)

KENDAL (*to* HARRY). Here ... see about my boots? Bloody stud missing last Thursday ... (*To* FIELDING) Suppose to check them every bloody week. Come up to training and nearly bust me bloody ankle. God Christ, they don't give a sod about bloody ought up here ... Patsy ...

PATSY. Kenny ... (*Having hung up his coat, starts taking off his jacket.*)

KENDAL (*to* FIELDING). Bought one of these electric tool-sets ...

FIELDING (*to* PATSY). Tool-sets ...
(PATSY *nods.*)

FIELDING. Got all the tools that I need, Kenny.

KENDAL. Bloody saw ... drill, bloody polisher. Just look.

FIELDING. What do you do with that? (*Picks out a tool.*)

KENDAL. Dunno.

PATSY. Take stones out of hosses' hoofs, more like.
(*They laugh.*
MORLEY *comes back in.*)

FIELDING. Dirty bugger. Pisses i' the bloody bath.

MORLEY. Been in that bog, then, have you? (*To* HARRY) You want to clean it out.

HARRY. That lavatory was new this season ... (*Indicating* FIELDING) He'll tell you. One we had afore I wouldn't have used.
(MORLEY *goes straight to the business of getting changed: coat off, sweater, then shoes and socks; then starts examining his ankle.*)

FIELDING. Harry doesn't use a lavatory, do you?

MORLEY. Piles it up behind the bloody posts.

FIELDING. Dirty bugger.

HARRY. Don't worry. It all goes down.

MORLEY. Goes down?
    (*They laugh.*)
Goes down where, then, lad?

PATSY. He's reporting it back, tha knows, to Moscow.

MORLEY. Moscow? Moscow?

HARRY. Somebody does, don't you bloody worry. Everything they hear.

FIELDING. Nay, Harry, lad. Thy should have warned us. (*Puts his arm round* HARRY'*s shoulder.*)

HARRY. Don't worry. You carry on. (*Breaks away from* FIELDING'*s embrace.*) You'll be laughing t'other side of your bloody face. (*Exits.*)

FIELDING (*holding jersey up*). Given me number four, an' all. I'll be all right jumping up and down i' middle o' yon bloody backs.

KENDAL. By God (*rubbing his hands at the fire*). I wouldn't mind being on the bloody bench today.
    (*Pause.* LUKE *comes in, wearing a track-suit and baseball shoes and carrying a large hold-all, plus a large tin of Vaseline; sets them down by the massage table. A small, middle-aged man, perky, brisk, grey-haired.*)

FIELDING. Nah, Lukey, lad. Got a drop o' rum in theer, then, have you?

LUKE. Aye. Could do with it today.

MORLEY. Lukey ...

KENDAL. Lukey ...

LUKE. Who's first on, then? (*Indicating the table.*) By Christ ... (*Rubs his hands.*)

PATSY. My bloody shoulder ...

LUKE. Aye. Right, then. Let's have a look. (*Rummaging in his bag; gets out crepe bandage.*)
    (PATSY *is stripped to his shirt by now; takes it off, hangs it and comes over in his vest and trousers. Sits on the edge of table for* LUKE *to strap him up.*)

MORLEY. Bloody ankle, Lukey ...

LUKE. Aye. All right.

FIELDING (*examining* PATSY's *shoulder*). By God, there's nowt theer, lad. Which shoulder wa're it?

MORLEY. Sprained it.

FIELDING. Sprained it.

MORLEY. Twisted it i' bed.

> (*They laugh.* PATSY *pays no attention. Holds his elbow as if one shoulder gives him great pain.*
> HARRY *comes back in with remaining jerseys.*)

LUKE. Right, then, lad. Let's have it off.

> (*Having got out all his equipment,* LUKE *helps* PATSY *off with his vest.*)

KENDAL (*to* MORLEY). Look at that, then, eh? (*Shows him his tool-kit.*) Sand-paper ... polisher ... circular saw ...

FIELDING (*stripping*). What're you going to mek with that, then, Kenny?

KENDAL. Dunno ... shelves.

MORLEY. What for?

KENDAL. Books.

FIELDING (*laughs*). Thy's never read a bleeding book.

KENDAL. The wife reads ... Got three or four at home.

> (MORLEY *laughs.*)

Cupboards ... Any amount o' things ... Pantry door. Fitments ...

FIELDING. Fitments.

> (*They laugh: look over at* KENDAL; *he re-examines the tools inside the parcel.*)

MORLEY. T'only bloody fitment thy needs, Kenny ... Nay, lad, thy weern't find wrapped up inside that box.

> (*They laugh;* FIELDING *sneezes.* KENDAL *begins to pack up his parcel.* HARRY *has gone out, having set the remaining jerseys. The door from the porch opens:* FENCHURCH, JAGGER *and* TREVOR *come in.*)

FENCHURCH *is a neatly groomed man, small, almost dainty; wears a suit beneath a belted raincoat. He carries a small hold-all in which he keeps his boots: self-contained, perhaps even at times a vicious man.*

JAGGER *is of medium height, but sturdy. He wears an overcoat, with an upturned collar, and carries a newspaper: perky, rather officious, cocky.*

TREVOR *is a studious-looking man; wears glasses, is fairly sturdily built. Quiet, level-headed: a schoolmaster.*)

FIELDING. Fenny.

MORLEY. Fenchurch.

FENCHURCH. Na, lad.

JAGGER. Come up in old Fenny's bloody car ... (*To* LUKE) By God: nearly needed thee there, Lukey ... Blind as a bloody bat is yon ... Old feller crossing the bleedin' road: tips him up the arse with his bloody bumper.

FENCHURCH. He started coming backwards. In't that right, then, Trevor?

TREVOR. Aye. He seemed to.

LUKE. Did he get your name?

JAGGER. Old Fenny gets out of the bleedin' car ... How much did you give him?

FENCHURCH. A bloody fiver.

TREVOR. A ten-bob note.

JAGGER. The bloody miser ...

TREVOR. Bends down, tha knows ...

JAGGER. He picks him up ...

TREVOR. Dusts down his coat ...

JAGGER. Asks him how he was ... Is that right? That's all you gave him?

FENCHURCH. Gone to his bloody head if I'd have given him any more.

(*They laugh.*)

96

TREVOR (*instructional*). You told him who you were, though, Fen.

JAGGER. Offered him his bloody autograph.

(*They laugh.*)

MORLEY. I went up to Fenny's one bloody night ... He said, 'I won't give you my address ... just mention my name to anyone you see ...' Stopped a bobby at the end of his bloody road: 'Could you tell me where Gordon Fenchurch lives? Plays on the wing for the bloody City?' 'Who?' he said. '*Who?*' 'Fenchurch.' 'Fenchurch? Never heard of him.'

(*They laugh.* FENCHURCH, *taking no notice of this, has merely got out his boots and begun to examine them.*
HARRY *has come in with boots.*)

JAGGER. Ay up, ay up. Ay up. He's here. Look what the bloody ragman's brought.

(WALSH *comes in: a large, somewhat commanding figure. He wears a dark suit with a large carnation in the buttonhole. He enters from the offices, pausing in the door. He's smoking a cigar. His age, thirty-five to forty. Stout, fairly weather-beaten. There are cries and mocking shouts at his appearance:* '*Ay up, ay up, Walshy, then.*' '*What's this?*')

WALSH. And er ... who are all these bloody layabouts in here?

FIELDING. The bloody workers, lad. Don't you worry.

WALSH. I hope the floor's been swept then, Harry ... Keep them bloody microbes off my chair ... (*Comes in.*) Toe-caps polished with *equal* brightness, Harry ... (*To* JAGGER) I hate to find one toe-cap brighter than the next.

JAGGER. White laces.

WALSH. White laces.

(HARRY *has set the boots down. Goes out.*)

MORLEY. Where you been, then, Walshy?

WALSH. Been?

FIELDING. Been up in the bloody offices, have you? (*Gestures overhead.*)

WALSH. ... Popped up. Saw the managing director. Inquired about the pitch ... Asked him if they could *heat it up* ... thaw out one or two little bumps I noticed. Sir Frederick's going round now with a box of matches ... applying a drop of heat in all the appropriate places ... Should be nice and soft by the time you run out theer.

FIELDING. Thy's not coming with us, then?

WALSH. Nay, not for bloody me to tell ...

MORLEY. It's up to more important folk than Walsh ...

WALSH. Not more important ... more influential ... (*Watching TREVOR*) Saw you last week with one of your classes, Trev ... Where wa're it, now, then. Let me think ...

TREVOR. Don't know.

WALSH. Quite close to the Municipal Park ... (*Winks to JAGGER.*) By God, some of the girls in that bloody school ... how old are they, Trev?

TREVOR. Fourteen.

WALSH. Fourteen. Could have fooled me, old lad. Could have bloody well fooled me entirely. Old Trevor: guides them over the road, you know ... *by hand.*

FENCHURCH. Where have you been, then, Walshy?

WALSH (*conscious of his carnation quite suddenly, then cigar*). Wedding.

JAGGER. A wedding.

WALSH. Not mine ... Sister-in-law's as a matter of fact.

TREVOR. Sister-in-law?

WALSH. Married to me brother. Just got married a second time. Poor lass ... Had to come away. Just got going ... T'other bloody team's arrived ...

JAGGER. Seen the bus? (*Gestures size, etc.*)

WALSH. Ran over me bloody foot as near as not ... 'Be thy bloody head next, Walsh' ... Said it from the bloody window! ... Said, 'Bloody well get out theer and tell me then' ... gesturing at the field behind.

(*They laugh.*)

Load o' bloody pansies. Tell it at a glance ... Off back theer, as a matter of fact. Going to give a dance ... Thy's invited, Jagger, lad. Kitted out ... Anybody else fancy a dance tonight? Champagne ... (*Belches: holds stomach.*) I'll be bloody ill if I drink owt else ...

LUKE. Thy doesn't want to let old Sandford hear you.

WALSH. Sandford. Sandford ... Drop me from this team, old lad ... I'd gi'e him half o' what I earned.

LUKE. One week's dropped wages and he's round here in a bloody flash.

WALSH. There was some skirt at that bloody wedding, Jagger ... (*To* TREVOR) Steam thy bloody glasses up, old lad.

JAGGER. You're forgetting now ... Trevor here's already married.

WALSH. She coming to watch, then, Trev, old lad?

TREVOR. Don't think so. No.

WALSH. Never comes to watch. His wife ... A university degree ... what wa're it in?

TREVOR. Economics.

WALSH. Economics ... (*To* FENCHURCH) How do you fancy being wed to that?

(FENCHURCH *goes off through bath entrance.*)

JAGGER. Wouldn't mind being married to bloody ought, wouldn't Fenny.

FIELDING. Tarts: should see the bloody ones he has.

(WALSH *has warmed his hands, rubbing.*)

WALSH. Kenny: how's thy wife keeping, then, old lad?

KENDAL. All right.

WALSH (*looking in the parcel*). Bought her a do-it-yourself kit, have you?

KENDAL. Bought it for meself.

MORLEY. Going to put up one or two shelves and cupboards ... and what was that, now?

FIELDING. Fitments.

MORLEY. Fitments.

WALSH. By Christ, you want to be careful theer, old lad ... Ask old Jaggers. He's very keen on fitments.

LUKE. Come on, Walsh. You'll be bloody well still talking theer when it's time to be going out ... Morley: let's have a bloody look, old lad.

(HARRY *has come in with last boots.*

LUKE *has strapped up* PATSY's *shoulder.* PATSY *goes back to finish changing, easing his shoulder.*

MORLEY *comes over to the bench: sits down on it, half-lying, his legs stretched out.* LUKE *examines his ankle: massages with oil; starts to strap it.*

WALSH *boxes with* JAGGER, *then goes over to his peg.*)

WALSH. Sithee, Harry: I hope thy's warmed up Patsy's jersey.

MORLEY. Don't want him catching any colds outside ...

(*They laugh.* PATSY *has taken his jersey over to the fire to warm, holding it in front of him.*)

FENCHURCH (*returning*). Seen that bloody bog?

JAGGER. Won't catch Sir Frederick, now, in theer.

FENCHURCH. Thy wants to get it seen to, Harry.

HARRY. Has been seen to ...

WALSH. Alus go afore I come. Drop off at the bloody peek-a-boo ... now what's it called?

JAGGER. Nude-arama.

WALSH. Best pair o' bogs this side o' town ... Lukey, gi'e us a rub, will you, when I'm ready?

(*Slaps* LUKE's *shoulder then backs up to the fire, elbowing* PATSY *aside.*

LUKE *is strapping* MORLEY's *ankle.*)

MORLEY. God Christ ... go bloody steady. (*Winces.*)

LUKE. Does it hurt?

MORLEY. Too tight.

TREVOR (*watching*). Don't worry. It'll slacken off.

(HARRY *goes off.*)

FIELDING (*calling*). What've you got on this afternoon, then, Jagger?

JAGGER (*looking at his paper*). A fiver.

FIELDING. What's that, then?

JAGGER. Two-thirty.

WALSH. Bloody Albatross.

JAGGER. You what?

WALSH. Seven to one.

JAGGER. You've never.

WALSH. What you got, then?

JAGGER. Little Nell.

(HARRY *has come in with shoulder-pads and tie-ups.*)

WALSH. Little Nell. Tripped over its bloody nose-bag ... now, when wa're it ...

JAGGER. See thy hosses home, old lad.

WALSH. About ten hours after the bloody start.

(*They laugh.*

HARRY *is taking shoulder-pads to* JAGGER, PATSY, FENCHURCH, *dropping the tie-ups for the stockings on the floor, then taking the last of the shoulder-pads to Stringer's peg.* SANDFORD *has come in through the office door. He's a man of about forty, medium build; he wears an overcoat, which is now open, and carries a programme with one or two papers clipped to a pen. Stands for a moment in the door, sniffing. The others notice him but make no comment, almost as if he wasn't there.*)

SANDFORD. I can smell cigar smoke ... (*Looks round.*) Has somebody been smoking bloody cigars?

(WALSH, *back to the fire, is holding his behind him.*)

JAGGER. It's Harry, Mr Sandford. He's got one here.

WALSH. That's not a bloody cigar he's got, old lad.

HARRY. I don't smoke. It's not me. Don't worry.

(*They laugh.*)

MORLEY. Come on, now, Harry. What's thy bloody got?

(HARRY *avoids them as* JAGGER *sets at him. Goes.*)

SANDFORD (*to* WALSH). Is it you, Ken?

WALSH. Me?

FIELDING. Come on, now, bloody Walsh. Own up.

WALSH. Wheer would I get a bloody cigar? (*Puts the cigar in his mouth; approaches* SANDFORD.) I was bloody well stopped five quid this week. Thy never told me ... What's it for, then, Sandy?

SANDFORD. Bloody language.

WALSH. Language?

SANDFORD. Referee's report ... Thy wants to take that out.

WALSH. Out? (*Puffs.*)

(SANDFORD *removes it; carefully stubs it out.*)

SANDFORD. You can have it back when you're bloody well dressed and ready to go home ... If you want the report you can read it in the office.

WALSH. Trevor: exert thy bloody authority, lad. Players' representative. Get up in that office ... (*To* SANDFORD) If there's any been bloody well smoked I shall bloody well charge thee: don't thee bloody worry ... Here, now: let's have it bloody back.

(*Takes it out of* SANDFORD's *pocket, takes* SANDFORD's *pencil, marks the cigar.*

They laugh.)

Warned you. Comes bloody expensive, lad, does that.

(*Puts cigar back. Goes over to bench to change.*)

SANDFORD (*to* MORLEY). How's thy ankle?

MORLEY. All right. Bit stiff.

LUKE (*to* SANDFORD). It'll ease up. Don't worry.

SANDFORD. Patsy: how's thy shoulder?

PATSY. All right. (*Eases it, winces.*) Strapped it up. (*He's now put on a pair of shoulder-pads and is getting ready to pull on his jersey.*)

> (*The others are now in the early stages of getting changed, though* WALSH *has made no progress and doesn't intend to, and* FENCHURCH *and* JAGGER *are reading the racing page of the paper, still dressed.*
>
> HARRY *has come in. Puts down more tie-ups; wanders round picking up pieces from the floor, trying to keep the room tidy. The door from the porch opens and* COPLEY *comes in, limping, barging against the door. He's followed in by* STRINGER. COPLEY *is a stocky, muscular man; simple, good-humoured, straightforward.* STRINGER *is tall and slim; aloof, with little interest in any of the others. He goes straight to his peg and checks his kit; nods briefly to the others as he crosses.* COPLEY *staggers to the fire.*)

COPLEY. God ... It's like a bloody ice-rink out theer ... Christ ... (*Pulls up his trouser-leg.*)

SANDFORD. Are you all right ...

COPLEY. Just look at that.

WALSH. Blood. Mr Sandford ... Mr Sandford. Blood.

COPLEY. You want to get some salt down, Harry ... (*To* SANDFORD) Thy'll have a bloody accident out theer afore tonight.

> (LUKE *crosses over to have a look as well. He and* SANDFORD *gaze down at* COPLEY'S *knee.*)

JAGGER. You all right, then, Stringer?

STRINGER. Aye.

JAGGER. No cuts and bruises.

STRINGER. No.

MORLEY. Get nowt out of Stringer. In't that right, then, Jack?

> (STRINGER *doesn't answer.*)

LUKE. Well, I can't see a mark.

COPLEY. Could'a sworn it wa' bloody cut.

WALSH. Wants to cry off there, Mr Sandford. (*To* COPLEY)
Seen the bloody pitch thy has.

COPLEY. Piss off.

    (*They laugh.*)

SANDFORD (*to* STRINGER). Jack, then. You all right?

STRINGER. Aye.

SANDFORD. Who else is there?

JAGGER. There's bloody Owens: saw him walking up.

FENCHURCH. Stopped to give him a bloody lift.

JAGGER. Said he was warming up.

WALSH. Warming up!

    (*Blows raspberry. They laugh.*)

JAGGER. Silly prick.

SANDFORD (*to* TREVOR). You all right?

TREVOR. Thanks.

SANDFORD. Saw your wife the other night.

TREVOR. So she said.

WALSH. Ay, ay. Ay, ay ...

FENCHURCH. Heard that.

WALSH. Bloody Sandford ...

JAGGER. Coach old Trevor, Sandy, not his wife.

SANDFORD. It was a meeting in the Town Hall, as a matter of
fact.

WALSH. Sithee—Harry: pricked up his bloody ears at that.

FIELDING. What was the meeting about, then, Mr Sandford?

SANDFORD. Just a meeting.

FENCHURCH. Town Hall, now: that's a draughty bloody
place, is that.

    (*They laugh.*

      HARRY *goes out.*)

WALSH. Come on, now, Trevor. What's it all about?

TREVOR. Better ask Mr Sandford.

WALSH. He'll have no idea. Can't spell his name for a bloody start.

> (*They laugh.*
> *The door opens:* ATKINSON *comes in, followed by* SPENCER, CLEGG *and* MOORE.)

ATKINSON. Jesus! Jesus! Lads! Look out! (*Crosses, rubbing hands, to fire.*)

CLEGG. How do. How do. (*Follows him over to the fire, rubbing hands.*) By God, but it's bloody freezing.

> (ATKINSON *is a tall, big-boned man, erect, easy-going. He wears a threequarter-length jacket and flat cap.*
> CLEGG *is a square, stocky, fairly small man, bare-headed, in an overcoat and scarf.*)

MORLEY. Here you are, then, Cleggy. I've gotten the spot just here, if you want to warm your hands.

> (*They laugh.*
> SPENCER *and* MOORE *are much younger men. They come in, nervous, hands in pockets.*)

How's young Billy keeping, then?

SPENCER. All right.

WALSH. Been looking after him, have you, Frank?

MOORE. Be keeping a bloody eye on thee, then, Walsh.

FIELDING. Babes in the bloody wood, are yon.

ATKINSON. Here, then. I hear that the bloody game's been cancelled.

FENCHURCH. Cancelled?

COPLEY. Cancelled?

FENCHURCH. Cancelled?

MORLEY. Here, then, Bryan: who told you that?

ATKINSON. A little bird ...

CLEGG. We were coming up ...

ATKINSON. Came over ...

CLEGG. Whispered in his ear ...

JAGGER. Give over ...

FENCHURCH. Piss off.

COPLEY. Rotten bloody luck.

(ATKINSON *and* SPENCER *laugh*.)

Sit on their bloody backsides up yonder.

MORLEY. Give ought, now, to have me hands in Sir Frederick's bloody pockets ...

WALSH. Dirty bloody sod ...

MORLEY. Warming. Warming ...

WALSH. Come on, now, Sandy. Let it out. (*To* ATKINSON *and* CLEGG) He's been having it off here, now, with Trevor's wife.

TREVOR. All right, Walsh.

LUKE. We've had enough of that.

SANDFORD. The meeting ... was about ... a municipal centre.

JAGGER. A municipal what?

FENCHURCH. Centre.

CLEGG. Centre.

SANDFORD. There you are. I could have telled you.

WALSH. Sir Frederick bloody Thornton.

JAGGER. What?

WALSH. Going to build it ...

SANDFORD. That's right.

WALSH. Votes for it on the bloody council ...

JAGGER. Puts in his tender ...

SANDFORD. He's not even on the council.

CLEGG. All his bloody mates are, though.

SANDFORD. He asked me to attend, as a matter of fact. There are more important things in life than bloody football.

CLEGG. Not today there isn't.

SANDFORD. Not today there, John, you're right ... Now, then, Frank: are you all right?

MOORE. Aye.

SANDFORD. Billy?

SPENCER. Aye. I'm fine.

SANDFORD. Right. Let's have you bloody well stripped off ...
None of you seen Clifford Owens, have you?

MOORE. No.

SPENCER. No ...

SANDFORD (*looking at watch*). By God: he's cutting it bloody
fine.

> (*With varying speeds, they've all started stripping off.*
> HARRY *has distributed all the kit and checked it.*
> LUKE, *after strapping* MORLEY's *ankle, has started strapping*
> STRINGER's *body, wrapping it round and round with tape,*
> STRINGER *standing by the table, arms held out.*)

WALSH (*to* SANDFORD). Here, then ... Get a bit of stuff on ...
Let's see you do some bloody work.

> (WALSH *lies down on the table.*
> LUKE *has put his various medicine bottles from his bag by the*
> *table.*
> SANDFORD *opens one, pours oil onto the palm of his hand*
> *and starts to rub* WALSH *down.*)

KENDAL. Is there anywhere I can keep this, Lukey?

COPLEY. What you got in there, Kenny?

MORLEY. He's bought an electric tool-kit, Luke.

KENDAL. Aye.

FIELDING. Show him it, Kenny. Let him have a look.

KENDAL. Drill ... electric polisher ... sandpaper ... electric saw
... Do owt with that.

> (*Shows it to* COPLEY. FENCHURCH *and* JAGGER *look at it*
> *as well.*)

COPLEY. We better tek it with us yonder, Kenny. Bloody well
mek use o' that today.

> (*They laugh.*)

STRINGER. I've got one of those at home.

KENDAL. Oh?

STRINGER. Aye.

JAGGER (*winking at the others*). Is that right, then, Jack?

STRINGER. Get through a lot o' work wi' that.

JAGGER. Such as?

KENDAL. Bookcases.

JAGGER. Bookcases?

STRINGER. I've made one or two toys, an' all.

KENDAL. Any amount of things.

STRINGER. That's right.

FENCHURCH. Who did you give the toys to, Jack?

STRINGER. What?

JAGGER. Toys.

STRINGER. Neighbour's lad ...

FENCHURCH. Your mother fancies you, then, with one of those?

STRINGER. She doesn't mind.

COPLEY. You ought to get together here with Ken.

ATKINSON. Bloody main stand could do with a few repairs.

(*They laugh.*)

WALSH. Take no bloody notice, Jack ... If thy's got an electric tool-kit, keep it to thysen ... Here, then, Sandy ... lower ... lower!

(*They laugh.*)

By God, I could do that better, I think, mesen.

LUKE. Kenny: leave it with me, old lad. I'll keep an eye on it ... Anybody else now? Fieldy: how's thy eye?

FIELDING. Be all right. A spot of bloody grease.

LUKE (*to* COPLEY). Barry. Let's have your bloody back, old lad. (*Gets out more bandage.*)

(STRINGER *and* FENCHURCH *have put on shoulder-pads.* PATSY, *changed and ready, crosses to the mirror to comb his hair and examine himself; gets out piece of gum, adjusts socks, etc.*

The tin of grease stands on the second table by the wall. After the players have stripped, got on their shorts, they dip in the tin and grease up: legs, arms, shoulders, neck, ears.

The stockings they fasten with the tie-ups HARRY *has dropped on the floor. A slight air of expectation has begun to filter through the room: players rubbing limbs, rubbing hands together, shaking fingers, flexing; tense.*

At this point CROSBY *comes in. He's dressed in a track-suit and enters from the office. A stocky, gnarled figure, late forties or fifties.)*

CROSBY. Come on ... come on ... half ready ... The other team are changed already ...

(*Calls of 'Ah, give over,' 'Get lost,' 'Silly sods,' etc.*)

SANDFORD. Clifford hasn't come yet, Danny.

CROSBY. He's upstairs.

WALSH. Upstairs?

CROSBY (*looking round at the others, on tip-toe, checking those present*). Bill? Billy?

SPENCER (*coming out*). Aye ... I'm here.

CROSBY. Frank?

MOORE. Aye ... I'm here.

CROSBY. On the bench today, then, lads.

(SANDFORD *slaps* WALSH *who gets up to finish changing.* CLEGG *lies down to be massaged.*

LUKE *is strapping* COPLEY's *body with crepe bandage and strips of plaster.*)

WALSH. What's old Owens doing upstairs?

CROSBY. Minding his own bloody business, lad.

CLEGG. Having a word with His Highness, is he?

CROSBY. Patsy. How's your shoulder, lad?

PATSY. All right ... stiff ... (*Eases it up and down in illustration.*)

CROSBY. Fieldy. How's thy eye?

FIELDING. All right.

CROSBY (*suddenly sniffing*). Bloody cigars. Who the hell's been smoking?

LUKE. What?

CROSBY. Not ten minutes afore a bloody match. Come on.

SANDFORD. Oh ... aye ... here ...

CROSBY. You know the bloody rule in here, then, Sandy?

SANDFORD. Yes. Aye. Sorry. Put it out.

LUKE. Is Clifford changed, then, Danny?

CROSBY (*distracted*). What?

LUKE. Need a rub, or strapping up, or ought?

CROSBY. Changed ... He's gotten changed already.

WALSH. Bloody well up theer? By God, then. Bridal bloody suite is that.

CROSBY. Jack? All right, then, are you?

STRINGER. Fine. Aye ... Fine. All right.

CROSBY. Trevor?

TREVOR. All right.

CROSBY. Bloody well hard out theer. When you put 'em down ... knock 'em bleeding hard.

WALSH. And what's Owens bloody well been up to? Arranging a bloody transfer, is he? Or asking for a rise?

(*They laugh.*)

CROSBY (*reading from a list*). Harrison's on the wing this afternoon, Patsy. Alus goes off his left foot, lad.

PATSY. Aye. Right. (*Rubs arms, legs, etc.*)

(*He and* CLEGG *laugh.*)

CROSBY. Scrum-half: new. Barry: when you catch him knock him bloody hard ... Morley?

MORLEY. Aye!

CROSBY. Same with you. Get round. Let him know you're theer ... Same goes for you, Bryan.

ATKINSON. Aye.

CROSBY. Kenny ... Let's see you bloody well go right across.

MORLEY. He's brought something to show you here, Mr Crosby.

CROSBY. What?

MORLEY. Kenny ... Show him your bloody outfit, Ken.

KENDAL (*after a certain hesitation*). Piss off!

(*They laugh.*)

WALSH. You tell him, Kenny, lad. That's right.

JAGGER (*to* KENDAL). Anybody gets in thy road ... (*Smacks his fist against his hand.*)

CLEGG. Ne'er know which is bloody harder. Ground out yon or Kenny's loaf.

(*They laugh.*)

CROSBY. Jack ... Jagger ...

STRINGER. Aye.

JAGGER. Aye ...

CROSBY. Remember what we said. Keep together ... don't be waiting theer for Trev ... If Jack goes right, then you go with him ... Trevor: have you heard that, lad?

TREVOR. Aye.

CROSBY. Use your bloody eyes ... John?

CLEGG. Aye?

CROSBY. Let's have a bit of bloody service, lad.

CLEGG. Cliff been complaining, has he?

CROSBY. Complained about bloody nowt. It's me who's been complaining ... Michaelmas bloody Morley ... when you get that bloody ball ... remember ... don't toss it o'er your bloody head.

WALSH. Who's refereeing then, old lad?

CROSBY. Tallon.

(*Groans and cries.*)

JAGGER. Brought his bloody white stick, then, has he?

FENCHURCH. Got his bloody guide-dog, then?

CROSBY (*undisturbed; to* COPLEY). Watch your putting in near your own line, Barry ... No fists. No bloody feet. Remember ... But when you hit them. Hit them bleeding hard. (*Looks at his watch.*) There's some gum. Walshy: how's thy back?

WALSH. She told me, Danny, she'd never seen ought like it.

(*They laugh.*

CROSBY *drops the packets of chewing-gum on the table.*

*Goes over to talk to the players separately, helping them
with jerseys, boots, etc.*

CLEGG *gets up from the table.* JAGGER *comes to have his leg
massaged by* SANDFORD.

*Faint military music can be heard from outside, and the low
murmur of a crowd.*

FIELDING *comes over to have his eye examined by* LUKE: *he
greases it over.* FIELDING *goes back.*)

CROSBY. Any valuables: let me have 'em ... Any watches,
ear-rings, anklets, cigarettes ...

ALL. Give over. Not bloody likely. Safer to chuck 'em out
o' bloody winder ...

(*Laughter.* CROSBY, LUKE *and* SANDFORD *take valuables
and put them in their pockets.*

OWENS *comes in through the office door, dressed in a
track-suit: bright red with* CITY *on the back; underneath
he's already changed. Medium build, unassuming, bright,
about thirty to thirty-two years old, he's rubbing his hands
together, cheerful. A shy man, perhaps, but now a little
perky.*)

OWENS. All right, then. Are we ready?

JAGGER. Sod off.

FENCHURCH. Give over.

FIELDING. Where you been?

(*Cries and shouts.*

HARRY *has come in with track-suits; gives them to* MOORE
to give out. Goes out.)

OWENS. Told me upstairs you were fit and ready. 'Just need
you, Cliff,' they said, 'to lead them out.'

WALSH. And how's Sir Frederick keeping, then?

OWENS. Asked me to come up a little early.

ALL. Ay, ay. Ay, ay. What's that? Give over.

OWENS. Fill him in on the tactics we intend to use today.

SANDFORD. That's right.

JAGGER. What tactics are those, then, Clifford?

OWENS. Told him one or two hand signals he might look out for, Jag.

(*They laugh.*

The players are picking up gum, tense, flexing. Occasionally one or other goes out through the bath entrance, returning a few moments later.

HARRY *has come in with buckets and bottles of water.*)

Freeze the eyeballs off a copper monkey, boy, today. By God ... (*Goes over to the fire.*) Could do with a bit more coal on, Harry.

SANDFORD. You want to keep away from that bloody fire ...

LUKE. Get cramp if you stand in front of that.

WALSH. Got cramp in one place, Luke, already.

(*They laugh.*)

OWENS. Just watch the ball today, boy. Come floating over like a bloody bird.

WALSH. If you listened to half he said afore a bloody match you'd never get out on that bloody field ... Does it all, you know, inside his bloody head ... How many points do you give us, then, today?

OWENS. Sod all. You'll have to bloody earn 'em, lad.

SANDFORD. That's the bloody way to talk.

CROSBY. Harry ... where's the bloody resin board, old lad?

JAGGER. Let's have a bloody ball, an' all.

(*Roar off of the crowd.*

HARRY *goes off through bath entrance.*)

MORLEY. What bonus are we on today, then, Danny?

CROSBY. All 'bonus thy'll get, lad, you'll find on t'end o' my bloody boot ... Now come on, come on, then, lads. Get busy ...

(CROSBY *is moving amongst the players; now all of them are almost ready: moving over to the mirror, combing hair, straightening collars, tightening boots, chewing, greasing*

*ears, emptying coat pockets of wallets, etc., and handing them
to* CROSBY, SANDFORD *or* LUKE.

TALLON *comes in: a soldierly man of about forty, dressed in
black referee's shorts and shirt.*)

TALLON. You all ready, then, in here?

SANDFORD. Aye. Come in, Mr Tallon. We're all ready, then.
All set.

TALLON. Good day for it.

CROSBY. Aye. Take away a bit o' frost.

TALLON. Right. I'll have a look. Make sure that nobody's
harbouring any weapons.

(*A couple of players laugh.*

TALLON *goes round to each player, examines his hands for
rings, his boots for protruding studs; feels their bodies for
any belts, buckles or protruding pads. He does it quickly;
each player nods in greeting; one or two remain aloof.*

As TALLON *goes round,* HARRY *comes back with the resin
board and two rugby balls; sets the board on the table against
the wall. The players take the balls, feel them, pass them
round, lightly, casual.*

HARRY *moves off, to the bath entrance. He takes the coal-
bucket with him.*

OWENS *takes off his track-suit to several whistles; exchanges
greetings, formally, with* TALLON.

*After each player's been examined he goes over to the resin
board, rubs his hands in the resin, tries the ball.*

SPENCER *and* MOORE *have pulled on red track-suits over
their playing-gear.*)

WALSH. By God, I could do with wekening up ... Lukey:
where's thy bloody phials?

OWENS. Off out tonight, then, Walshy, lad?

WALSH. I am. Two arms, two legs, one head. If you pass the
bloody ball mek sure I'm bloody looking.

(*They laugh.*)

OWENS. Ton o' rock there, Walshy, lad.

WALSH. Second bloody half ... where wa're it? ... 'Walshy! Walshy! Walshy!' ... Passes ... Fastening me bloody boot, what else.

JAGGER. Never looks.

WALSH. Came down like a ton o' bloody lead.

(They laugh.

LUKE has got out a tin of ammonia phials. The players take them, sniff, coughing, flinging back their heads; pass them on to the others. Several of the backs don't bother. WALSH takes his, breathes deeply up either nostril: no effect.)

JAGGER. Shove a can o' coal-gas up theer: wouldn't make much bloody difference.

WALSH. Mr Tallon! Mr Tallon! You haven't inspected me, Mr Tallon!

(They laugh. TALLON comes over, finishing off.)

TALLON. All right, then, Walshy. Let's have a look.

(WALSH, arms raised, submits ponderously to TALLON's inspection.)

WALSH. Count 'em! Count 'em! Don't just bloody look.

(The players laugh.

TALLON finishes, goes over to the door.)

TALLON *(to the room)*. Remember ... keep it clean ... play fair. Have a good game, lads. Play to the whistle.

ALL. Aye. All right.

TALLON. All right, then, lads. I'll see you. May the best team win. Good luck.

(An electric bell rings as TALLON goes out.)

CROSBY. Okay. Five minutes ... Forr'ads. Let's have you ... Billy? Frank? You ready?

MOORE. Aye.

SPENCER. Aye ...

CROSBY. Over here, then. O'd these up.

(CLEGG *raises his arms;* WALSH *and* FIELDING *lock in on either side, casual, not much effort.*

ATKINSON *and* KENDAL *bind together and put their heads in-between the three in front.*)

FIELDING. Ger off. Ger off!

WALSH. A bit lower there, then, Kenny ... Lovely. Beautiful.

CLEGG. Just right.

(*They laugh.*)

CROSBY (*holding the forwards with* SPENCER *and* MOORE).
All right. All right.

(MORLEY *leans on* ATKINSON *and* KENDAL, *then, at* CROSBY's *signal, puts his head between them as they scrum down.*

SPENCER, MOORE *and* CROSBY *are linked together.*)

Let's have a ball ... Cliff ... Barry ... Number four: first clear scrum we get: either side ... (*Takes the ball* SAND-FORD's *brought him.*) Our possession, theirs ... Clifford ... Jagger ... Jack ... that's right.

(*The rest of the players take up positions behind:* COPLEY *immediately behind, then* OWENS, *then* STRINGER, JAGGER *and* PATSY *on one side,* FENCHURCH *on the other.* TREVOR *stands at the back.*)

Right, then? Our ball, then ...

(CROSBY *puts the ball in at* CLEGG's *feet. It's knocked back through the scrum to* COPLEY; *then it's passed, hand to hand, slowly, almost formally, out to* PATSY. *As each player passes it, he falls back; the scrum breaks up, falls back to make a line going back diagonally and ending with* FENCHURCH.)

WALSH. From me. To you ...

(*Laughter.*)

CROSBY. All right. All right.

(*When the ball reaches* PATSY *he passes it back: to* JAGGER, *to* STRINGER, *to* OWENS, *to* COPLEY, *each calling the*

Christian name of the one who hands it on, until it reaches
FENCHURCH.)

WALSH. Run, Fenny! Run!

JAGGER. Go on. Go on! It'll be t'on'y bloody chance thy has.
(*They laugh.*)

WALSH. I never know whether it's bloody speed or fear with
Fenny ... The sound of a pair of bloody feet behind.
(WALSH *catches his backside. They laugh.*)

CROSBY. All right. All right ... Trev: number six.

SANDFORD. Come up on your positions, lads: remember that.
(*They get down as before, though this time* MORLEY
stands out and takes COPLEY's *place.* COPLEY *falls back;*
OWENS *falls back behind him.* JAGGER *and* PATSY *stand on
one side of* OWENS, STRINGER *and* FENCHURCH *on the
other;* TREVOR *stands immediately behind him.*)

CROSBY. Remember: first time up ... Cliff'll give his signal ...
our head; their put in ... doesn't matter ...
(CROSBY *puts the ball in the scrum as before. The forwards
play it back between their feet.* MORLEY *takes it, turns,
passes it back to* COPLEY; COPLEY *passes it back to* OWENS,
OWENS *to* TREVOR, *who runs and mimes a drop kick.*)

JAGGER. Pow!
(HARRY *has come in with coal-bucket.*)

WALSH. Now thy's sure thy won't want thy glasses, Trev?
(*One or two laugh.*)

TREVOR. Just about.

WALSH. If you can't see the posts just give a shout.
(*They laugh.*)

JAGGER. Walshy here'll move 'em up.
(*Laughter.*)

CROSBY. All right. All right. I'll say nowt else ...
(*The door from the office has already opened.*
THORNTON *comes in: tall, dressed in a fur-collared overcoat.
A well-preserved man of about fifty.*)

He's accompanied by MACKENDRICK, *a flush-faced man of about sixty. He wears an overcoat, a scarf and a dark hat.*)

THORNTON. Hope I'm not intruding, Danny.

CROSBY. No, no. Not at all.

THORNTON. Thought I'd have a word.

SANDFORD. That's right.

(SANDFORD *gestures at the players. They move round in a half-circle as* THORNTON *crosses to the centre.*)

THORNTON. Chilly in here. That fire could do with a spot of stoking ...

MACKENDRICK. Harry ... spot o' coal on that.

HARRY. Aye ... Right ... (*Mends the fire.*)

THORNTON. Just to wish you good luck, lads.

PLAYERS. Thanks ...

THORNTON. Fair play, tha knows, has always had its just rewards.

SANDFORD. Aye ...

THORNTON. Go out ... play like I know you can ... there'll not be one man disappointed ... Now, then. Any grunts and groans? Any complaints? No suggestions? (*Looks round.*)

JAGGER. No ...

FENCHURCH. No, Sir Frederick ...

CROSBY. No.

SANDFORD. No, Sir Frederick ...

THORNTON. Right, then ... Mr Mackendrick here'll be in his office, afterwards ... if there's anything you want, just let him know ... Good luck. Play fair. May the best team win ... Cliff. Good luck.

OWENS. Thanks. (*Shakes his hand.*)

MACKENDRICK. Good luck, Cliff ... Good luck, lads ...

PLAYERS. Aye ... Thanks.

THORNTON. Danny.

CROSBY. Aye. Right ... Thanks.

THORNTON. Good luck, lads. See you later.

MACKENDRICK. Danny ...

> (THORNTON *waves, cheerily, and followed by* MAC-
> KENDRICK, *goes.*
> *Silence. Broken finally by* HARRY, *stoking fire.*
> *Crowd roars off; fanfare music; the opposing team runs on.*
> *A bell rings in the room.*)

CROSBY. Right, then, lads ... Cliff? Ought you'd like to add?

OWENS. No. (*Shakes his head.*) Play well, lads ...

PLAYERS. Aye ...

> (*The players, tense, nervous, start to line up prior to going*
> *out.*
> OWENS *takes the ball. He heads the column.*
> *Crowd roars again; loudspeaker, indecipherable, announces*
> *names.*)

WALSH. Harry: make sure that bloody bath is hot.

> (HARRY *looks across. He nods his head.*)

 Towel out, tha knows ... me bloody undies ready ...

CROSBY. Bloody Walsh ... come on. Line up ...

> (*Groans, moans; the players line up behind* OWENS (6).

TREVOR (1)
PATSY (2)
JAGGER (3)
STRINGER (4)
FENCHURCH (5)
COPLEY (7)
WALSH (8)
CLEGG (9)
FIELDING (10)
ATKINSON (11)
KENDAL (12)
MORLEY (13)

SPENCER (15) *and* MOORE (14), *in red track-suits with*
CITY *on the back, are helping* LUKE *and* SANDFORD

*collect the various pieces of equipment: spare kit, track-suits,
sponges, medical bag, spare ball, bucket.*

CROSBY *holds the door.*)

OWENS. Right, then?

ALL. Right. Ready. Let's get off. (*Belches, groans.*)

CROSBY. Good luck, Trev ... good luck, lad ... good luck ...
Good luck, Mic ...

(*He pats each player's back as they move out. Moments
after* OWENS *has gone there's a great roar outside.*

CROSBY *sees the team out, then* SPENCER *and* MOORE *in
track-suits, then* LUKE *and* SANDFORD. *He looks round,
then he goes, closing the door.*

The roar grows louder. Music.

HARRY *comes in, wanders round, looks at the floor for
anything that's been dropped, picks up odd tapes, phials.
Goes to the fire; puts on another piece of coal, stands by
it, still. The crowd roar grows louder.*

Then, slowly, lights and sound fade.)

ACT TWO

The same. About thirty-five minutes later.

The dressing-room is empty, the light switched off. There's a faint glow from the fire.

The roar off of the crowd: rising to a crescendo, fading.

The door from the porch opens. THORNTON *enters, rubbing his hands, followed by* MACKENDRICK.

THORNTON. By God ... (*Gasps, shudders, stumbling round.*) Where's the light switch?

MACKENDRICK. Here ...
 (*Light switched on.*)

THORNTON. How much longer?

MACKENDRICK (*looks at his watch*). Twelve ... fifteen minutes.

THORNTON. Could do with some heating in that bloody box ... either that or we watch it from the office. (*Crosses to the fire and warms his hands.*) Anybody in here, is there?

MACKENDRICK (*looks into the bath entrance*). Don't think so.

THORNTON. Got your flask?

MACKENDRICK. Empty. (*Shows him.*)

THORNTON (*rubbing his hands*). Send up to the office.

MACKENDRICK (*calls through the bath entrance*). Harry! (*Listens: no answer. Goes to office entrance.*)

THORNTON. You go, Mac ... He'll be up in the bloody canteen, that lad. (*Has settled himself in the chair in front of the fire.*)
 (*The crowd roars off.*)

MACKENDRICK. Shan't be a second.

THORNTON. Second cabinet on the right: my office.

MACKENDRICK. Right. (*Hesitates, goes off through office door.*)

(THORNTON *settles himself in front of the fire. Crowd roars off. He raises his head, listens.*

The roar dies. He leans forward, puts piece of coal on the fire.

Door bangs off; stamping of feet; coughs, growls, clearing of throat, sighs.

HARRY *comes in from the bath entrance, muffled up: balaclava, scarf, cap, ex-army overcoat, gloves.*)

HARRY. Oh ... Oh ... (*On the way to the fire sees* THORNTON *and stops, about to go back.*)

THORNTON. That's all right. Come in, Harry ... Taking a breather.

HARRY. I just nipped up to the er ...

THORNTON. That's all right, lad.

HARRY. Cup o' tea.

THORNTON. Pull up a chair, lad. (*Moves his own over fractionally.*)

(HARRY *looks round. There's no other chair. He remains standing where he is.*)

Nowt like a coal fire. Hardly get it anywhere now, you know ... Synthetic bloody fuel. Like these plastic bloody chickens. Get nought that's bloody real no more.

HARRY (*sways from one foot to the other*). Aye ...

THORNTON. Water's hot, then, is it?

HARRY. What?

THORNTON. For the bath.

HARRY. Oh. Aye ... (*Pause.*) I've just stoked up.

THORNTON. I'd have given you a hand myself if I'd have known. By God, that box ... like ice ... (*Takes hands out of his gloves.*) Can't feel a thing.

HARRY. It comes fro' Russia.

THORNTON. What?

HARRY. The cold.

THORNTON. Oh ...

HARRY. East wind ... Blows from the Russian steppes.

THORNTON (*looks up*). More north-west today, I think.

HARRY. Over the Baltic ... Norway ...

> (THORNTON *has raised his hand. The crowd's roar rises; he listens.* HARRY *waits. The roar dies down.*)

THORNTON. Them, I think ... Score today, our lads: they'll raise the bloody roof.

HARRY. I've read it in a book.

THORNTON. What?

HARRY. The Russians ... when the wind blows to the west — spray it with a special gas.

THORNTON. Good God.

HARRY. Without anybody knowing ... Breathe it ... Take it in ... (*Breathes in.*) Slows down your mind ... (*Illustrates with limp arms and hands.*) Stops everybody thinking.

THORNTON. I think our lads've had a drop of that today. By God, I've never seen so many bloody knock-ons ... dropped passes ...

HARRY. I've been a workman all my life.

THORNTON. Oh ... Aye.

HARRY. I used to work in a brickyard afore I came up here.

THORNTON. It's a pity you're not back theer, Harry lad. Bloody bricks we get. Come to pieces in your bloody hand ... Had a house fall down the other day. Know what it was ... ? Bricks ... crumbled up ... Seen nothing like it ... Still ...

HARRY. Knew your place before. Now, there's everybody doing summat ... And nobody doing owt.

THORNTON. Still. Go with it, Harry.

HARRY. What ...

THORNTON. Can't go against your times ... (*Twists round.*) Sent Mac up for a bloody snifter ... Had time to mek the bloody stuff by now.

> (*Crowd's roar rises; reaches crescendo; dies. Booing.*)

Don't know why they do that job, you know. Refereeing.
Must have a stunted mentality, in my view. To go on
with a thing like that.

HARRY. Be all communist afore long.

THORNTON. Aye. (*Pokes fire.*) If the Chinese don't get here
afore.

HARRY. It's happening all the time. In the mind ... Come one
day, they'll just walk in. Take over ... There'll be nobody
strong enough to stop them. They'll have all been brain-
washed ... You can see it happening ...

THORNTON (*calls*). *Mac!* Takes that man a fortnight to
brew a cup of tea. Accountant ... He'll be up there now,
counting the bloody gate receipts. I don't think he's at all
interested in bloody football ... He's never slow, you
know, to tell us when we've made a bloody loss.

    (*Banging outside.* MACKENDRICK *comes in with the bottle.*)
Thought you'd been swigging the bloody bottle.

MACKENDRICK. It wasn't in the cabinet ... I had to get it
from the bar ... Got to sign about four receipts ... Anybody gets a drink in this place they bloody well deserve it,
lad.

THORNTON. No glasses?

MACKENDRICK. Here. (*Takes two from his pocket.*)

THORNTON. Was that a score?

MACKENDRICK. Penalty. Missed.

THORNTON. Them? Or us.

MACKENDRICK. Seven, two. Them. It'll take some pulling
back ... Harry. (*Nods.*)

HARRY. Mr Mackendrick.

MACKENDRICK. Wrapped up for the weather, Harry.

HARRY. Aye.

THORNTON. Been telling me: comes from Russia.

MACKENDRICK. Russia.

THORNTON. Weather.

MACKENDRICK. Weather!

THORNTON. Might have bloody guessed ... (*To* HARRY) Got a cup, then, have you? Try a drop o' this.

HARRY. Don't drink. Thanks all the same, Sir Frederick.

THORNTON. Nay, no bloody titles here, old lad. Freddy six days o' the week. (*To* MACKENDRICK) Sir Frederick to the wife on Sundays.

(THORNTON *and* MACKENDRICK *laugh.*
THORNTON *drinks.*)

By God. Brings back a drop of life, does that.

MACKENDRICK (*drinks, gasps*). Grand ... Lovely.

(*Roar of the crowd, huge, prolonged. They listen.*)

THORNTON. Have a look. Go on. Quick. You've missed it ...

(MACKENDRICK *goes to the porch; disappears outside.*)

How do you think they compare to the old days, Harry?

HARRY. Players? ... Couldn't hold a bloody candle ... In them days they'd do a sixteen-hour shift, *then* come up and lake ... Nowadays: it's all machines ... and they're *still* bloody puffed when they come up o' Sat'days. Run round yon field a couple of times: finished. I've seen 'em laking afore with broken arms, legs broke ... shoulders ... Get a scratch today and they're in here, flat on their bloody backs: iodine, liniment, injections ... If they ever played a real team today they wouldn't last fifteen bloody seconds. That's my view. That's what I think of them today. Everywheer. There's not one of them could hold a candle to the past.

(*Roar and cheering from the crowd.* THORNTON *twists round and listens.*)

They'll wek up one morning and find it's all too late ...

(MACKENDRICK *comes back in.*)

MACKENDRICK. Scored.

THORNTON (*pleased*). Try?

MACKENDRICK. Converted.

THORNTON. Who wa're it?

MACKENDRICK. Morley.

THORNTON. By God. Bloody genius that lad.

(MACKENDRICK *pours a drink*.)

MACKENDRICK. Harry ... ?

HARRY. No thanks, Mr Mackendrick.

THORNTON. Harry here's been enlightening me about the past ... Nothing like the old days, Mac.

HARRY. Aye!

MACKENDRICK. Bloody bunkum.

THORNTON. What's that? (*Laughs: pleased.*)

MACKENDRICK. God Christ ... If this place was like it was twenty years ago—and that's not *too* far back—you wouldn't find me here for a bloody start ... As for fifty years ago. Primeval ... Surprised at thee, then, Harry lad.

HARRY. Aye ... (*Turns away.*)

MACKENDRICK. Have another snifter.

THORNTON. Thanks.

(MACKENDRICK *pours it in*.)

MACKENDRICK (*to* HARRY). I'd have thought thy'd see the difference, lad.

(HARRY *doesn't answer, turns away.*)

Washed i' bloody buckets, then ... et dripping instead o' bloody meat ... urinated by an hedge ... God Christ, bloody houses were nobbut size o' this—seven kiddies, no bloody bath: no bed ... fa'ther out o' work as much as not.

HARRY. There's many as living like that right now!

MACKENDRICK. Aye. And there's a damn sight more as not.

THORNTON. I never knew you had strong feelings, Mac.

MACKENDRICK. About one or two bloody things I have.

(*He pours himself another drink. A faint roar from the crowd.*)

I suppose you're more on his side, then?

THORNTON. Nay, I'm on nobody's bloody side, old lad ... I

had a dream the other night ... I was telling Cliff afore the match ... I came up here to watch a match ... looked over at the tunnel ... know what I saw run out? (*Laughs.*) Bloody robots. (*Laughs again.*) And up in the bloody box were a couple of fellers, just like Danny, flicking bloody switches ... twisting knobs. (*Laughs.*) I laugh now. I wok up in a bloody sweat, I tell you.

> (*Roar from the crowd, applause.*
> *Noises off: boots, shouting.*)

Ay up. Ay up ... (*Springs up.*)

HARRY. You'll wake up one day ... I've telled you ... You'll wek up one day ... You'll find it's bloody well too late. (*Goes off through bath entrance.*)

MACKENDRICK. Aren't you staying to see them in?

THORNTON. I'll pop in in a couple of jiffies, lad ... You stay and give 'em a bloody cheer ... (*Slaps his shoulder.*) Shan't be long ... (*Calls through to bath entrance*) Harry ... I'll pursue that argument another time. (*Nods, winks at* MACKENDRICK, *then goes out smartly through the office door.*)

> (MACKENDRICK *moves the chair from in front of the fire just as the players start to come in.*
> FENCHURCH *comes in first, shaking his hand violently. He's followed by* LUKE *carrying his bag.*)

FENCHURCH. Jesus! Jesus! Bloody hell.

LUKE. Here ... Let's have a look. Come on.

JAGGER (*following him in*). It's nothing ... bloody nothing ...

FENCHURCH. Bloody studs, you see ... Just look!

> (*He holds it up, wincing, as* LUKE *takes it. He groans, cries out, as* LUKE *examines it.*
> *The others are beginning to flood in: stained jerseys, gasping, bruised, exhausted.*
> HARRY *brings in two bottles of water; the players take swigs from them and spit out into* LUKE'S *bucket which* MOORE *has carried in.*)

LUKE. Nothing broken. It'll be all right.

SANDFORD. Do you want me to bind it for you, then?

FENCHURCH. No, no. No ... No.

JAGGER. Can't hold the ball with a bandage on.

COPLEY. Have you off to hospital, Fenny, lad. Match o'er: don't worry. Operation. Have it off. Not going to have you troubled, lad, by that.

FENCHURCH. Sod off.

(*They laugh.*
WALSH, *groaning, collapses on the bench.*)

WALSH. I'm done. I'm finished. I shall never walk again. Sandy ... Bring us a cup o' tea, old lad.

SANDFORD. You'll have a cup o' bloody nothing. Have a swab at that.

(*Splashes a cold sponge in* WALSH's *face and round his neck.* WALSH *splutters, groans; finally wipes his face and neck.* CROSBY *has come in with the remainder of the players.*)

CROSBY. Well done. Well done. Start putting on the pressure in the second half.

JAGGER. Pressure?

FENCHURCH. Pressure ...

JAGGER. That *was* the bloody pressure. Anything from now on is strictly left-overs, Danny lad ... I'm knackered. Look at that. Use hammers on that bloody pitch out theer ...

MACKENDRICK. Well done, then, lads. Well done.

FIELDING. You watching in here, then, Mr Mackendrick, are you?

MACKENDRICK. Out there, old lad. I wouldn't miss it.

CLEGG. See that last try ... ?

MACKENDRICK. ... Go down in the bloody book will that.

SANDFORD. Keep moving. Don't sit still.

CROSBY. That's right. Keep moving ... Walshy. Get up off your arse.

(WALSH *takes no notice, drinks from bottle.*)

Bryan? How's your ankle?

ATKINSON. All right. I think. It'll be all right.

FIELDING. Just look at that. Can't move me bloody finger.

CROSBY. Keep away from that bloody fire ... Sandy: keep 'em moving round, old lad.

(LUKE *and* SANDFORD *are examining individual players.* MOORE *and* SPENCER *are helping out with laces, tightening boots, handing round the bottles.*)

Any new jerseys? Any new shorts?

(*A couple of players call:* 'No ... No thanks.')

COPLEY. Over here, lads ... I'll have one ...

CROSBY. Trevor? How's your hands?

TREVOR. All right. (*Holds them up, freezing.*)

CROSBY. Keep moving, lad. Keep shifting.

TREVOR. Be all right. (*He is quite cold: hands and arms folded, then rubbing himself, trying to get warm.*)

CROSBY. Barry?

COPLEY. No. No. All right.

STRINGER. Bloody cold out theer. I read it i' the paper. Seven degrees of frost last night.

SANDFORD. Bloody well move faster, lad.

STRINGER. I am moving faster. It bloody catches up with you.

KENDAL. Ears, look. Can't bloody feel 'em.

JAGGER. Still on, then, Kenny, are they?

KENDAL. Aye. Think so. Better have a look. (*Crosses to mirror.*)

(*They're gradually getting over their first shock of entering the warmer room: sucking sponges, rinsing their mouths from the bottle, rubbing on more grease, adjusting boot-fastenings and socks. Those on the move move quite slowly, tired, panting.*)

FENCHURCH. What's the bloody score, then, lads?

FIELDING. Never notices on the bloody wing.

COPLEY. Picking his bloody nose.

FIELDING. Talking to the crowd.

MOORE. Seven–seven, Fenny, lad.

CLEGG (*to* MOORE *and* SPENCER). Bloody cold, you lads, out
theer.

SPENCER. Freezing.

MOORE. Fro'zen.

WALSH. Mr Crosby, sir.

CROSBY. What's that?

WALSH. Isn't it time we had a substitute out theer. These lads
are dying to get on and lake.

CROSBY. They'll get on in *my* bloody time, not yours. Now
get up. Come on. Get moving. I've told thee, Walsh,
before.

> (PATSY *is sitting down, having his leg 'stretched' by* SAND-
> FORD: PATSY's *leg stretched out before him,* SANDFORD
> *pressing back the toe of his boot.*)

(*To* PATSY) You all right?

PATSY. Bloody cramp. God ... (*Groans, winces.*)

WALSH. Another bloody fairy ...

CLEGG. Go on. Give him summat, Sandy ...

WALSH. Here. Let's have a bloody hold.

PATSY. S'all right. S'all right. S'all right. (*Springs up, flexes leg.*)

WALSH. S'all in the bloody mind, tha knows ... Here. Have
a look at my bloody back, then, will you?

> (SANDFORD *lifts his jersey at the back.*)

SANDFORD. Got a cut.

WALSH. How many stitches?

SANDFORD. Twenty or thi'ty. Can't be sure.

WALSH. Go on. Go on. Get shut ...

> (*Players laugh.*)

Fieldy: have a bloody look, old lad.

> (FIELDING *lifts* WALSH's *shirt and looks; slaps* WALSH's
> *back.* WALSH *goes over to the bucket, gets sponge, squeezes
> it down his back.*)

LUKE (*calling, with liniment, etc.*). Any more for any more?

JAGGER. Any bruises, cuts, concussions, fractures ...

COPLEY. One down here you could have a look at, Lukey.
(*Opens shorts: players laugh.*

THORNTON *has come in from the porch entrance.*)

THORNTON. Well played, lads. Well done ... Morley:
bloody fine try was that, young man.

MORLEY. Thank you, sir.

THORNTON (*to* CROSBY). Not often we see a run like that ...

CROSBY. No. That's right.

THORNTON. Good kick, Clifford. Good kick was that.

OWENS. Aye. (*During this period he has been out, through the
bath entrance, to wash his face and hands, almost like an
office worker set for home. Has come in now, drying face and
hands.*)

THORNTON. Trevor: dropped goal: a bloody picture.

TREVOR. Thanks.

THORNTON. How're your hands?

TREVOR. Frozen.

THORNTON. Saw you catch that ball: didn't know you'd got
it. (*Laughs.*)

TREVOR. Numb ... (*Laughs: rubs his hands.*)

THORNTON. Kenny.

(KENDAL *nods.*)

WALSH. Sir Frederick: how d'you think I managed, then?

THORNTON. Like a dream, Walshy. Like a dream.

JAGGER. Bloody nightmare, I should think, more likely.

(*The players laugh.*)

CROSBY. He could bloody well do wi' wekening up ...
There's half on you asleep out yon ... Fieldy ... Bryan ...
move across. Go with it ... It's no good waiting till they
come ... Bloody hell ... Trevor theer: he's covering all
that side ... Colin: *bloody interceptions*: it's no good going
in, lad, every time ... they'll be bloody well waiting for it

soon ... three times that *I* saw, Jack here had to take your man ...

WALSH. Billy?

SPENCER. Aye?

WALSH. Go eavesdrop at their door, old lad.

SPENCER (*laughs*). Aye!

WALSH. Find out all their plans.

(*They laugh.*)

CROSBY. As for bloody Walsh. A boot up the backside wouldn't go astray. I'll swear at times thy's running bloody backwards, lad.

WALSH. I am. I bloody am ... Too bloody cold today for running forr'ad.

(*They laugh.* WALSH *claps his cold hands either side of* SANDFORD's *face.* SANDFORD, *saying, 'Gerroff,' steps back.*

CROSBY *goes into private, whispered conversation with individual players.*)

MACKENDRICK. How're you feeling, Trevor, lad?

TREVOR. All right.

MACKENDRICK. Cut your ear there, lad ... (*Examines it.*) Not bad ... Sandy? ... Put a spot o' grease on that.

(SANDFORD *comes across.* TREVOR *winces.*)

Take care of the professional men, you know. These lot — (*gestures round*) bloody ten a penny.

(*Jeers.* MACKENDRICK *takes no notice.*)

Have you ever tried playing i' mittens, then?

TREVOR. No.

MACKENDRICK. Some players do, you know. Particularly in your position ... In the amateur game, you know ... Still. No need to tell you that, I'm sure.

TREVOR. Aye ... I'll ... just pop off in theer. Shan't be a minute.

MACKENDRICK. Aye ... aye! (*Slaps his back.*)

(TREVOR *goes off through bath entrance.*
Electric bell rings.)

CROSBY. All right. All right. I'm saying no more. Quick score
at the beginning: be all right ... Cliff. At the fourth tackle,
Cliff, try number five. (*To the rest*) Have you got that?

PLAYERS. Aye.

CROSBY. Be bloody ready ... Patsy?

PATSY. Aye.

CROSBY. Fenny?

FENCHURCH. Aye. All right.

CROSBY. Get *up* there! Bloody well stuck in.

FENCHURCH. Aye.

CROSBY. Bryan ...

ATKINSON. Aye.

CROSBY. Harder. *Harder* ... Kenny?

KENDAL. Aye?

CROSBY. *Bang 'em!* You're not tucking the buggers up in
bed.

KENDAL. Aye.

CROSBY. Let's bloody well see it, then ... I want to *hear* those
sods go down ... I want to feel that bloody stand start
shaking ... Johnny: have you got that, lad?

CLEGG. Aye.

CROSBY. Good possession ... If their hooker causes any
trouble let *Walshy* bang his head.

WALSH. I already have done, lad. Don't worry.

(*They laugh.*)

CROSBY. Cliff? Ought you want to add?

OWENS. No. No. Mark your man. Don't wait for somebody
else to take him.

(*Roar of the crowd off.*
They look to THORNTON, *who's been going round to
individual players, nodding formally, advising, giving praise.*
TREVOR *comes back in.*)

THORNTON. Good luck, lads. Keep at it. Don't let the pressure drop. Remember: it's thy advantage second half. Away from home, for them: it always tells.

CROSBY. Aye ...

THORNTON. Good luck.

PLAYERS (*uninterested*). Aye ... thanks ...

THORNTON. Go up and shake them lads out o' the bloody boardroom, Mac ... They'll watch the match from up theer if they get half a chance ...

MACKENDRICK. Aye ... Good luck, lads. Don't let up.

PLAYERS. No ... Aye ...

MACKENDRICK. See you after. Keep it up. Well done ... (*On his way out*) Well done ... Well done, Trev. (*Slaps* TREVOR's *back as he goes.*)

(THORNTON *smiles round, nods at* CROSBY, *then follows* MACKENDRICK *out.*)

CROSBY. Watch Tallon near your line.

PLAYERS (*moving off*). Aye ... aye.

OWENS. All right, then, lads. We're off ...

CROSBY. Barry ...

COPLEY (*on move out, hands clenched*). Aye.

CROSBY. Are you listening ...

COPLEY. Aye. Aye. Don't worry.

CROSBY. Right, then ... Fieldy: how's thy eye?

FIELDING. All right.

CROSBY. It's bloody well opened. (*To* LUKE) Look.

FIELDING. Aye. Aye. It'll be all right. (*Dismisses it, goes.*)

CROSBY. Remember ... Fenny ... Patsy ...

PLAYERS (*filing out*). Aye ... aye ... All right.

(*They go.* CROSBY *nods to each one at the door, advising, slapping backs.*

LUKE *and* SANDFORD *start collecting the kit to take out.* MOORE *and* SPENCER *still in their track-suits, pick up a bucket and a bag between them, waiting to follow* CROSBY

out after the players have gone.
Roar of the crowd off as the players go out.
HARRY *has come in to collect the towels, tapes, bottles, etc.,*
left lying around.)

LUKE (*packing his bag*). See you out theer, Danny ...

CROSBY. Right ... Frank ... Billy?

SPENCER. Aye.

CROSBY. Right ...

> (*They go.*
>
> SANDFORD, LUKE *and* HARRY *are left.*)

LUKE. Well, then, Harry ... How's t'a barn?

HARRY. All right.

LUKE. Been warming up in here, then, have you?

HARRY. I bloody haven't.

SANDFORD (*warming hands at fire*). I'm not so sure I wouldn't
prefer it here meself.

> (*Crowd roars off.*)

Ay up. Ay up. That's it. We're off. (*He zips up his track-*
suit top, pulls his scarf round his neck.)

LUKE. Be with you in a sec, old lad.

SANDFORD. All right. (*Goes.*)

> (LUKE *and* HARRY *work in silence for a moment.*)

LUKE. Do you ever back on matches, Harry?

HARRY. What?

LUKE. Bookies.

HARRY. I don't.

LUKE. Nor 'osses?

HARRY. Nowt.

LUKE. What do you do in your spare time, then?

HARRY. I don't have any spare time.

LUKE. What do you do when you're not up here, then?

HARRY. I'm alus up here.

LUKE. Sleep up here, then, do you?

> (*Roar off.* LUKE *raises head, listens: packs his bag.*)

135

HARRY. I sleep at home.

LUKE. Where's home?

HARRY. Home's in our house. That's where home is.

LUKE. A damn good place to have it, lad.

HARRY. Bloody keep it theer, an' all.

LUKE. Thornton here, then, was he: first half?

HARRY. Aye.

LUKE. Crafty ... He'll never put himself out, you know, unduly.

HARRY. And Mackendrick.

LUKE. Where one goes his shadder follows.

HARRY. It's his place ... He can do what he likes ... He can sit in here the whole afternoon if he bloody likes.

LUKE. I suppose he can.
    (*Roar off.*)
F'un him up here, you know, one night.

HARRY. What's that?

LUKE. Sir Frederick ... Came back one night ... Left me tackle ... Saw a light up in the stand ... Saw him sitting theer. Alone. Crouched up. Like that.

HARRY. His stand. Can sit theer when he likes.

LUKE. Ten o'clock at night.

HARRY. Ten o'clock i' the bloody morning. Any time he likes.
    (LUKE *fastens his bag.*)

LUKE. Is it true, then, what they say?

HARRY. What's that?

LUKE. Thy's never watched a match.

HARRY. Never.

LUKE. Why's that?

HARRY. My job's in here. Thy job's out yonder.

LUKE. They ought to set thee on a pair o' bloody rails. (*Goes over to the door.*)

HARRY. Most jobs you get: they're bloody nowt ...
    (LUKE *pauses at the door.*)
Don't know what they work for ...

LUKE. What?

HARRY. Not any more. Not like it was ...

LUKE. Well, thy works for the bloody club.

HARRY. I work for Sir Frederick, lad: for nob'dy else.

(LUKE *looks across at him.*)

I mun run the bloody bath. (*He goes.*)

(LUKE *watches from the door, then looks round for anything he's forgotten. Comes back in, gets scissors. Sound off, from the bath entrance, of running water. He crosses to the door and goes.*

HARRY *comes back a moment later. He gets towels from the basket and lays them out on the bench, by each peg. At one point there's a roar and booing from the crowd, trumpets, rattles. It dies away to a fainter moan.* HARRY *turns on the Tannoy.*)

TANNOY (*accompanied by roaring of the crowd*). ' ... Copley ... Clegg ... Morley ... Fenchurch! ... inside ... passes ... Jagger ... Stringer ... Tackled. Fourth tackle. Scrum down. Walsh ... Fielding ... Walsh having words with his opposite number! Getting down. The scrum is just inside United's half ... almost ten yards in from the opposite touch ... put in ... some rough play inside that scrum ... Referee Tallon's blown up ... free kick ... no ... scrum down ... not satisfied with the tunnel ... ball in ... Walsh's head is up ... (*Laughter.*) There's some rough business inside that scrum ... my goodness! ... Ball comes out ... Morley ... Copley ... Owens ... Owens to Trevor ... *Trevor is going to drop a goal* ... too late ... He's left it far too late ... They've tried that once before ... Kendal ... '

(HARRY *switches the Tannoy off.*

Great roar outside.

HARRY *has crossed to the fire; more coal; pokes it. Goes off to the bath entrance.*

A moment later the door from the porch opens: SANDFORD
comes in.)

SANDFORD (*calling*). Luke? ... Luke?

HARRY (*re-emerging*). He's just gone ...

SANDFORD. Oh, Christ ...

HARRY. Anything up?

SANDFORD. Gone through the bloody tunnel ... Missed him.
    (*Roar increasing off.* SANDFORD *hurries out.* HARRY
    *stands in the centre of the room waiting. Baying of the crowd.
    A few moments later, voices off:* 'Hold the bloody door.'
    'This side.' 'This side.' 'Take his shoulder.' 'I'm all right.
    I'm all right. Don't worry.'
    The door opens: KENDAL *comes in, supported by* CROSBY
    and MOORE.)

KENDAL. It's all right ... It's bloody nowt ... Where is it?
    Where's he put it?

CROSBY. Get him down ... no, over here. Over here. On this.
    (*They take him to the massage table.*)

KENDAL. Now, don't worry. Don't worry ... Don't worry.
    I'll be all right ...

MOORE. S'all right, Kenny, lad. All right.

CROSBY. Doesn't know where he is ... Now, come on. Lie
    down, Kenny, lad. Lie down.

KENDAL. S'all right. S'all right.

CROSBY. Where's bloody Lukey ... Frank: get us a bloody
    sponge. Harry: o'd him down.
    (CROSBY *tries to hold* KENDAL *down: having been laid on
    the table, he keeps trying to sit up.*
    HARRY *comes over to the table. He watches, but doesn't help.*)

HARRY (*to* MOORE). Over theer ... that bucket.
    (MOORE *goes off to the bath entrance.*)

CROSBY. Come on, Kenny. Come on ... Lie down, lad.

KENDAL. S'all right ... S'all right ... I'll go back on.

CROSBY. You'll go nowhere, lad ... Come on ... Come on,

then, Kenny, lad. Lie still. I want to bloody look ...
Come on ...

(*The door opens:* SANDFORD *comes in, followed by* LUKE
with his bag.)

LUKE. How is he? ... Don't move him ... Let's have a look.

CROSBY. Where's thy been? ... On thy bloody holidays,
hast tha?

LUKE. Let's have a look ... I was coming up ...

CROSBY. Nose ...

(*Steps back,* SANDFORD *takes hold.*

CROSBY *gets a towel, wipes his hands.*)

KENDAL. Nose ... It's me nose, Lukey ...

LUKE. Lie still, lad, now. Lie still.

KENDAL. I can't bloody see, Lukey ...

LUKE. Now just lie still ... That's it ... That's right ...

(MOORE *has brought the sponge.*)

Get some clean water, lad. That's no good ...

SANDFORD. Here ... here ... I'll get it. (*To* MOORE) Come
round here. Get o'd o' this.

(MOORE *takes* SANDFORD's *place.*

SANDFORD *goes off to bath entrance.*

LUKE *has looked at* KENDAL's *wound.* KENDAL's *face is
covered in blood.* LUKE *sponges round his cheeks and mouth,
then stoops down to his bag, gets out cotton-wool.* KENDAL
is still trying to get up.)

MOORE. It's all right, Kenny, lad. All right.

KENDAL. Can't see ...

LUKE. Now just keep your eyes closed, lad ... Harry: can you
get a towel?

MOORE. I don't think Ken wa' even looking ... His bloody
head came down ... bloody boot came up ...

(HARRY *has passed over a towel.* MOORE *takes it.*)

LUKE. Shove it underneath his head ... Kenny? Keep your
head still, lad.

(SANDFORD *has brought in a bowl of water.*

LUKE *wipes away the blood with cotton-wool, examines the damage.* SANDFORD *pours a drop of disinfectant from the bottle into the bowl of water.* LUKE *dips in the cotton-wool, wipes* KENDAL'*s nose.*

CROSBY, *not really interested, having wiped the blood from his hands and his track-suit, looks on impatiently over* LUKE'*s back.*)

KENDAL. A bit o' plaster: I'll go back on.

LUKE. Nay, lad. The game's over for you today.

KENDAL. I'll be all right ... I'll get back on ...

CROSBY. He's off, then, is he?

LUKE. Aye ...

SANDFORD. Aye ... (*Gestures up.*) I'll take him up.

CROSBY. Right ... Frank. Come on. Not have you hanging about down here.

SANDFORD. Who you sending on?

CROSBY (*looks round; to* FRANK). Do you think you can manage, then, out theer?

MOORE. Aye!

CROSBY. Come on, then. Let's have you up.

(MOORE, *quickly, jubilantly, strips off his track-suit.*)

Lukey ...

LUKE. Aye.

CROSBY. As soon as you've done. Let's have you up ... Kenny: do you hear that, lad?

KENDAL (*half-rising*). Aye ...

CROSBY. Well done, lad ... Just do as Lukey says ...

KENDAL. Aye ...

CROSBY (*to* MOORE). Come on. Come on. Not ready yet ...

(*Has gone to the door.* MOORE *scrambles out of the suit.* CROSBY *goes.* MOORE, *flexing his legs, pulling down his jersey, etc., hesitates.*

He goes.)

LUKE. Theer, then, Kenny ...

> (LUKE *has finished washing the wound and has dressed it*
> *with a plaster. He now helps* KENDAL *up with* SANDFORD'S
> *assistance.*)

If there's ought you want, just give a shout.

KENDAL. There's me electric tool-kit, Luke ...

LUKE. I've got it here, old lad ... Thy'll be all right ...

KENDAL. Fifteen quid that cost ... just o'er ...

SANDFORD. Here, then. Come on ... Let's have you in the
bath. Come on. Come on, now ... It wouldn't do you
much good if you dropped it in ...

> (KENDAL *has got up from the table.*
>
> SANDFORD *helps him over to the bath entrance.*
>
> LUKE *finishes packing his bag.*
>
> *The porch door opens:* MACKENDRICK *comes in.*)

MACKENDRICK. How is he?

LUKE. He'll be all right.

MACKENDRICK. Too bloody old, you know. If I've said it
once, I've said it ...

LUKE. Aye.

MACKENDRICK (*calls through*). How're you feeling, Kenny, lad.

KENDAL (*off*). All right.

MACKENDRICK. All right, Sandy?

SANDFORD (*off*). Aye. I'll have him in the bath.

MACKENDRICK. Taking him up ... ? (*Gestures up.*)

SANDFORD (*off*). Aye.

MACKENDRICK. I'll see about a car.

SANDFORD (*off*). Shan't be long.

MACKENDRICK (*to* LUKE). I'll go up to the office.

LUKE. Tool-kit. (*Shows him.*)

> (MACKENDRICK *looks in.*)

Bloody shelves ...

MACKENDRICK. Poor old Kenny ...

LUKE. Bloody wife.

MACKENDRICK. Like that, then, is it?

LUKE. Been round half the teams i' the bloody league ... one time or another. (*Packs his bag and goes over to the bath entrance.*) I'll get on up, then, Sandy, lad.

SANDFORD (*off*). Aye.

LUKE. Be all right, then, Kenny, lad?

KENDAL (*off*). Aye ...

    (LUKE *collects his bag.*)

LUKE. You'll see about a taxi, then?

MACKENDRICK. Aye.

    (*Roar off.*
    They lift their heads.)

LUKE. Another score.

MACKENDRICK (*gestures at bath entrance*). I'll get up and tell Sir Freddy, then.

    (MACKENDRICK *goes out by the office entrance,* LUKE *by the porch.*

    HARRY *is left alone. He's cleared up the bits of cotton-wool and lint; he collects the used towels.*

    SANDFORD *brings in* KENDAL's *used kit, drops it on the floor. Gets a towel.*)

SANDFORD. Take care of that, then, Harry ...

HARRY. Aye.

SANDFORD. Them his clothes?

HARRY. Aye.

    (SANDFORD *gets them down. He goes to the bath entrance with the towel.*)

SANDFORD (*off*). Come on, then, Kenny ... Let's have you out.

    (HARRY *retidies the massage table, resetting the head-rest which, for* KENDAL's *sake, has been lowered.*

    A moment later KENDAL's *led in with a towel round him.*)

    Can you see ought?

KENDAL. Bloody dots ...

SANDFORD. No, this way, lad, then. Over here.

KENDAL. Is the game over, Sandy ... ?

SANDFORD. Just about. Sit theer. I'll get you dried ...

> (KENDAL *sits on the bench.* SANDFORD *dries his legs and feet, then he dries his head.*
> HARRY *looks on.*)

Pass his shirt, then, will you?

> (HARRY *passes* KENDAL'*s shirt and vest over.*
> *There's a roaring of the crowd off.*)

KENDAL. Are we winning?

SANDFORD. Come on, then ... Get your head in this.

KENDAL. Can't remember ...

> (SANDFORD *pulls his vest and shirt round his head.* KENDAL *dazedly pushes in his arms.*)

HARRY. What's he done?

SANDFORD. Nose.

HARRY. Bro'k it, has he?

SANDFORD. Aye.

KENDAL. Remember shopping.

SANDFORD. We've got it here, old lad. Don't worry.

KENDAL. Bloody fifteen quid ...

HARRY. F'ust one this year.

SANDFORD. Come on, then, lad ... Let's have you up.

> (SANDFORD *helps* KENDAL *to his feet.*
> HARRY *watches, hands in pockets.*
> KENDAL *leans on* SANDFORD. SANDFORD *pulls on his trousers.*)

HARRY. Three collar-bones we had one week ... Two o' theirs ... the last un ours ... Ankle ... Bloody thigh-bone, once ... Red hair ... He never played again.

SANDFORD (*to* KENDAL). Come on, come on, then, lad ... o'd up.

KENDAL. Steam-boilers, lad ... Bang 'em in ... Seen nothing like it. Row o' rivets ... Christ ... Can hardly see ought ... Sandy?

SANDFORD. Here, old lad. Now just hold tight ... Come on.

Come on, now. Let's have you out of here ... (*To*
HARRY) Will you see if Mr Mackendrick's got that car? ...
(*As* HARRY *goes*) Harry: can you find me coat as well?
> (HARRY *goes, stiffly, leaving by office entry.*
> *Roar off, rises to peak, applause, bugles, rattles.*
> KENDAL *turns towards sound, as if to go.*)

Nay, lad: can't go with nothing on your feet.
> (*Sits* KENDAL *down, puts on his socks and shoes.*)

KENDAL (*dazed*). Started lakin' here when I wa' fifteen, tha
knows ... Intermediates ... Then I went out, on loan,
to one of these bloody colliery teams ... bring 'em up at
the bloody weekend in bloody buckets ... play a game o'
bloody football...booze all Sunday...back down at the coal-
face Monday ... Seen nothing like it. Better ring my wife.

SANDFORD. What?

KENDAL. She won't know.

SANDFORD. She's not here today, then?

KENDAL. No ...

SANDFORD. I'll see about it, lad. Don't worry.

KENDAL. If I'm bloody kept in, or ought ...

SANDFORD. Aye. It'll be all right.

KENDAL. The woman next door has got a phone.

SANDFORD. Aye. I'll see about it, lad. All right. (*Gets up.*)
Let's have your coat on. Won't bother with your tie.
> (KENDAL *stands.* SANDFORD *helps him into his raincoat.*)

KENDAL. I wa' going to get a new un ... until I bought this
drill ...

SANDFORD. Aye! (*Laughs.*)

KENDAL. Start saving up again ...

SANDFORD. That's right.
> (HARRY *comes in through the office door. He brings in*
> SANDFORD's *overcoat.*)

HARRY. There's one outside already.

SANDFORD. Good.

HARRY (*watches* SANDFORD'*s efforts*). Alus one or two out theer.

SANDFORD. Yeh.

HARRY. Sat'days.

SANDFORD. Could alus use Sir Frederick's, then.

HARRY. Aye ...

SANDFORD. How're you feeling, lad?

KENDAL. All right.

SANDFORD. Come on, then, lad ... Just fasten this ...

(KENDAL *holds his head up so* SANDFORD *can fasten on the dressing Luke has left. It covers his nose and is fastened with plaster to his cheeks.*)

KENDAL. Is it broke?

SANDFORD. There's a bit of a gash, old lad.

KENDAL. Had it broken once before ...

SANDFORD. Can you manage to the car? (*Collects his coat.*)

KENDAL. Wheer is it, then? (*Turns either way.*)

SANDFORD. Here it is, old lad ... (*Hands him his parcel.*)

KENDAL. Have to get some glasses ... hardly see ...

SANDFORD (*to* HARRY). Looks like bloody Genghis Khan ... Come on, then, Kenny ... Lean on me. (*To* HARRY) Still got me bloody boots on ... I'll get them in the office ... See you, lad.

(HARRY *watches them go.*

He waits. Then he picks up the used towel, takes it off to dump inside the bath entrance.

He comes back, looks round, switches on the Tannoy.)

TANNOY. (*Crowd roar.*) ' ... to Walsh ... reaches the twenty-five ... goes down ... plays back ... (*Roar.*) ... Comes to Clegg to Atkinson ... Atkinson to the substitute Moore ... Moore in now, crashes his way through ... goes down ... Walsh comes up ... out to Owens ... Owens through ... dummies ... beautiful move ... to Stringer, Stringer out to Patsy ... Patsy out to Trevor, who's come up on the wing ... kicks ... Copley ... Fenchurch ... Fielding ... *Morley* ...

(*Roar.*) Ball bounces into touch ... scrum ... (*Pause, dull roar.*) Growing dark now ... ball goes in, comes out, Tallon blows ... free kick ... scrum infringement ... one or two tired figures there ... can see the steam, now, rising from the backs ... Trevor's running up and down, blowing in his hands ... Kick ... good kick ... (*Crowd roar.*) Finds touch beyond the twenty-five ... (*Crowd roar.*)

(HARRY *sits, listening.*
Fade: sound and light.)

ACT THREE

The same.

Noise: shouting, singing, screeching, cries off. The Tannoy is playing music.

PATSY, *a towel round his waist, is drying himself with a second towel, standing by his clothes. He does it with the same care with which he prepared himself for the match.*

HARRY *is picking up the mass of discarded shorts, jerseys, jock-straps, and putting them on the basket.*

A pile of towels stands on the rubbing-down table.

SPENCER *is half-dressed in trousers and shirt, combing his wet hair in the mirror.*

CROSBY *is going round checking boots, putting pairs together by the massage table to be collected up.*

CROSBY (*to* SPENCER). Up there waiting for you, is she, Billy?

SPENCER. Aye. All being well. (*Combing in mirror.*) Bloody expecting me to play today, an' all.

CROSBY. Ne'er mind. Next week: might be in luck.

SPENCER. Bloody away next week!

CROSBY. Maybe she'll have to bloody travel.

SPENCER. Not the travelling kind, you know.

CROSBY. Can't win 'em all, old lad. Don't worry ... (*Calls*) Come on. Let's have you out o' there ... (*Switches off Tannoy, moves on. To* PATSY) How're you feeling, then, old lad?

PATSY. All right. Bit stiff. (*Winces: eases arm.*)

CROSBY. How's thy shoulder?

PATSY. All right.

CROSBY. Bloody lovely try. Worth any amount o' bloody knocks is that.

PATSY. Aye.

CROSBY. Couple more next week ... should be all right.

PATSY. Aye. (*Doesn't respond, drying himself, turns to check his clothes.*)

(JAGGER *comes bursting in from the bath.*)

JAGGER. Dirty bugger ... dirty sod ... Danny: go bloody stop him. (*Snatches towel, rubs his hair vigorously.*) Walshy— pittling in the bloody bath.

SPENCER (*calling through*). Thy'll have to disinfect that bloody water ... (*Laughing.*)

WALSH (*off*). This *is* disinfectant, lad.

CROSBY. Come on, Walshy: let's have you out ...

(*Takes a towel and dries* JAGGER's *back.*)

JAGGER. Dirty bugger: dirty sod!

WALSH (*off*). Come on, Jagger. You could do with a bloody wash.

JAGGER. Not in that, you dirty sod ... Set bloody Patsy onto you, if you don't watch out.

(*Water comes in from the bath.*)

Dirty! Dirty! ...

(*Dances out of the way: laughter and shouting off.*)

CROSBY. Come on, Trevor. Teach 'em one or two manners, then ... Bloody college-man ... going to go away disgusted with all you bloody working lads.

(*Another jet of water.* CROSBY *lurches out of the way.*)

Bloody well be in there if you don't watch out.

(*Jeers, cries.*)

COPLEY (*off*). Too bloody old!

CLEGG (*off*). Come on, Danny. Show us what you've got.

CROSBY. Got summat here that'll bloody well surprise you, lad ...

(*Laughter, cries.*)

And you!

148

(*Laughter off.*)

Sithee ... Billy. Go in and quieten 'em down.

SPENCER. Nay ... gotten out in one bloody piece. Not likely. Send Harry in. He'll shift 'em out.

(HARRY *looks up: they laugh. He doesn't respond. Singing starts off, then all join in from the bath.* LUKE *comes in.*)

CROSBY. Got through, then, did you?

LUKE. He'll be all right ...

JAGGER. Kenny?

LUKE. Broken nose.

JAGGER. Keeping him in, then, are they?

LUKE. Aye.

JAGGER. Give his missus chance to bloody roam.

LUKE (*goes over to* PATSY). How's it feel, old lad?

PATSY. All right. (*Eases his shoulder, stiffly.*)

LUKE. Come in tomorrow: I'll give you a bloody rub.

PATSY. Right.

LUKE. Need a drop of stuff on theer. (*Goes to his bag.*)

(TREVOR *has come in, wiping himself down with a towel.*)

TREVOR. Just look ... just beginning to get up circulation ... (*Flexes his fingers.*)

JAGGER. Circulate a bit lower down for me.

(CROSBY *has a towel and now dries* TREVOR'S *back.*)

TREVOR. Bloody shaking, still. Just look. (*Holds out his hands, trembling.*)

CROSBY. Don't worry. This time tomorrow ...

(*Flicks towel to* SPENCER, *who finishes rubbing* TREVOR'S *back.*)

SPENCER. What's thy teach, then, Trev?

TREVOR. Mathematics.

SPENCER. Maths ...

TREVOR. One of your subjects, is it?

SPENCER. One ... (*Laughs.*)

LUKE. T'other's bloody lasses, Trev.

SPENCER. Nay, I gi'e time o'er to one or two other things, an' all.

(*They laugh.*)

JAGGER. Here ... Got the two-thirty, Lukey, have you?

LUKE. Somewheer ... (*Tosses the paper over from his pocket.*)

SPENCER (*to* TREVOR). That kind o' mathematics, Trev.

(*Slaps* TREVOR's *back: finished drying.*)

TREVOR. Shoulda known. (*Turns away to get dressed.*)

JAGGER. Let me see ... (*Examines stop-press.*) One-thirty ...
(*To* SPENCER) Quite a bit fastened up in that ... (*Reading*)
Two o'clock ... Two-thirty ... No ...

CROSBY. What's that, Jagger, lad?

(JAGGER *tosses paper down. Goes to his clothes.*)

SPENCER. Let's have a look.

JAGGER (*to* LUKE). Don't say a word to bloody Walsh.

LUKE. Shan't say a word. (*Laughs.*) Not a sausage.

(LUKE *has dabbed an orange-staining antiseptic on* PATSY's
arm; now he crosses to TREVOR. *As* TREVOR *starts to dress
he moves round him, dabbing on antiseptic with cotton-wool.*)
Hold still. Hold still.

(CLEGG *comes in, drying.*)

CLEGG. Bit lower down there, Lukey.

LUKE. Aye. (*Laughs.*)

SPENCER (*reading*). Bloody Albatross. Seven to one.

JAGGER. What d'you back, Billy, lad?

SPENCER. Same as you, Jag. Little Nell. (*To* LUKE) Tipped
the bloody 'oss himself.

JAGGER. Bloody Walsh ... Never hear the end.

CLEGG. What's that?

(JAGGER, *dry, has started to dress.*

SPENCER *has taken the towel from* CLEGG *and is drying his
back.*)

JAGGER. Albatross: come up ... (*Gestures off.*)

CLEGG (*to* SPENCER). What's that?

SPENCER. I'm saying nowt.

> (*Flicks the towel to* CLEGG, *picks up another.*
> COPLEY *has come in, followed by* FENCHURCH. SPENCER
> *goes to dry* COPLEY's *back,* CROSBY *to dry* FENCHURCH's.)

COPLEY. Sithee, there ought to be a special bloody bath for those dirty bloody buggers: I'm muckier now than when I bloody well went in.

WALSH (*off, siren-call*). Barry! Barry! *We can't do without you, Barry!*

COPLEY (*calling*). Sod off.

MORLEY (*siren, off*). *Barr...y!*

WALSH (*siren, off*). Barr...y ...

MORLEY (*off*). Barr...y! ... We're *waiting*, Barry!

COPLEY (*calling*). Piss off!

CROSBY. Come on, Fieldy ... Keep those ignorant sods in line.

FIELDING (*off*). I'm in the bloody shower. I'm not in with those mucky bloody sods.

JAGGER. How're you feeling, Fenny, lad?

FENCHURCH. All right ... (*Indicating paper*) Results in theer, then, are they?

CLEGG (*has picked it up to read*). Aye. (*Reads*) 'Latest score: twelve–seven.' Patsy: they didn't get thy try ... Sithee: pricked up his bloody ears at that.

> (*They laugh.* PATSY, *having turned, goes back to dressing.*)

FENCHURCH. Fifteen–seven ...

JAGGER. Fifteen–seven.

FENCHURCH. Put a good word in with Sir Frederick, then.

CROSBY. Good word about bloody what, then, lad?

FENCHURCH. Me and Jagger, Danny boy ... Made old Patsy's bloody try ... In't that right, then, Jagger lad?

PATSY. Made me own bloody try. Ask Jack ...

> (STRINGER *has come in, shaking off water.* CROSBY *goes to him with a towel: dries his back.*)

MORLEY (*off*). Any more for any more?
  (*Laughter off.*)
WALSH (*off*). Barry...y! *We're waiting, Barry!*
FENCHURCH. Take no notice. Silly sod.
STRINGER. Where's Cliff, then?
JAGGER. Up in the directors' bath, old lad.
STRINGER. Is that right, then?
CROSBY. Captain's privilege, lad.
STRINGER. Bloody hell ... (*Snatches towel, goes over to the bench to dry himself.*)
  (LUKE *is still going round, dabbing on antiseptic.*)
LUKE. Any cuts, bruises: ought that needs fastening up?
JAGGER. I've a couple of things here that need a bit of bloody attention, Lukey ...
LUKE. What's that?
  (*Goes over;* JAGGER *shows him.*
  They all laugh.
  PATSY *has crossed to the mirror to comb his hair.*)
PATSY. Did you see a young woman waiting for me up there, Danny?
  (*Groans and jeers from the players.*)
CLEGG. How do you do it, Patsy? I can never make that out.
FENCHURCH. Nay, his girl-friend's a bloody schoolmistress. Isn't that right, then, Patsy?
  (PATSY *doesn't answer: combs his hair, straightens his tie.*)
JAGGER. Schoolmistress?
FENCHURCH. Teaches in Trevor's bloody school ... Isn't that right, then, Trev?
  (TREVOR *nods, doesn't look up: gets on with his dressing.*)
JAGGER. What do you talk about, then, Patsy?
  (*They laugh.* PATSY *is crossing to his coat. With some care he pulls it on.*)
CLEGG (*having gone to him*). The moon in *June* ... Is coming out quite *soon!*

WALSH (*off*). Barr...y! *Where are you, Barr...y!*

COPLEY. Piss off, you ignorant sod.

MORLEY (*off*). Barr...y! *We're waiting, Barr...y!*
> (*Laughter off.*)

LUKE. Sithee ... Can you sign these autograph books: there's half a dozen lads outside ... Clean forgot. (*Takes them from his pocket, puts them on the table.*)

JAGGER. By God: just look at that!
> (PATSY *has already crossed to the table.*)

Pen out in a bloody flash ...
> (PATSY *takes out a pen clipped to his top pocket. Writes.* JAGGER *stoops over his shoulder to watch.*)

He can write, an' all ... 'Patrick Walter Turner.' Beautiful. Bloody beautiful is that.

PATSY. Piss off.

JAGGER. Here, now. Bloody language, Trev! ... Hears that, she'll never speak again.

FENCHURCH. Put you down in her bloody book ...

JAGGER. Black mark.

FENCHURCH. A thousand lines ...

JAGGER. 'I must not bloody swear, you cunt.'
> (*They laugh.*
> FIELDING *comes in, picks up a towel.* SPENCER *goes over to dry his back.*)

FIELDING. They're going to be in theer a bloody fo'tnight ... Harry—go in and pull that bloody plug.

HARRY. Aye. (*Doesn't look up.*)
> (*Burst of laughter. Shouts off: 'Give over! Give over! You rotten bloody sod!'*)

STRINGER. They could do with putting in separate bloody showers in theer.

CROSBY. What's that, Jack?

STRINGER. Separate showers. It's not hygienic, getting bathed together.

CLEGG. It's not. He's right. That's quite correct.

FENCHURCH. Put a bit o' colour in your cheeks, old lad.

STRINGER. I've got all the colour theer I need.

JAGGER. Played a grand game today, though, Jack. (*Winks at the others.*)

STRINGER. Aye. (*Mollified.*)

JAGGER. Marvellous. Bloody fine example, that.

STRINGER. Aye. Well ... I did my best.

JAGGER. Them bloody forwards: see them clear a way.

> (*They laugh.* STRINGER *dries his hair, rubbing fiercely.*
> ATKINSON *comes in from the bath, limping.*
> CROSBY *gets a towel, dries his back.*)

LUKE. Let's have you on here, Bryan. Let's have a look.

> (LUKE *waits by the table while* ATKINSON *gets dry.*)

MORLEY (*off*). Barry! *Where are you, Barry!*

WALSH (*off*). Barry! *We're waiting, Barry ...*

> (COPLEY *looks round: sees one of the buckets: takes it to the bath entrance: flings the cold water in.*
> *Cries and shouts off.*
> *The players laugh.*)

CROSBY. Go on. Here ... Here's a bloody 'nother.

> (COPLEY *takes it, flings the water in.*
> *Cries, shouts off.*
> *The players laugh, looking over at the bath entrance.*
> ATKINSON *is dry now and, with a towel round him, he lies down on the massage table.* LUKE *examines his leg.*
> PATSY, *having got on his coat, has returned to the mirror. Final adjustments: collar, tie, hair ...*
> STRINGER *continues getting dressed.* TREVOR *joins* PATSY *at the mirror.*
> FENCHURCH, JAGGER *and* CLEGG *are almost dressed,* FIELDING *just beginning.*)

JAGGER. Go on, Barry! Ought else you've bloody got!

> (COPLEY *looks round, sees nothing.*)

CROSBY. Here ... Come on ... Turn on that bloody hose.

(*He picks up the end of the hose by the bath entrance, turns the tap. They spray the water into the bath entrance.*

Cries and shouts from the bath.

The players call out: 'More! More! Go on! All over!'

Cries and shouts off. A moment later MOORE *and* MORLEY *come running in, shaking off water, the players scattering.*)

MOORE. Give over! Give over! Ger off!

(*They grab towels, start rubbing down.*)

WALSH (*off*). More! More! Lovely! Lovely! ... That's it, now, lads ... No. No. Right ... Lovely. Lovely ... Bit lower, Barry ... Lovely! Grand!

(*The players laugh.*)

CROSBY (*to* COPLEY). All right ...

LUKE. That's enough ...

CROSBY. Nowt'll get through that bloody skin, I can tell you. (*Calls through*) We're putting the lights out in ten minutes, lad ... You can stay there all night if tha bloody wants.

(COPLEY *turns off the tap.*

The players go back to getting dressed.)

STRINGER. All over me bloody clothes. Just look.

FIELDING. Here ... here, old lad. I'll mop it up ... Grand game today, then, Jack.

STRINGER. Aye ... All right.

(CROSBY *dries* MOORE's *back.* SPENCER *dries* MORLEY's.)

CROSBY. What's it feel like, Frank?

MOORE. Grand ... Just got started.

FIELDING. Knows how to bloody lake, does Frank ... ten minutes ...

MOORE. Nearer thi'ty.

FIELDING. Just time to get his jersey mucky ...

CROSBY. He'll bloody show you lads next week ...

FIELDING. Can't bloody wait to see, old lad.

WALSH (*off*). Barry ... *I'm waiting,* Barry!
  (*The players laugh.*)
COPLEY. Well, I'm bloody well not waiting here for thee!
  (*They laugh.*
  The door from the office has opened.
  THORNTON, *followed by* MACKENDRICK, *comes in.*)
THORNTON. Well done, lads ... Bloody champion ... well
  done ... They'll not come here again in a bloody hurry ...
  not feel half so bloody pleased ... How's thy feeling,
  Patsy, lad?
PATSY. All right, sir.
THORNTON. Lovely try ... Bloody text-book, lad ... Hope
  they got that down on bloody film ... Frank? How's it
  feel, young man?
MOORE. Pretty good. All right.
CROSBY. Just got started ...
FIELDING. Just got into his stride, Sir Frederick.
THORNTON. Another ten minutes ... he'd have had a bloody try.
  (*They laugh.*)
  Set 'em a bloody fine example, lad, don't worry. Well
  played there, lad. Well done.
MACKENDRICK. Well done, lad.
THORNTON. How's your leg, then, Bryan?
ATKINSON. Be all right.
  (ATKINSON *is still on the table.* LUKE *is massaging the leg*
  with oil.)
THORNTON. Nasty bloody knock was that.
ATKINSON. Went one way ... Me leg went t'other.
THORNTON (*to* TREVOR). How's your hands now, then, lad?
TREVOR. All right. Fine, thanks. (*Has pulled on his club blazer.*
  Looks up from dusting it down.)
THORNTON (*to* FIELDING). I hope you're going to get your
  eye seen to there, old lad.
FIELDING. Aye.

THORNTON. Bad news about old Kenny.

PLAYERS. Aye ...

WALSH (*off*). Barr...y ... I am *waiting*, Barry!

THORNTON. Who's that, then? Bloody Walsh?

CROSBY. Aye.

THORNTON (*going to the bath entrance*). And who's thy waiting for, then, Walshy?

(*Pause.*)

WALSH (*off*). Oh, good evening, Sir Frederick ...

THORNTON. I'll give you Sir bloody Frederick ... I'll be inside that bath in a bloody minute.

WALSH (*off*). Any time, Sir Frederick, any time is good enough for me.

(*The players laugh.*

MACKENDRICK *has moved off amongst the players, going first to* PATSY, *then to* TREVOR, *slapping backs: 'Well done. Good match.'*

THORNTON *turns back to the players.*)

THORNTON. I think we ought to charge Walsh bloody rent: spends more time here than he does at home.

CROSBY. Thy had five quid off him here last week: swearing to the referee.

MACKENDRICK. That's right. We did!

(*They laugh.*)

THORNTON. No luck this week, then, I fancy?

CROSBY. Shouldn't think so. Tallon's not above bloody answering back.

THORNTON. Shifty bugger is old Walshy ... Grand try in the first half, Mic. Good game.

MORLEY. Thanks.

(MORLEY, *his back dried by* SPENCER, *is now getting dressed.*)

THORNTON. Bloody well stuck to you in the second half, I noticed.

MORLEY. Aye ... Hardly room to move about.

THORNTON. Was Kenny's an accident, then ... Or someb'dy catch him?

MORLEY. A bit slow, I think, today.

ATKINSON. Too cold ...

MORLEY. It went right through you.

THORNTON. There's a bloody frost out theer already ... Shouldn't be surprised if it snows tonight ... Jagger: grand game, lad. Well done.

JAGGER. Thanks, Sir Frederick.

THORNTON. Shook their centre a time or two, I saw.

JAGGER. Always goes off the bloody left foot.

THORNTON. So I noticed ... (*To* STRINGER) Well done there, Jack. Well played.

STRINGER. Thanks, Sir Frederick.

THORNTON. One of your best games for a long time, lad ... Not that the others haven't been so bad. (*Laughs.*) Liked your tackling. Stick to it ... Low, low!

STRINGER. Aye! That's right!

THORNTON. Any knocks, bruises?

STRINGER. No. No. Be all right.

THORNTON. Come up tomorrow if you're feeling stiff. Lukey here'll be doing his stuff.

LUKE. Aye ... That's right.

(*He slaps* ATKINSON *who gets up and starts to dress.*)
Gi'e us a couple o' hours i' bed ... mek it ten o'clock, old lad.

(*After wiping his hands* LUKE *starts to check his bottles, cotton-wool, etc., packing them in his bag.*)

THORNTON. Bloody gossip shop is this on a Sunday morning ... Isn't that right, then, Mac?

MACKENDRICK. Aye. It is.

PATSY. I'll ... er ... get off, then, Sir Frederick ... See you next week, then, all being well.

THORNTON. Your young lady waiting, is she?

PATSY. Aye ... I think so.

THORNTON. Grand game. Well done.

PATSY. Thanks, Sir Frederick ... See you next week, Mr Mackendrick.

MACKENDRICK. Aye. Aye. Well done, young man.

PATSY. Bye, lads!

PLAYERS (*without much interest*). Aye ... bye ... cheerio.

MORLEY. Gi'e her a big kiss, then, Patsy, lad.
(*Chorus of laughter.*)

JAGGER. Gi'e her one for me, an' all.

FENCHURCH. And me.

COPLEY. And me.

FIELDING. And me.

ATKINSON. And me.

CLEGG. And me.

MOORE. And me.

SPENCER. And me, an' all.
(*They laugh.*
PATSY *goes: leaves through the porch entrance.*)

MACKENDRICK. Bloody good example there is Pat ... Saves his bloody money ... Not like some.

CLEGG. Saves it for bloody what, though, Mac?

MACKENDRICK. He's got some bloody brains has Pat ... puts it i' the bank, for one ...

FIELDING. Big-headed sod.

CROSBY. What's that?

LUKE. He's got some good qualities has Pat.

FIELDING. I don't know where he keeps them, then.
(*They laugh.*)

THORNTON (*to* MACKENDRICK). Nay, don't look at me, old lad. (*Laughs. Has gone over to the fire to warm his hands.*)

JAGGER (*calling*). Sing us a song, then, Jack, old love.

STRINGER. Sing a bloody song thysen.

(*They laugh.*

OWENS *has come in from the office, dressed in a smart suit: a neat, cheerful, professional man.*)

OWENS. Look at this. Bloody opening-time. Not even dressed.

MORLEY. Where's thy been, then, Cliff?

JAGGER. Up in Sir Frederick's private shower-room, have you?

OWENS. I thought it might be crowded, lads, today. What with that and the bloody cold ... (*Winks, crosses to the massage table. Loudly*) Got a bit o' plaster, have you, Lukey?

PLAYERS. Give over! Give over! Get off!

OWENS. Got a little cut here ...

PLAYERS. Give over! Give over! Get off!

(OWENS, *winking, goes over to the fire to warm his hands.*)

JAGGER. Give him a bloody kiss, Sir Frederick ... that's all he bloody wants.

(*They laugh.*

WALSH *appears at the bath entrance, a towel around his middle.*

He stands in the bath entrance, nodding, looking in.)

WALSH. I thought I could hear him ... (*To* OWENS) Come to see the workers, have you? How long're you going to give us, lad?

OWENS. I'll give thee all the time thy wants, old love.

(*The others laugh.*)

WALSH (*gestures back*). I've been waiting for you, Barry ...

(*The others laugh.*)

FENCHURCH. What's thy want him for, then, Walsh?

CROSBY. What's he after, Barry? What's he want?

WALSH. He knows what I've been waiting for.

(*They laugh.*)

LUKE. We're bloody well closing shop in a couple o' minutes,

WALSH. You want to hurry up. You'll be turned out without thy bloody clothes.

ATKINSON. T'only bloody bath he gets is here.

(*They laugh.* WALSH *still stands there, gazing in, confronted.*)

COPLEY. Come on, then, Walshy. Show us what you've got.

WALSH. I'll show thee bloody nowt, old lad. (*Moves over towards his clothes.*) Keeping me bloody waiting ... sat in theer.

(*They laugh.*)

I was *waiting* for you, Barry ...

(*They laugh.*)

CLEGG. Come on, then, Walshy, lad ...

FENCHURCH. Gi'e us a bloody shock.

MORLEY. Mr Mackendrick, here: he's been hanging on for hours.

(*They laugh.*)

MACKENDRICK. Nay, don't bring me into it, old lad. I've seen all of Walshy that I bloody want.

(WALSH, *with great circumspection, the towel still around him, has started to put on his clothes: vest and shirt.*)

WALSH. Tell my bloody wife about you, Jagger ... Dirty bloody sod ...

CROSBY (*to all of them*). Come on, come on, then. Let's have you out ...

HARRY (*entering*). Have you all finished, then, in theer?

(*Most of the players now are dressed; one or two have started to smoke.* OWENS *and* THORNTON *stand with their backs to the fire, looking on.*

HARRY *has collected up the jerseys, stockings, shorts and towels. He's worked anonymously, overlooked, almost as if, for the players, he wasn't there. Having taken out some of the boots, he comes back in.*)

WALSH. What?

HARRY. Have you finished with that bath?

WALSH. What do you want me to bloody do? Sup the bloody stuff, old lad?

(*They laugh.*)

HARRY. I'll go and empty it, then.

FENCHURCH. Mind how you touch that water, lad.

FIELDING. Bloody poisonous, is that.

(HARRY, *without any response, goes to the hose, takes it in to the bath, reappears, turns the tap, goes off to the bath.*

TALLON *has put his head in from the office entrance. He's dressed in an overcoat and scarf, and carries a small hold-all.*)

TALLON. Just say goodnight, then, lads.

PLAYERS. Aye ... aye ... Goodnight ... Goodnight ...

TALLON. A good game, lads.

CROSBY. Aye.

TALLON. Both sides played very well. And in very difficult conditions, too.

CROSBY. Aye. Aye. That's right.

TALLON. Sorry about Kendal ... I hear they've taken him off.

LUKE. Aye ... He'll be all right.

TALLON. Keeping him in, then, are they?

MACKENDRICK. Aye. That's right.

TALLON. Say goodnight, then, Mr Mackendrick ... See you soon.

(*Crosses, shakes hands with* MACKENDRICK.)

MACKENDRICK. I don't think you've met Sir Frederick.

TALLON. No. No. I haven't.

THORNTON. Admired your refereeing very much.

TALLON. Thank you. Thank you very much, sir.

THORNTON. See you up here again, then, soon, I hope.

TALLON. Aye. Aye. Our job, though, you never know.

THORNTON. If you bring the same result with you, you can come up every bloody week, tha knows.

(*They laugh.*)

Going upstairs, then, are you? (*Mimes drink.*)

TALLON. No. No. I've to catch me train. Otherwise I would. This weather. You can never chance your luck ... Well, goodbye. It's been a pleasure.

(*Nods to* OWENS, *ducks his head to the others, goes.*)

WALSH. Anybody heard the bloody two-thirty?

JAGGER. No.

FENCHURCH. No.

SPENCER. No.

LUKE. No.

FIELDING. No.

MOORE. No.

WALSH (*back to them, getting dressed*). By God, sunk me bloody week's wages theer ... You haven't got a paper, Mac?

MACKENDRICK. No. No. Haven't had a chance.

COPLEY. Let's see. Now here's one ... What wa're it, now?

WALSH (*dressing*). Two-thirty.

COPLEY (*reading*). 'One o'clock ... one-thirty ... two o'clock ... two-fifteen ...'

WALSH. Come on, come on, come on ...

(JAGGER *points it out.*)

COPLEY. Two-thirty! ... Let's see now. What d'thy bet?

WALSH. Just tell us the bloody winner. Come on. Come on.

COPLEY. What's this, now? ... Can't see without me glasses ... Little ... what is it?

WALSH. Oh, God.

COPLEY. Nell.

WALSH. Hell fire ... Can't bloody well go home tonight.

COPLEY (*still reading*). Worth having something on, was that.

WALSH. Tell bloody Jagger: don't tell me.

JAGGER. And Fenny (*winking*).

WALSH. And Fenny ... Here. Let's have a look.

(*They wait, watching, suppressing their laughter as* WALSH, *eyes screwed up, short-sighted, reads.*)

Here! ... Here! ... What's this ... (*Eyes screwed, still reads.*)
(*They burst out laughing.*)

Just look at that. Bloody Albatross! *Seven to one!*
(*Shows it to* ATKINSON *to be confirmed.*)

ATKINSON. That's right.

WALSH. I've won, I've won.
(*Embraces* STRINGER, *who's standing near him, fastening his coat.*)

STRINGER. Go on. Go on. Ger off!
(*The players laugh.*)

WALSH. By God. That's made my bloody day, has that.

MACKENDRICK. More interested in that than he is in bloody football.

WALSH. I am. I am, old lad ... More bloody brass in this for a bloody start. (*Laughs, finishes his dressing.*) By God, then: see old Barry now ... Wish thy'd washed my bloody back, then, don't you?

COPLEY. I think I bloody do. That's right.
(*They laugh.*)

FIELDING. Well, then, lads. I'm off ...

PLAYERS. See you, Fieldy ... Bye.

LUKE. Watch that bloody eye.

FIELDING. Aye. Aye. It'll be all right.

THORNTON. Bye, Fieldy. Well done, lad.

FIELDING. Aye ... (*Goes.*)

JAGGER. Fenny ... Ar' t'a barn, then? ... Trev?

FENCHURCH (*packing his bag*). Aye ...

TREVOR. Aye.

WALSH. Lukey ... where's my bloody cigar, old lad!
(*They laugh.* LUKE *gets out the cigar.*

JAGGER *and* TREVOR *have gone to the door. They're joined by* FENCHURCH *carrying his bag.*)

JAGGER. See you, lads, then.

ALL. Aye.

TREVOR. Bye.

ALL. Bye ... See you.

MACKENDRICK. Well done, Trevor, lad.

TREVOR. Aye ...

>(*They go.*
>
>WALSH *is lighting up.*)

THORNTON (*going*). Mind you don't choke on that, then, Walshy.

WALSH. Don't bloody worry ... From now on ... Trouble free! (*Blows out a cloud of smoke for his amusement.*)

THORNTON. Bye, lads ... Clifford?

OWENS. Aye. Shan't be a minute.

THORNTON Time for a snifter, lads, tha knows ... (*Gestures up.*)

ALL. Aye ...

COPLEY. Bye, Sir Frederick ...

>(THORNTON *goes through the office entrance.* MACKEN-DRICK, *nodding, follows.*
>
>CROSBY, *picking up a couple of remaining boots, goes off through the bath entrance.*)

STRINGER. Well, I've got everything, I think. I'm off.

COPLEY. Enjoyed yourself today, then, Jack?

STRINGER. Aye. All right.

CLEGG. They tell me your mother was here this afternoon, then, Jack.

STRINGER. As likely.

COPLEY. T'only bloody fan he's got.

STRINGER. I've got one or two more, an' all.

>(*They laugh.*)

ATKINSON. Give you a lift into town, Jack, if you like.

STRINGER. No ... no ... I like to walk. (*He goes.*)

>(*They laugh.*)

WALSH. Here ... Here you are, then, Cliff.

>(WALSH, *having finished dressing, adjusted his buttonhole*

and combed his hair in the mirror, gets out another cigar.
The others watch in amazement.)

OWENS. Thanks, Walshy ... Thanks very much ... Won't
smoke it now. (*Smells it appreciatively.*)

WALSH. Save it.

OWENS. Appreciate it later.

WALSH. Not like these ignorant bloody sods ...

COPLEY. Well, bloody hell ...

WALSH. Come today, tha knows ... All gone tomorrer.

CLEGG. Bloody hell.

COPLEY. The stingy bugger ...

> (WALSH *laughs: a last look round: coat.*
> CROSBY *comes back in through bath entrance.*)

CROSBY. Come on. Come on. Let's have you out. (*Claps his
hands.*)

CLEGG. A bloody fistful ...

WALSH. Just one. Just one. (*Puffs at his own.*) Just the odd one,
old son.

COPLEY. Greasing round the bloody captain, Danny.

WALSH. Keep in wi' me bloody captain. Never know when
you might need a bloody favour. Isn't that right, then,
Cliff?

OWENS. That's right.

> (*They laugh, going.*)

ATKINSON. Well, then, Walshy ... (*Gestures up.*) Gonna buy
us one?

WALSH. I might ...

> (*They've moved over to the office door, except for* OWENS,
> CROSBY *and* LUKE.
> MOORE *stands to one side.*)

Barry here, o' course, will have to do without ... (*To*
CROSBY) Never came when I bloody called ... As for the
rest ... I might stand a round ... Might afford it ... And
one for thee, old lad. All right?

SPENCER. All right.

WALSH (*looking back*). What was Jagger's horse, now?

LUKE. Little Nell.

WALSH. Little Nell! (*He laughs.*)

CLEGG. Are you coming, Frank?

MOORE. Aye. Aye. I will.

WALSH (*to* MOORE). Thy's kept bloody quiet, old lad ...

MOORE. Aye ...

WALSH. Don't let these bloody lads upset you.

MOORE. No. No. (*Laughs.*)

WALSH (*puts his arm round* MOORE'*s shoulder, going*). Sithee,
Barry ... first flush o' bloody success is that.

COPLEY (*leaving*). Mic?

MORLEY. Aye. Just about.

> (*They go, laughing. Burst of laughter and shouts outside.
> Silence.* LUKE *has packed his bag; he zips it up.* CROSBY *is
> picking up the rest of the equipment: odd socks, shirts.*
> OWENS *gets out a cigarette; offers one to* CROSBY *who takes
> one, then offers one to* LUKE *who shakes his head.*
> There's a sound of* HARRY *singing off: hymn.*
> OWENS *flicks a lighter. Lights* CROSBY's *cigarette, then
> his own.*)

CROSBY. Not two bloody thoughts to rub together ...
(*Gestures off.*) Walshy.

OWENS. No. (*Laughs.*)

CROSBY. Years ago ... ran into a bloody post ... out yonder
... split the head of any other man ... Gets up: looks
round: says, 'By God', then ... 'Have they teken him
off?'

> (*They laugh.* LUKE *swings down his bag.*)

LUKE. I'm off.

CROSBY. See you, Lukey.

LUKE. Cliff ...

OWENS. Thanks, Lukey.

LUKE (*calls*). Bye, Harry ...
    (*They wait. Hymn continues.*)
CROSBY. Wandered off ... (*Taps his head: indicates Harry off.*)
LUKE. Aye ... See you, lads. (*Collects autograph books.*)
OWENS. Bye, Lukey.
    (LUKE *goes with his bag through the porch entrance.*
    CROSBY *picks up the last pieces. Hymn finishes.*)
CROSBY. How're you feeling?
OWENS. Stiff.
CROSBY. Bloody past it, lad, tha knows.
OWENS. Aye. One more season, I think: I'm finished.
    (CROSBY *laughs.*)
  Been here, tha knows, a bit too long.
CROSBY. Nay, there's nob'dy else, old lad ...
OWENS. Aye ... (*Laughs.*)
CROSBY. Need thee a bit longer to keep these lads in line.
OWENS. Aye. (*Laughs.*)
CROSBY. Did well today.
OWENS. They did. That's right.
CROSBY. Bloody leadership, tha see, that counts.
OWENS (*laughs*). Aye ...
CROSBY (*calls through to bath*). Have you finished, then, in theer ...
    (*No answer.*)
    (*To* OWENS) Ger up yonder ...
OWENS. Have a snifter ...
CROSBY. Another bloody season yet.
    (*Puts out the light.*)
  Poor old Fieldy.
OWENS. Aye.
CROSBY. Ah, well ... this time tomorrer.
OWENS. Have no more bloody worries then.
    (*They laugh.* CROSBY *puts his arm round* OWENS. *They go.*

Pause.
HARRY *comes in, looks round. He carries a sweeping brush.*
Starts sweeping. Picks up one or two bits of tape, etc. Turns
on the Tannoy: light music.
Sweeps.
The remaining light and the sound of the Tannoy slowly
fade.)

CURTAIN

MOTHER'S DAY

This play was first presented at the Royal Court Theatre, London, on 22 September 1976, directed by Robert Kidd. The cast was:

Judy	JANE CARR
Edna	PATRICIA HEALEY
Lily	SUSAN PORRETT
Mrs Johnson	BETTY MARSDEN
Gordon	ALUN ARMSTRONG
Mr Johnson	BRYAN PRINGLE
Farrer	COLIN FARRELL
Harold	GORDEN KAYE
Peters	DAVID RYALL
Mr Waterton	PETER MYERS
Mrs Waterton	DOROTHEA PHILLIPS

CHARACTERS

JUDY
EDNA
LILY
MRS JOHNSON
GORDON
MR JOHNSON
FARRER
HAROLD
PETERS
MR WATERTON
MRS WATERTON

ACT ONE

Scene 1

The living-room of a council house: there's an atmosphere of decayed affluence; the furniture, a three-piece suite and a dining-table with four upright chairs, might in the distant past have graced an interior of much grander pretensions. There's an oil painting on the wall of a pastoral scene, heavily framed, and a second, smaller picture. The fireplace is more like a conventional kitchen range, with grate, oven, metal top, surmounted by a high mantelshelf. There are two windows opening respectively on the rear and the front of the house.

The door opens and JUDY *comes in. She's a young, well-dressed girl who, though only seventeen, looks older: still slightly gauche, however, untried, but perhaps high-spirited, selfish, cold. She carries a suitcase which, in its newness, contrasts sharply – as do her clothes – with the decayed atmosphere of the room. The place, however, is not a slum.*

JUDY *looks round with a mixture of surprise and apprehension.*

She's followed in by EDNA. *She's a woman of thirty-five, small, sharp, with almost bird-like features. She wears a coat (slightly too large for her) which, as she comes in, she begins to take off, going to the fire, poking it, getting cigarettes from the mantelpiece: alert, pert, snappy.*

EDNA. How long have you been waiting at the door?

JUDY. Oh ... About five minutes. (*Looking round.*)

EDNA. You were knocking, were you?

JUDY. Yes ...

EDNA. My mother's told me nothing about the room.

JUDY. Thirty-four.

EDNA. That's us. (*Looks overhead. Then:*) My name's Edna.

JUDY. Oh.

175

EDNA (*waits*). Johnson ... My father's named Johnson. And my mother's named Johnson.

JUDY. Oh ... I'm Mrs Farrer.

EDNA. On your own?

JUDY. There's my husband ...

EDNA. Got tired of waiting, did he?

JUDY. He was coming this evening ... (*Pause.*) Or perhaps tomorrow morning.

EDNA. That's the back field out there ... council houses left and right ... That's what we call 'the orchard' ... Apples.

JUDY. Oh.

EDNA. Six trees ... They look nice in spring. They're beginning to lose their leaves now ... the kids come over at night and take the fruit ... We're not supposed to let rooms. You've got to be a relative.

JUDY. I see.

EDNA. Or a friend.

JUDY. Oh.

(*Pause.*)

EDNA. You want to leave your case down. (*Gestures overhead.*) You might decide to leave.

JUDY. I arranged to meet my husband here. He arranged for the room. And told me the address.

EDNA. How long have you been married?

JUDY (*hesitates. Then:*) Not long.

EDNA. I should leave it down. There may be nowhere to put it when you get it up.

(*She goes out.* JUDY, *after gazing round at the room once more, follows her.*

A few moments later LILY *puts her head round the door. She's a tall, gangly woman in her late thirties, simple if not actually defective, her hair loose, her figure draped in an ill-fitting cardigan and skirt.*

*She comes over to the case; examines it; tries to open it.
Finds it locked. Hears a door close off and feet stamping; goes
quickly out.*

MRS JOHNSON *enters.*

*She's a small, wiry, sharply-featured woman: the one from
whom* EDNA *evidently gets her looks, but in this instance –
the original – everything is more pronounced; she's in her
early sixties, dressed with some pretensions to 'elegance' –
a long coat, in the style of perhaps some twenty years ago, a
fox fur, and a hat – not eccentric but marking someone of
a 'stylish' disposition – gloves, and a bag which serves both
as a handbag and a shopping bag.*

*She comes in the room; stops and listens, but less to sound out
what's going on in the house than as an automatic reflex:
someone registering that they're not 'out there' any more but
have come indoors.)*

MRS JOHNSON (*calls*). Edna ... ? ... Lily ... ?

(*Goes to fireplace; puts kettle on, against the coals; doesn't
take off her coat or hat.*

LILY *enters. Pauses; watches* MRS JOHNSON'S *stooped
back. Then, as she straightens:*)

LILY. Yes, Mother.

MRS JOHNSON. You were hiding in that cupboard.

LILY. I wasn't.

MRS JOHNSON. *Liar.*

LILY. I was cleaning up.

MRS JOHNSON. Where? (*Looks about her.*)

LILY. All over.

MRS JOHNSON. Liar! (*Runs her hand over table.*) Just look at
this.

(LILY *begins to cry: a low moan, dolorous, her hand to her
eyes.*

MRS JOHNSON, *hand on mantelpiece, but without interest.*
LILY'S *crying is so much a regular feature that* MRS JOHN-

177

SON *pays it no attention; stoops to the fire again; sets kettle more firmly.*)

Where's the tea-caddy? I'm dying for a cup.

LILY. There's somebody in the house.

MRS JOHNSON. Where?

LILY. In Gordon's room.

MRS JOHNSON. Not Gordon?

LILY. A lady.

MRS JOHNSON. What's she doing in Gordon's room?

LILY. Looking at it, Mummy.

MRS JOHNSON. Is anybody with her?

LILY. Edna. (*Bang overhead.*) She's trying to shift the bed.

MRS JOHNSON (*goes to the door. Calls: high, demented*). Edna!
     (*Pause.*)

EDNA (*heard, calling*). Mam?
     (MRS JOHNSON *doesn't answer; turns straight back to
     the room.*
     Sound of EDNA's *feet on the stairs.*)

MRS JOHNSON. Is that her case?

LILY. I don't know.

MRS JOHNSON. Liar. (*Tries the lock herself.*)
     (EDNA *enters.*)

EDNA. She's coming down.

MRS JOHNSON. Who is it?

EDNA. Mrs Farrer. (*Pause: no effect.*) Her husband, Mother,
     wrote you a letter.

MRS JOHNSON. Mr Farrer ...

EDNA. This is his wife.

MRS JOHNSON. He didn't say he had a wife. (*Looks in-
     effectually: mantelpiece, pockets of her coat, bag; quickly,
     without interest.*)

EDNA. She says the bed's too narrow.

MRS JOHNSON. It *is* too narrow.

LILY. It's a three-quarter bed.

EDNA. Three-quarters of what? A cat couldn't turn round in that.

MRS JOHNSON. It's meant for one ... Though I suppose they'll pay for two.

EDNA. You better ask her.

MRS JOHNSON. Does she want any tea? *She's* lost the caddy.

LILY. I haven't. (*Weeps again.*)

MRS JOHNSON. *Liar!*

EDNA. She was on the step. She'd been waiting, she said, five minutes. Knocking.

MRS JOHNSON. *She'll* never open the door, will you? Hiding in the cupboard.

LILY. I wasn't.

MRS JOHNSON. Liar.

EDNA. The caddy's been put away again.

MRS JOHNSON. Where?

EDNA. Where have you put it this time?

MRS JOHNSON. I put it somewhere so I should remember ... It'll be boiling and no tea to mash.

(JUDY *enters.*)

EDNA. This is the young woman, Mother. Mrs Farrer.

MRS JOHNSON. How old are you?

JUDY. Eighteen.

MRS JOHNSON. Where's your husband?

JUDY. He said he'd meet me here this evening ...

EDNA. Or tomorrow morning ... This is my mother, Mrs Johnson.

MRS JOHNSON. How do you do? (*She shakes* JUDY's *hand perfunctorily.*) We're looking for the caddy.

EDNA. My mother's hidden it ... Lily makes tea otherwise, when we're out.

LILY. I don't.

MRS JOHNSON. Liar!

(LILY *smiles at* JUDY, *however, nodding.*)

EDNA. And this is Lily. My eldest sister.

JUDY. Hello, Lily.

LILY. ... Hello, Missis.

MRS JOHNSON. I put it somewhere so I should remember ... You found it, didn't you, Lily?

LILY. No.

MRS JOHNSON. Liar!

EDNA. Hidden it in the usual, Mother. (*Takes it out from beneath a cushion. To* JUDY) What's your first name?

JUDY. Judy.

EDNA. Short for Judith.

JUDY. That's right.

MRS JOHNSON. Do you want a cup of tea? It comes inclusive. Bed, breakfast, no lunch, and supper.

EDNA. What does your husband do?

JUDY. He works.

    (*They wait.*)

EDNA. What's his job?

JUDY. He's an executive.

MRS JOHNSON. Of what?

JUDY (*hesitates. Then:*) I'm not sure, really.

EDNA. They've only been married ... how long did you say?

JUDY. Not long.

    (*Pause.*)

MRS JOHNSON. No children, have you?

    (JUDY *shakes her head.*)

MRS JOHNSON. You better be my niece. I'm your aunty.

EDNA. When the rent man comes.

MRS JOHNSON. Not supposed to let rooms. Not without permission.

EDNA. And they never give permission.

MRS JOHNSON. Not to council tenants.

EDNA. Take your coat off. Lily wants to see it.

JUDY. Oh ... (*Aware of* LILY's *scrutiny.*)

(EDNA *helps her off with her coat.*)

MRS JOHNSON. You're very pretty ... Your husband like you, does he?

JUDY. Yes.

EDNA. Lily's very fond of clothes ... Aren't you, Lily?

LILY. Yes. (*Continues to gaze at* JUDY, *however, even though her coat has been removed.*)

MRS JOHNSON. Lovely material. (*Feeling it.*) Where do you get it?

JUDY. Oh . . . at home.

MRS JOHNSON. Where's home?

JUDY. It changes, you see, quite often.

EDNA. Home is here for the moment, Judy. Do you want me to take your case up?

JUDY. Yes.

EDNA. You can leave your coat down here if you like.

LILY (*seizes the case*). I'll carry it.

MRS JOHNSON. I've been shopping. That's why you missed me.

JUDY. Did my husband write to you as a matter of fact?

MRS JOHNSON. No.

EDNA. I thought he had.

MRS JOHNSON. He came to the door.

JUDY. Here?

MRS JOHNSON. Two days ago.

JUDY. He said he'd written.

EDNA. Are you telling the truth, then, Mother?

MRS JOHNSON. You can twist my arm behind me if you want to ... You can tear my tongue out ... You can give me electric torture ... Is he a well-built man?

JUDY. Medium.

MRS JOHNSON. With sandy hair.

JUDY. Light-coloured.

MRS JOHNSON. Name of Farrer.

JUDY. He's called Farrer.

MRS JOHNSON. First name John.

JUDY. Patrick.

MRS JOHNSON. That's the man.

LILY. Shall I take it up?

MRS JOHNSON. Take it up, then.

LILY. It's not as heavy as it looks.

MRS JOHNSON. Liar!

(LILY *goes; after a moment's hesitation over leaving her coat,* JUDY *follows her.*)

Did she want a cup?

EDNA. She didn't say.

MRS JOHNSON. Gordon hasn't been, then, has he?

EDNA. I've only been in five minutes.

MRS JOHNSON. He said he might call today ... Haven't seen the teapot, have you?

EDNA. Have you looked in the usual?

MRS JOHNSON. All over. (*Since* JUDY'*s departure* MRS JOHNSON *has been searching the room.*)

EDNA. I don't know why you can't use the kitchen.

MRS JOHNSON. I've cooked all your meals on that ... Ever since you were how old?

EDNA. You must have hidden it.

MRS JOHNSON. Lily's had it.

EDNA. She doesn't touch anything while you're out.

MRS JOHNSON. 'Cept food.

EDNA. She won't eat while you're in ... It's only while you're out she can get anything at all. If you stayed in all the time she'd starve.

MRS JOHNSON. Might do that.

EDNA. It's not kind.

MRS JOHNSON. She should have been put to sleep before she was born. She's a living reproach to me, that woman. I can't believe I ever gave birth to her ... Nor to you, if it comes to that ... It's only Gordon I can believe I ever gave birth to ... and that's how many years ago?

EDNA. Thirty-two ...

MRS JOHNSON. My baby.

EDNA. You're not being fair, Mother.

MRS JOHNSON. It's her father she gets it from ... (*Finally produces teapot from cupboard.*) If we find some milk we can have some tea ... Though where I put it, I can't be sure.

BLACKOUT

Scene 2

The room is empty.

After a moment JUDY *comes in. She's changed from her dress of the first scene to a skirt and blouse; she's freshly washed and made-up.*

Looks round; sits down.

Gets up again quickly; retrieves kettle from behind a cushion.

Looks for somewhere to put it; places it finally in the hearth.

Sits again. Waits; gazes abstractedly at fire.

Door opens quietly.

GORDON *enters: 32, slightly built, dark; a dark, somewhat battered suit.*

He gazes into the room a moment.

JUDY, *half-aware of someone entering, refrains from turning.*

A neckerchief he uses as a scarf, GORDON *lifts up and masks his face.*

He leaps on JUDY *and attempts to choke her.*

She screams; he goes through the violent motions of attempting to strangle her, kneeling over her in the chair, his movement increasingly agitated.

Eventually, pausing, he gets off her.

JUDY, *gasping, overwhelmed, lies back in the chair.*

GORDON. I'm Gordon.

JUDY. Where's ... Mrs Johnson?

GORDON. Are those real?

JUDY. Leave me alone.

GORDON. I don't live here ... I did live here. I don't live here any longer.

JUDY. Who are you?

GORDON. Gordon ... Mrs Johnson's Gordon.

JUDY. Are you her son?

GORDON. Youngest ... I've an older brother. (*Taps his head.*) That's to say: he's in the R.A.F. Been there eighteen years. Keeps signing on. Never got a stripe. What's your name?

JUDY. Mrs Farrer.

GORDON. First name?

JUDY. Judith ... My husband's due here any time. (*Tries to look at her wristwatch.*)

(GORDON *has sat cross-legged, directly facing her, on the floor. He picks up a poker.*)

GORDON. You've met my mother?

(JUDY, *after a moment, nods.*
A door bangs, off.
Silence: tense.)

My brother's name is Harold. He comes home on leave sometimes but never stays for long. Lily is the eldest, then Edna, then Harold; lastly, yours truly ...

(*The door opens: a lean man enters, 60s, lined face, heavy-featured: slender build. He has on a jacket over a pair of paint-stained overalls.*
He stands at the door a moment, gazing in: first at JUDY, *who has her back to him, in the chair, and then* GORDON.)

GORDON. This is my father.

(GORDON *doesn't get up, however, and* MR JOHNSON *continues to gaze in at* JUDY.
JUDY *turns in her chair, afraid to rise.*)

Mr Johnson.

MR JOHNSON. Gordon. (*Acknowledges him with a nod of the head.*)

GORDON. Mr Johnson paints houses.

MR JOHNSON. Who's this?

GORDON. Mrs Farrer.

MR JOHNSON. Is your mother in?

GORDON. She's out.

MR JOHNSON (*to* JUDY). Are you staying here?

JUDY. I'm waiting for my husband.

MR JOHNSON. Is there any tea, then?

GORDON. She usually hides it.

MR JOHNSON. There's nothing in the kitchen . . .

GORDON. Where's Lily?

MR JOHNSON. She's in her cupboard.

GORDON. My father paints houses ... It takes three years, can you imagine, to work from one end of the estate to the other. When he's finished he starts again. He paints the same houses year after year.

MR JOHNSON. I paint new houses as well ... (*To* JUDY) The insides in winter. The outsides in the spring. Don't believe anything he tells you. (*Goes to hearth; lifts kettle.*) Here's her kettle.

GORDON. I shouldn't use it. She might come in.

MR JOHNSON. I'll get my own ... I'll use the gas.

GORDON. She's probably gone out to get your supper.

MR JOHNSON (*to* GORDON). How long are you staying?

GORDON (*looking at* JUDY). Not long.

(MR JOHNSON *goes.*)

My mother comes from a titled family. She's the daughter of a famous Lady. Her father was a Lord. They lived in a large house in the country. One day my father – younger than he is now – came to paint the windows. He put the ladder up one morning, saw my mother lying naked on her bed: climbed in, fucked her, and two nights later they eloped. Her father disowned her. They've been together ever since. Harold, if he was recognized, would have had a title. I would too. So would Edna. So would Lily. The fact of the matter is, we probably have, though none of us has gone into it.

JUDY. I think I'll go to my room.

GORDON. Back room?

JUDY. Yes.

GORDON. That's the back field out there. Where Harold flies his gliders ... He had a duration record once. Twenty-five minutes for a model glider ... It was on his Royal Air Force station ... He's a servant of the Queen ... Can I come up?

JUDY. No.

GORDON. I have a book here: do you want to read it?

JUDY. No.

GORDON. Written by myself. (*Has taken out notebook.*) It's mainly my sexual fantasies ... all my fantasies are sexual. I have this uncontrollable urge to make love to women: I want to bury my head between their legs, devour them, stroke them. Time spent with me you'll find different to time spent with anybody else ... Lots of women have said that to me ... There's a lot a girl of your age wouldn't even know about. It takes years of experience to get to the stage I'm at. For instance, if I threatened you with this would you let me touch you?

JUDY. No.

(JUDY *goes back into the chair.*

GORDON *has held up the poker, kneeling now in front of her.*)

GORDON. I could come up to your room ...

JUDY. You better not come near me.

GORDON. If you threaten me it makes me worse.

JUDY. Keep away ...

GORDON. One night, quite shortly, I'm going to kill my father ...

JUDY. I want to go ...

GORDON. Won't you let me?

JUDY. No.

GORDON. I won't hurt ...

JUDY. No! (*Leaps back in her chair.*) Keep off!

(*The door opens.* MR JOHNSON *comes in, carrying a plate of food and a pot of tea.*)

MR JOHNSON. I'll eat in here. That fire needs mending. Mrs Johnson said we're having guests.

JUDY. My husband.

MR JOHNSON. Not here, then?

JUDY. No.

(MR JOHNSON *has sat down at the table.*)

MR JOHNSON. He attacked a man one night ... The police came. His description, but couldn't prove anything. He had a knife.

GORDON. I never used it.

MR JOHNSON. Who was to know that, though?

GORDON (*to* JUDY). You'd know. Wouldn't you?

JUDY. I'll go up, if you don't mind.

GORDON. I'll come with you: show the way.

(JUDY *stays where she is.*)

Is she going or isn't she?

JUDY. I want my coat ...

MR JOHNSON. It'll be in Mrs Johnson's room: she keeps everything in there: coats, food, teaspoons ... do you know I've got to go upstairs to stir my tea? (*Takes teaspoon out of his overall breast pocket.*)

JUDY. Which is Mrs Johnson's room?

MR JOHNSON. It's locked ... I sleep in there. Let in and out at certain times. He'll tell you. He's seen it all. The long, doleful history of my life.

JUDY. Would you ask your son to stay here while I go up, Mr Johnson?

MR JOHNSON. He's his own master ... I can ask him: I can plead with him: I can beseech him. Nothing I say to him has any effect.

GORDON. There's no lock on that door. I took it off. Was my

room at one time. And Harold's. If you look under the
bed you'll find one of his gliders. The wings are packed in
tissue ... Spent hours building them at that table. Ask Mr
Johnson.

JUDY. If I can't go up alone I shall stay down here.

GORDON. I know what you look like ... I know what's
underneath those clothes. What've you got to hide that I
don't already know about?

JUDY. I'd like to wait up there until my husband comes.

GORDON. Won't be coming tonight. (*Looks at a watch on his
wrist.*) No transport into town, not from any distance
now ... He's not walking, is he?

JUDY. He'll be coming by car.

MR JOHNSON. Got a car, has he?

JUDY. I believe he has.

GORDON. You don't know much about him.

JUDY. He may come by car ... He may come by train.

GORDON. He won't be coming by train.

JUDY. May I go up to my room, Mr Johnson?

MR JOHNSON. I'll keep an eye on him, don't worry.

(JUDY *goes to the door.*
GORDON *doesn't move.*)

I should shove your bed against the door. It takes some
shifting when it's wedged in tight.

(*Still uncertain,* JUDY *goes.*
Pause.*)

You want to leave her alone.

GORDON. She doesn't mind.

MR JOHNSON. I'd mind – waving that about. Where are you
living? (*Eating.*)

GORDON. I've got a room.

MR JOHNSON. In town?

GORDON. It's in the town. Where no one knows except
myself.

(*Listens.*)

She's trying Mrs Johnson's room.

MR JOHNSON. No luck.

GORDON. If she comes back down I'll grab her.

MR JOHNSON. I shouldn't bother.

GORDON (*still listening*). There's someone up there with her.

MR JOHNSON. Lily.

GORDON. She was in her cupboard.

MR JOHNSON. Came out when I arrived.

GORDON. This family needs looking into, I can tell you that.

MR JOHNSON. Want any supper?

GORDON. No thanks.

MR JOHNSON. You live in Clarendon Street.

GORDON. How do you know that?

MR JOHNSON. Got a room on the second floor.

(*No answer.*)

Can you see the Cathedral clock from there? Your mother
and I lived there forty years ago. Had a room with a
blanket across to hide the bed. From our window you
could only see the chimneys opposite ... It's the oldest part
of the town is that: narrow streets, gas, just under the
Cathedral wall. It's where the ecclesiastics lived ... until
they moved to houses in the country ... There she is ... A
man who works with me saw you coming out.

(*Door off has slammed. Room door opens.*

MRS JOHNSON *enters: bag, paper.*)

GORDON. Hello, Mother.

MRS JOHNSON. Hello, my darling.

(GORDON *embraces her.*)

I thought you might be coming this evening. (*Sees the
poker.*)

GORDON. Your guest is trying to leave.

MR JOHNSON. Wanted her coat. Trying your room door a
minute ago.

MRS JOHNSON. Her husband not arrived yet?

GORDON. I don't think she has a husband.

MR JOHNSON. Gordon was trying to frighten her, Elsie.

MRS JOHNSON. Gordon wouldn't frighten anyone. Would you, love?

MR JOHNSON. I told her to put the bed against the door.

MRS JOHNSON. Edna's bringing in the supper ... (*To* MR JOHNSON) Not for you.

MR JOHNSON. I've had it ... Tea as well.

MRS JOHNSON. I hope you used your kettle.

MR JOHNSON. I did.

MRS JOHNSON. Do you want a cup of tea, my love?

GORDON. No thanks, Mother.

MRS JOHNSON. Edna's bringing it all in hot ... (*To* GORDON) Do you want to call her?

(GORDON *goes to the door.*)

GORDON (*calls*). Judith ... supper's ready! (*Pause.*) I'll go up. I don't think she heard me, Mother. I won't be long. (*Goes.*)

MR JOHNSON. When you've unlocked the door I'll go to bed.

MRS JOHNSON. You can go when I'm ready. I'm not having you on your own up there.

MR JOHNSON. It's cold in that room without a fire.

MRS JOHNSON. The fire's in safe-keeping.

MR JOHNSON. I saw it in Charlesworth's window ... Five guineas.

MRS JOHNSON. Nobody will ever buy it; and by the time Mr and Mrs Farrer have been here a week I'll buy it back.

EDNA (*entering with tray*). Supper's up! Hello, Father.

MR JOHNSON, Hello, Edna.

EDNA. Finished, darling?

MR JOHNSON. Finished: just.

EDNA. What's he had?

MR JOHNSON. Tins: I opened them. I heated them. I brewed tea in my own cup.

MRS JOHNSON. Doesn't use a teapot.

MR JOHNSON. No point, for one.

MRS JOHNSON. Primitive.

MR JOHNSON. She thought I was primitive when I swept her off her feet.

MRS JOHNSON. Swept me never ... And certainly never off my feet.

MR JOHNSON. When I married your mother she was just sixteen.

MRS JOHNSON. Would have appeared in court if my family hadn't have wanted to avoid a scandal.

MR JOHNSON. Not the scandal: just the expense of bringing you up.

MRS JOHNSON. We had a palace in the country.

MR JOHNSON. A mansion.

MRS JOHNSON. A palace compared to the reduced circumstances I've had to live in. (*Weeps.*) All my life.

MR JOHNSON. Could have left.

MRS JOHNSON. Admitted I was wrong? Never. Not to them.

MR JOHNSON. They're dead now.

EDNA. Supper's ready. (*Having set the plates and glasses.*)

MRS JOHNSON. My brothers and sisters are titled people, living on their vast estates.

MR JOHNSON. You live on a vast estate.

MRS JOHNSON. A *council* estate.

MR JOHNSON. Beaumont estate is larger than all your family's put together.

MRS JOHNSON. My family's estates extended over thirteen thousand acres.

MR JOHNSON. In seventeen hundred and twelve.

MRS JOHNSON. My father's motto is 'Truth Before All'.

MR JOHNSON. 'And Justice Never'.

MRS JOHNSON. Look at what I've had to suffer for one impulsive moment: forty-five years of this. Will God ever forgive me. Will my father, looking down, ever extend his hand to greet me. Will my mother ever dry her tears?

MR JOHNSON. Her father's father was a bastard.

MRS JOHNSON. He was not.

MR JOHNSON. He was illegitimate.

MRS JOHNSON. He was legitimized much later – and came into, as it happens, the family wealth.

(EDNA *has gone to the door.*)

EDNA (*calls*). Gordon ...

GORDON (*entering*). They won't come down.

EDNA. Are you stopping them or something, Gordon?

GORDON. They won't let me in.

EDNA. Who won't let you in? (*No answer.*) Who won't let you in? (*To* MRS JOHNSON) Gordon has Mrs Farrer in a state of siege.

GORDON. Lily and Judith won't let me in.

MRS JOHNSON. What's Lily doing up there?

GORDON. She went up to protect her.

MRS JOHNSON. From whom?

GORDON. From me.

EDNA. I'll go up and tell her. (*Goes.*)

MR JOHNSON. This food is getting cold.

MRS JOHNSON. Don't you touch it!

(*She sits down to eat it.*)

Do you want a portion, darling?

GORDON. No thanks.

(LILY *has appeared at the door.*)

LILY. Can I come in, Mother?

MRS JOHNSON. Stand over there.

(LILY *crosses immediately to the opposite corner of the room.*)

MR JOHNSON. How are you, Lily?

LILY. I'm poorly, Daddy.

MRS JOHNSON. She's never been fitter in her life.

MR JOHNSON. Have some supper of mine, if you like. I left it in a tin.

LILY. No thank you, Daddy.

MRS JOHNSON. Is that woman coming down or not?

LILY. Gordon frightened her, Mummy.

MRS JOHNSON. Liar! Gordon's frightened no one in his life ... Have you, Gordon?

GORDON. Never, Mummy.

MRS JOHNSON. Gordon is my youngest. Gordon is my best. Gordon's always loved me. More than all the rest.

(GORDON *kisses her as she sits at the table.*)

(*To* LILY) Don't stand there ... *There.* Where I don't have to look at you ... Horrible, dirty, terrible, greedy, treacherous, loathsome child.

LILY. I love you, Mummy.

MRS JOHNSON. I don't love Lily. Lily is the one I've *never* loved!

(LILY *weeps loudly into her hand.* EDNA *comes in, followed by* JUDY.)

EDNA. Mrs Farrer didn't want to eat, Mother. I asked her to come down, all the same.

MRS JOHNSON. Won't you eat, Mrs Farrer? It's on the bill.

JUDY. Have you had any message from my husband?

MRS JOHNSON. Edna and I have been out to buy your supper. There's a shop at the corner sells it ready cooked. Here. (*Indicates the cardboard container in which the food has been brought in.*)

JUDY. No thanks.

MRS JOHNSON. Those who don't eat will never be happy.

GORDON. Mrs Farrer's in love.

MRS JOHNSON. She's missing her husband, I can see that.

JUDY. I thought I'd go out and look for him. I can't find my coat.

MRS JOHNSON. Going out this weather without a coat is taking a risk ... This chicken is cooked to a secret recipe ... My family had many secret recipes.

MR JOHNSON. Toilet manufacturers ... De John.

MRS JOHNSON. The family's name is de John. I don't believe I've mentioned that before.

MR JOHNSON. They've even got an original in the Science Museum. Hence the euphemism, handed down from Elizabethan times ... My own family, on the other hand, are descended from the celebrated Doctor Johnson. Of Lichfield. The first lexicographer in the English language.

MRS JOHNSON. Doctor Johnson had no family. He can tell you that. (*Indicates* GORDON.)

MR JOHNSON. On his father's side ... The first dictionary, embodying the beauties of the English language – the foremost language of our contemporary world – was conceived and executed by a member of my family. All *your* family has done has been to oppress, disfigure and finally humiliate the struggling classes, with which I am, through no fault of my own, at present identified.

MRS JOHNSON. You've been a house-painter all your life. You were a house-painter when I married you. God forgive me. (*To* JUDY) We ran away to Gretna Green.

GORDON. And married on the anvil.

MR JOHNSON. In those days you could. It was like Las Vegas in North America.

MRS JOHNSON. Many of my ancestors went to North America: made considerable fortunes, founded an Empire: none of it's ever come to me.

GORDON. Would you like to read my notes?

JUDY. No thanks.

MRS JOHNSON. Make a seat for Mrs Farrer.

>(EDNA *has got on with her supper.* LILY *eyes the spare one hungrily.*

195

GORDON *holds a chair, but* JUDY *won't sit down.*)

JUDY. I'd like my coat, Mrs Johnson.

MRS JOHNSON. I don't unlock the door, Mrs Farrer (*looks at a watch pinned to her*) for half an hour.

MR JOHNSON. That's when she lets me in to sleep.

MRS JOHNSON. Don't give any of that food to greedy Lily. (EDNA *has offered* LILY *some food.*)

JUDY. I really would like to go out, Mrs Johnson.

MRS JOHNSON. This food is really lovely ... (*To* LILY) Has Mrs Farrer's bed been aired?

LILY. No, Mummy.

MRS JOHNSON. I suppose you were hiding in your cupboard.

LILY. No, Mummy.

MRS JOHNSON. Liar! (*To* JUDY) Lily hides in the cupboard by the back door. The latch, I don't need to tell you, is on the *outside*. When she's been *very* naughty, she sits there for a day *and* a night.

MR JOHNSON. The de Johns were noted for their barbarity.

MRS JOHNSON. For their discipline, their order, their circumspection.

MR JOHNSON. She left school when she met me. Everything she's learnt I've taught her ... grammar, syntax. Everything, in fact, that I've taught myself.

MRS JOHNSON. He's been a house-painter all his life.

MR JOHNSON. I've read Greek. I've read Latin ... I taught myself algebra, geometry, astronomy, geology; subjects that would give me an insight into the modern world.

MRS JOHNSON. You wouldn't think a man with interests as wide as that would be living on the pittance that he and his children do.

GORDON. I'm self-employed.

MRS JOHNSON. Gordon has always been reliable, Mrs Farrer. He's the only one with a sense of humour. For example, he left school when he was fifteen and joined a circus.

GORDON (*to* JUDY). I became a clown.

MRS JOHNSON. Shortly after that he became a teacher ... then a bus-conductor, and, for a little while, an assistant keeper in a museum.

GORDON (*to* JUDY). I purloined several of the exhibits and sold them for personal profit.

MRS JOHNSON. It was never proved.

GORDON. After that I became a writer.

MRS JOHNSON. Show them your black book, Gordon.

GORDON. This is my black book. In it I set down all my secret thoughts.

MRS JOHNSON. Mrs Farrer, will you be wanting any of this? I'll heat it up in that case for tomorrow's dinner.

LILY. Can I have anything to eat, then, Mam?

MRS JOHNSON. Nothing.

LILY. I've had nothing to eat all day.

MRS JOHNSON. Liar! (*To* JUDY) What Gordon turns into works of the imagination, Lily turns into common lies.

(LILY *weeps.*)

Don't cry. Don't snivel. I can't stand people who cry and snivel. Go upstairs and air the bed.

LILY. What shall I air it with?

MRS JOHNSON. Lie down, for God's sake, until you feel the damp come out. (*To* JUDY) These houses are very wet, Mrs Farrer. The Corporation takes no care of them. *He*'s the Corporation. He takes no care of them.

MR JOHNSON. I am employed by the Corporation. I'm not responsible for their decisions, nor for their policy ... In the great aeons of time by which we're surrounded the Corporation plays a very small part indeed.

MRS JOHNSON (*to* LILY). What're you still standing there for? Move!

(LILY, *after gazing at* JUDY, *finally goes.*)
Edna, have you finished chewing?

EDNA. Almost ...

MRS JOHNSON. Father ... put out your pipe. (*To* JUDY) The smoke affects Gordon's lungs. His enunciation is perfect in smokeless air. Round here pollution is rampant. It's a condition I've been obliged to live with all my married life ... I was a beautiful young girl. He'll tell you. He deflowered me. He inserted the poisonous seed that came out as that unfortunate child.

MR JOHNSON. In the great aeons of time by which we're surrounded my love for you will be seen to be very small beer indeed ... and the de Johns' love even less ... Unless, of course, they use toilets yonder: then the de Johns' name will have been venerated down the ages.

MRS JOHNSON. My father's mother was a de Courcey ... even *her* mother was ashamed when she married my father, and his family were here before them.

MR JOHNSON. John-son and the de Johns may very well be related. Johnson is the son of John. We may all be incestuously related.

MRS JOHNSON. Gordon, would you read to us from your secret book? (*To* JUDY) A publisher offered him a considerable sum of money just to read it.

GORDON (*to* JUDY). My work is directed to posterity: no one else.

MR JOHNSON. Posterior I should think's more like it.

MRS JOHNSON. Mr Johnson was an inexperienced and vulgar man when he deflowered me, and vulgarity has been a plant that has flourished, vigorously, in the manure of his existence.

GORDON (*clears his throat: examines book*). 'It's my contention that happiness is only bought at other people's expense. For instance, the other day, I was walking down a street in our tiny provincial town, dreaming great visions of what it must be like to live in a metropolitan city – and concluding that we all do live in a metropolitan city wherever we happen to be domiciled – when I saw a young woman coming towards me with legs of the kind to which, for as long as I remember, I have been peculiarly addicted, and was thinking what I might do with her (no one, I am quite sure, would have interfered), when a man came out of a shop doorway to my right and said, "Warm day, isn't it? For this time of the year," and, raising his hat to the woman in question, took her arm. My one thought was ...'

MR JOHNSON. Isn't this very boring?

EDNA. I'll take the plates into the kitchen and wash up, Mother.

MRS JOHNSON. I want you to listen to Gordon's thoughts.

GORDON. 'My one thought was: What does it matter what I do as long as I restore to more reasonable proportions the object which, at the present moment, is causing me the most considerable embarrassment – making it no longer a source of potential terror to any young woman or old woman, who happens to be passing.'

JUDY. I'd like my coat now, otherwise I'll go out as I am, Mrs Johnson.

MRS JOHNSON. Lily's airing your bed. It'll be ready to go to any time now. Perhaps in a few minutes your husband will be here. What shall I say to him if you're out and he's missed you. 'Has she gone for good?'

JUDY. I'd just like some fresh air. I'd like to go to the corner. You've no right to lock up my possessions.

MRS JOHNSON. How do I know you won't walk out of here without paying? You've occupied that room for half a day. I let your room to a young man and no one else. He said nothing about a wife ... For instance: *Are* you his wife? How long have you been married? Do you even know him? Does he even know you're here? You'd be surprised at some of the people I've come across. Ask Gordon. Ask Edna. I'd say ask Mr Johnson if he didn't tell so many lies. Lily gets her lying from him. From his polluted seed grew Lily: the final flowering of the Johnson line.

MR JOHNSON. Gordon was the final flowering: Lily was the first.

MRS JOHNSON. You weren't the only man who fascinated me.

JUDY. Mrs Johnson, I'm going now, coat or no coat, and when my husband discovers how you've treated me he'll be very angry.

MRS JOHNSON. Are you leaving your baggage behind?

JUDY. Yes, I am.

MRS JOHNSON (to EDNA). Was there anything in her case?

EDNA. I've no idea.

JUDY. I can pay you now if it's money you want.

MRS JOHNSON. Oh, you have the money, do you?

(They all look at her purse.)

JUDY. How much do you want?

MRS JOHNSON. I'm afraid I can't accept your money, Mrs Farrer. It was Mr Farrer I let the room to. It wouldn't be ethical, in his absence, to let it to someone else. Even if it was someone who said they were his wife.

JUDY. I'm going to the end of the road.

GORDON. Watch the hedges. The estate is full of people like me.

JUDY. Oh!

(JUDY covers her face, cries, and hurries from the room.)

EDNA. Now, you see, you've gone and upset her.

MRS JOHNSON. Has she gone out?

GORDON. She's gone up to her room ... I'll go up and comfort her if that's all right.

MRS JOHNSON. Go up and comfort her, Gordon ... That's what she needs: a man's affection.

(GORDON *going.*)

Will you take your black book with you?

GORDON. Yes, Mam.

MRS JOHNSON. You can read something to her ... Send Lily down. That bed should be warm enough by now.

(GORDON *goes.*)

When the family are here we have such an entertaining evening.

EDNA. Is it all right to take this out?

MRS JOHNSON. Have you finished eating?

EDNA. All I wish to have.

MRS JOHNSON. You may.

(EDNA, *having cleared the table, carries out the tray.*)

There's your father's there ... He can take his own things out. We are not his servants. He *was* my parents': hired to paint the windows.

(EDNA *goes.*)

He's never stopped painting since that day ... and attempting to seduce his employer's daughter.

MR JOHNSON. Four fucks: four children. The saint of perpetuity must be looking down.

(*Silence.*

They sit apart, paying each other no attention. Then:)

MRS JOHNSON (*calling*). Is Lily in there, Edna?

EDNA (*pause. Then, calling*). Yes, Mother.

MRS JOHNSON. Put her in her cupboard, please.

EDNA (*pause. Then, calling*). Yes, Mother.

MRS JOHNSON. That child would be a raving lunatic if I didn't watch her.

MR JOHNSON. She is a raving lunatic.

MRS JOHNSON. There: you see. All my care for nothing.

(*Pause.*)

MR JOHNSON. In the great aeons of time by which we're surrounded Lily's anguish will be seen to be very small beer indeed.

MRS JOHNSON (*sighs*). Everyone seems settled ... (*Listens.*) No sounds from Mrs Farrer's room ... I don't think her husband will be coming ... Not tonight.

MR JOHNSON. Time for bed.

MRS JOHNSON. Another five minutes. (*Checks her watch.*)

MR JOHNSON. Time for one more fuck, before the light's extinguished.

MRS JOHNSON. Now that *is* a Johnson talking: that I recognize at least.

FADE

ACT TWO

Scene 1

Morning.

MR FARRER *enters: medium build, debonair; striped silk scarf tucked into his collar, bright shirt, sports jacket, neat trousers.*

FARRER. Anybody at home!

> *(Comes in: gazes round.*
> *Looks at his watch.)*
> *(Calls cheerily.)* Hello?
> *(Listens.)*

Hello there! Anybody about!

> *(Looks at his watch again; shakes it.*
> *Disturbed by a sound outside the door, quickly opens it.)*

I say: I thought there must be someone in ... *Miss* Johnson, is it?

> *(LILY enters: gazes at him, entranced.)*

LILY. My name's Lily.

FARRER. Are you Mrs Johnson's daughter?

LILY. Can't tell you.

FARRER. What?

LILY. Can't tell you.

FARRER. Why not?

LILY. *Can't tell you.*

FARRER. Is Mrs Johnson in?

LILY. Out.

FARRER. Haven't seen a young lady, have you? Name of Farrer. I called three days ago, to be precise. Booked a room.

LILY. Your wife's here.

FARRER. I say ... Plan going to schedule! Smashing!

LILY. In bed.

FARRER. All right, is she?

LILY. Upstairs.

FARRER. What time's breakfast?

LILY. My mother's had it. Edna's had it. Mr Johnson's gone to work.

FARRER. Damned difficult getting rooms at all. Which one is it?

LILY. Back.

FARRER. Back. (*Stretches.*) Hardly slept a wink last night. If Mrs Johnson comes in, tell her I've arrived ... *Farrer.*

LILY Yes.

FARRER. *Farrer.* Okey-doke?

> (FARRER *goes: spritely.*
> LILY *stands and waits: doesn't look up.*
> After a few moments FARRER comes back in.*)

Back, left hand; or back, right?

LILY. This one. (*Her left hand.*)

FARRER. Left ... Right!

> (*Goes.*
> LILY *waits.*
> After a few moments FARRER comes back in.*)

FARRER. Locked.

LILY. It hasn't got a lock.

FARRER. Are you sure she's there?

LILY. She went up last night.

FARRER. I'll try again.

> (*Goes.*
> After a few moments MRS JOHNSON enters, dressed in coat, fur, hat, etc.*)

MRS JOHNSON. You're not supposed to feel the warm in here. Your cupboard's for feeling warm in ... Where's my kettle?

LILY. I don't know, Mam.

MRS JOHNSON. Liar!

LILY. That man's come, Mummy.

MRS JOHNSON. What man?

LILY. The one who was coming with the woman.

MRS JOHNSON. Where is he?

LILY. He's gone up, Mummy.

MRS JOHNSON. He's never up there, then, is he?

LILY. She's pushed the bed up behind the door.

MRS JOHNSON. If my Gordon's there he'll never get inside. My Gordon can protect the ones he loves.

LILY. It's his wife, Mummy.

MRS JOHNSON. Have you been eating while I've been out?

LILY. No, Mummy.

MRS JOHNSON (*takes off her coat.* LILY *stands there*). Don't stand there. Get inside.

(LILY *goes.*

FARRER *comes in.*)

FARRER. Mrs Johnson ... Good morning! My room appears to be fastened. I understand my wife's inside.

MRS JOHNSON. She'll be fast asleep.

FARRER. I can't get in.

MRS JOHNSON. She had such a tiring night ... Brought any luggage, have you?

FARRER. As a matter of fact my wife has it.

MRS JOHNSON. One case?

FARRER. I left the remainder at the station.

MRS JOHNSON. What train did you come on?

FARRER. Quite early.

MRS JOHNSON. You've had your breakfast?

FARRER. Up with the larks – my job: on the move, quite often, day and night.

MRS JOHNSON. Mrs Farrer's breakfast was here and ready. Only I didn't wake her. She was missing you very much last night.

FARRER. No phone; otherwise I could have sent a message.

MRS JOHNSON. Mr Johnson did contemplate at one stage having one installed. The neighbours round here, Mr Farrer, are avaricious. If we had a telephone then everyone would assume they had a right to use it. Defending one's rights in a case like that can take up all your time: saying no to one, yes to another ...

FARRER. It's a beautiful coat.

MRS JOHNSON. The fur came with it.

FARRER. And the hat.

MRS JOHNSON. Your wife has very beautiful clothes. I noticed that particularly when she arrived.

FARRER. There's been no one else ... enquiring about our arrival, then?

MRS JOHNSON. This is a private house, Mr Farrer. As I explained when you called three days ago: what goes on in here is entirely our own concern and no one else's.

FARRER. An Englishman's home is his castle, Mrs Johnson.

MRS JOHNSON. My parents owned a very large mansion in the country. If I hadn't have been disinherited by my father I wouldn't be plain Mrs Johnson, but Lady Elizabeth de John-Johnson.

FARRER. I'm very susceptible to titles, Mrs Johnson, myself. A nephew – on my father's side – married a Lady Mac-Gregor. A Scottish family, related to the Scottish Royal Line.

MRS JOHNSON. Shipping?

FARRER. No, no. Royalty, you know.

MRS JOHNSON. My father's sister was the Duchess of Calder and Strathscommon.

FARRER. An aunt, on my mother's side, has a second cousin – widowed now – who was married, for a brief period of her life, to the High Sheriff and Chief Proclamator of Northern Ireland ... He married again, subsequently, and his wife ran over him in a remarkable motoring accident wherein, having got out of his car to pick up a child who had fallen in the road, she inadvertently allowed the car to roll forward and crush his head – from which incident he never recovered. The case created numerous precedents and is frequently referred to in the courts of law.

MRS JOHNSON. What business are you in, Mr Farrer?

FARRER. I'm employed – in an executive capacity – to look after the interests of certain companies who – for reasons of trade etiquette and business decorum – prefer to have their names unknown, except to certain privileged clients. Perhaps you'll become one of them, Mrs Johnson, and I can let you into the secret too!

MRS JOHNSON. Mr Farrer.

FARRER. I know a beautiful woman, Mrs Johnson, when I see one. A woman of breeding and sensibility. You, Mrs Johnson, come from a very distinguished line.

MRS JOHNSON. My husband, Mr Johnson, is a descendant, on the father's side, from the celebrated Doctor Johnson of Lichfield, the first compiler of an English Dictionary.

FARRER. This little house has quite a history.

MRS JOHNSON. It contains many remarkable secrets, Mr Farrer: much anguish and sorrow, and also, correspondingly, much joy.

GORDON (*entering in vest and trousers*). Morning, morning, morning. How are we, Mother!

MRS JOHNSON. This is my son. My youngest son, Arthur.

GORDON. Gordon, Mother.

MRS JOHNSON. Gordon. My first son died. Shortly before my eldest daughter was born.

FARRER. Lily.

MRS JOHNSON. That's quite correct. *His* name was Arthur. Say how do you do to Mr Farrer, Gordon.

GORDON. I've just been fucking your wife upstairs. I fucked her everywhere I could. I fucked her up the front, then I fucked her up the back, then I fucked her in the throat, then I fucked her between her breasts, then I fucked her between her thighs. She's resting now. It's been quite a night.

MRS JOHNSON. Gordon always was active as a child.

GORDON. Not too late for breakfast, Ma?

FARRER. I say ... Is this true? Your son's been with my wife?

MRS JOHNSON. Gordon has a room of his own in town ...

GORDON. In Clarendon Street.

MRS JOHNSON. In Clarendon Street. It's one of the older parts of town.

GORDON. Georgian.

MRS JOHNSON. Georgian. Immediately beneath the walls of our Cathedral. You can see its spire from the station when you arrive.

FARRER. Is Judy up there?

GORDON. I shouldn't disturb her. Needs time to recover. My mother – God bless her – is a little eccentric. I wouldn't believe everything she says.

MRS JOHNSON. Gordon's always had a disposition, Mr Farrer, to use his imagination. He has a notebook in which he keeps his secret thoughts. He was reading it to us as a matter of fact last night, entertaining your wife, my husband, Mr Johnson, and myself.

GORDON. Fucking's my main interest. I'll fuck anything. I draw a line at men. I've tried them in my time, but a woman is better than any man. I'm a great believer in female supremacy. The female is the superior of man in all departments: better cunts, bigger breasts, more to get into, more to get hold of.

MRS JOHNSON. Gordon has a great appetite for life. He's been like it since a child.

GORDON. Anything for breakfast? After all that fucking I'm feeling parched.

MRS JOHNSON. Call Lily from her cupboard. She'll get it for you, dear.

GORDON. I'll fuck her too if I'm not too tired. Edna's gone to work, then, has she?

MRS JOHNSON. I think she has. (*To* FARRER) He's also – you may have noticed – a sense of humour. I'm very proud of my youngest child. (*Kisses him.*)

GORDON (*to* FARRER). Give her five minutes, then go on up. (*Goes.*)

MRS JOHNSON. His father's side: a disposition to ideas and spectacular statements. It's all there in his antecedents. Coming as he does, from two such parents, his antecedents are very strong.

FARRER. Look here, I better go up. You don't mind if I bang on the door and rouse her?

MRS JOHNSON. Not in the least. Treat this house as you would your home.

> (FARRER *gazes at her for a moment: then goes.*
> MRS JOHNSON *hunts around: cushions; looks under chairs and table; cupboards. She still wears her hat.*)

Where are you, kettle? Kettle: come to me. Oh.

> (*Stooping, she slowly straightens: standing in the door is* HAROLD: *a tall, thin man, 34 or 35, though he might easily be taken for someone ten years older. He's dressed in a Royal Air Force uniform, of the lowest rank.*)

HAROLD. Hello, Mother.

MRS JOHNSON. Hello, Harold.

HAROLD. Got forty-eight hours.

MRS JOHNSON. That girl has been the death of me. Ever since Arthur died I've had bad luck – and she was the confirmation of it. Conceived on the night of wedlock, Arthur was.

HAROLD. I came on home because I had nowhere else to go.

MRS JOHNSON. You could go back.

HAROLD. They'll wonder why I left if I go back now.

MRS JOHNSON. How are your aeroplanes?

HAROLD. All right, Mother.

MRS JOHNSON. Brought any with you?

HAROLD. I left them all at camp.

MRS JOHNSON. There's that glider under your bed. But the lodgers are sleeping there. They're my niece and her husband if the rent man comes.

HAROLD. I could always sleep down here.

MRS JOHNSON. We'll have to see, love. The house can only hold so many.

(FARRER *enters*.)

Your wife all right, then, is she?

FARRER. She's coming down.

MRS JOHNSON. I told you she needed rest.

(FARRER *is gazing at* HAROLD.)

This is my second youngest: Harold. He's in the Royal Air Force.

HAROLD (*comes to attention, salutes*). The Royal Air Force. (*Holds out his hand.*)

(*After a moment* FARRER *shakes it.*)

FARRER. Where's your other son, Mrs Johnson?

MRS JOHNSON. He's in the kitchen getting his breakfast.

HAROLD. He's in the cupboard, as a matter of fact, with Lily. I heard them when I came in the back door.

FARRER. I don't know whether he's been near my wife; but I ought to warn you, Mrs Johnson, I'll get it out of him if I have to kill him.

HAROLD. He was going to kill my father: he wrote me a letter.

MRS JOHNSON. Mr Johnson?

HAROLD. That is my father?

MRS JOHNSON (*to* FARRER). Mr Johnson is out at work. He

seduced me when I was only sixteen ... discovering me
one morning lying naked and inexperienced on my single
bed. Two nights later we absconded, stopping on the way
while he seduced me once again. It was beneath a tree of
heaven: the only one for miles around: an import into
England in the nineteenth century, with very long leaves.
Its normal climate is the Mediterranean.

FARRER. Excuse me a moment while I step into the kitchen.
(*Bows stiffly. Leaves.*)

HAROLD. He's very upset.

MRS JOHNSON. Men have all the worries: women, children,
jobs. But we ladies have our sorrows: not to be dismissed
for not being mentioned. There you are, my dear. Your
husband has just stepped into the kitchen.

(JUDY *enters: dressing-gown over nightie.*)

JUDY. I've seen him. We're not speaking at the moment.

MRS JOHNSON. Allow me to introduce you to my other son
– my eldest, Arthur, died when he was only two years old.
Scarcely that. It was nearer eighteen months. Or was it
nine? He never spoke a word. Or had he? It might have
been Lily: she spoke quite early on.

HAROLD. My name's Harold.

MRS JOHNSON. He's a member of Her Majesty's Royal Air
Force.

HAROLD. I'm home on leave for forty-eight hours.

MRS JOHNSON. Harold's stationed at a very remote aero-
drome in the north of Scotland.

HAROLD. It takes me nearly all my forty-eight hours to travel
home: that's to say: I can only stay until this evening, then
I have to set off back again.

MRS JOHNSON. Harold's a Cancerian: home-loving is one of
their principal qualities.

HAROLD. Could I have something to eat, then, Mother?

MRS JOHNSON. I'll see what's in the kitchen, love.
(*Goes.*
Pause. Then:)

HAROLD (*clears his throat*). How do you like staying here?

JUDY. It's ... very nice.

HAROLD. You've met my sisters?

JUDY. Yes.

HAROLD. And my other brother?

JUDY. Yes.

HAROLD. He was born in January. He's been preoccupied nearly all his life with sex. When he was thirteen he assaulted his teacher. He stripped her naked and laid her on the desk. When the case went to court the judge dismissed it because they couldn't prove she hadn't provoked him. He was under age, and apparently she could have landed herself in very deep waters. Do you want to see my glider?

JUDY. I think I'd prefer my breakfast first.

HAROLD. It must be very strange being in someone else's house ... Which is someone's home as well.
(FARRER *comes in.*)

FARRER. I can't get him out of that cupboard ... When I do, and even if half of what I suspect is true, I'll kill him.

HAROLD. My brother has sexual compulsions he can't control. He does something to women different from anyone else.

FARRER. What's that?

HAROLD. I've never asked him.

FARRER. It's not half as bad as what I'm going to do to him when he comes out of that cupboard. What's he do in there?

HAROLD. He talks to Lily. Sometimes he talks to Edna too.

FARRER. Does he have sexual relations with his sisters?

HAROLD. Nearly always if he can't get anything else.

FARRER (*to* JUDY). What sort of house have you landed us in?

JUDY. It was you who booked it. I only came here as per *arrangement*. You weren't here, no message, nothing.

FARRER. Hadn't you better get out of that? Get dressed?

JUDY. If we're going to stay here I might as well get used to living here as well.

FARRER. I didn't say we were living here. Not after last night at least.

JUDY. Where else are we going to go?

FARRER. I've no idea.

HAROLD. It's cheap. My mother charges me very little.

FARRER. She charges you for coming home?

HAROLD. I take up space. I breathe the air. I sometimes feel the fire when they have it lit.

FARRER (*to* JUDY). If he didn't sleep in our room, which room did he sleep in?

JUDY. I jammed the bed against the door.

FARRER. Why didn't you move it when I knocked?

JUDY. I was awake nearly all the night: I only fell asleep when daylight came. I never heard you knock.

FARRER. I'll kill him. I'll kill him even if I only thought he'd touched you.

JUDY. He doesn't live here. He'll be going soon, I'm sure of that.

MRS JOHNSON (*entering*). There you are, my darling. (*Sets down a tray at the table.*) Gordon is eating in Lily's cupboard. (*To* FARRER) I think he's a bit frightened of you. Even as a child he was very sensitive. Harold, I can't find anything for you, my dear. If you'd like to go to the shop – if you've got some money. They're bound to be open now, my love.

HAROLD. I'll go up and look at my glider if that's all right.

JUDY. It's not very tidy.

HAROLD. I won't disturb anything. It's underneath the bed.

(*Goes.*)

MRS JOHNSON. He's such a conscientious man. He came home to protect his father. Gordon had sent him a message saying he was going to murder him. (*To* JUDY) He's in the Royal Air Force. They come down very hard on violence.

(JUDY *has set to with a passion.*

FARRER *watches her eating, suspiciously.*)

(*To* FARRER) Your wife has a beautiful dressing-gown ... She's got the figure for it. I had beautiful breasts when I was a girl: before Mr Johnson deflowered me. Shortly after that they began to fall; then later, with so many children, they virtually collapsed. A woman's lot isn't to be envied, Mr Farrer. I like to see someone with an appetite. Those who eat a lot can love a lot. Two weeks in advance, was that it?

(FARRER *nods.*)

Non-returnable. And your luggage is at the station.

FARRER. I thought we'd bring it later.

MRS JOHNSON. Don't want it cluttering up all the room before you've had a chance to settle.

FARRER. Are you eating all that, Judith?

JUDY. I thought I would.

MRS JOHNSON. She had scarcely any supper.

JUDY. I had none at all.

MRS JOHNSON. She was so excited. Expecting you all evening.

FARRER. I've explained my delay to her, Mrs Johnson. I hope – all other things considered – our stay will pass without any further misunderstanding. Will your youngest son be staying, Mrs Johnson?

MRS JOHNSON. He has a job to go to ... He works in an insurance office. Insuring people against disaster.

(*She goes.*)

JUDY. What's the hurry?

FARRER. I thought we might go up to bed.

JUDY. Bed?

FARRER. I've been travelling here all night.

JUDY. That's what you said.

FARRER. Anyone would think you weren't pleased to see me.

JUDY. I thought you'd be getting here last night. You *said* you'd be getting here last night. The alternative, of getting here this morning, was so remote, you said, that it was scarcely to be considered.

FARRER. I did the best I could. Business of the sort I'm in can't easily be delayed.

JUDY. What sort of business are you in?

FARRER. The export business.

JUDY. I thought you said it was an import business.

FARRER. It imports as well. Every export business is an import business. It's the life-blood of the nation. Do you want me to give that up for a matter of twelve hours in bed?

JUDY. I've given up a lot more for a matter of twelve hours in bed.

FARRER. We needn't go into that, my love.

JUDY. I'm prepared to go into it any time you want.

FARRER. All I want is to go to bed. I've been travelling all night: you've been awake all night.

JUDY. I had a very sound sleep this morning.

FARRER. So I've noticed.

JUDY. Harold is still up there.

FARRER. He can bring his glider out.

JUDY. Perhaps he doesn't want to fly it.

FARRER. You know a great deal about this house: you seem to be very sympathetic to its inhabitants.

JUDY. I've had to learn a great deal about them in a very short space of time. For instance: how did you come across this house in the first place?

FARRER. I read an advertisement in a local paper. The

description didn't fit this, but at least I thought it was anonymous.

JUDY. It's anonymous all right. There isn't one person in this house who isn't crazy.

FARRER. Were you followed here?

JUDY. Not that I'm aware of.

FARRER. As far as I know, then, we'll be all right. It's cheap. It's well hidden, from the beaten track.

JUDY. What beaten track?

FARRER. Where people in our predicament might easily go.

JUDY. There aren't many people in our predicament. How can you say there's a beaten track? Do you mean you've done this sort of thing before?

FARRER. I've only been married once before. I'm not likely to undertake another lightly.

JUDY. I missed you. (*Puts her arms round his neck.*)

FARRER. I missed you, too.

JUDY. Let's go up and make me warm.

FARRER. I was ready hours ago.

JUDY. Lift me in your arms, my love.

FARRER. Isn't the staircase narrow, dear?

JUDY. Not if you're feeling very strong.

FARRER. Oh, I feel strong enough, my love.

JUDY. Then up we go to bed, my dove.

(*He lifts her.*
They go.)

FADE.

Scene 2

The same scene.

Late afternoon. The light is fading.

HAROLD *lies on the settee, apparently asleep; the glider lies on the floor beside him.*

MR JOHNSON *comes in from work: overalls, jacket, cap. Puts on light.*

HAROLD *wakes.*

MR JOHNSON. Anybody in?

HAROLD. Hello, Father.

MR JOHNSON. What're you doing here?

HAROLD. I'm home on leave.

MR JOHNSON. You haven't been on leave for over three years.

HAROLD. Gordon wrote me a letter saying he was going to kill you.

MR JOHNSON. You came home for that?

HAROLD. I've got a forty-eight-hour pass.

MR JOHNSON. He'll have to do it soon, then, won't he? (*Looks at the clock.*)

HAROLD. I thought I might risk it and get back late.

MR JOHNSON. Why?

HAROLD. I can't pack my glider.

MR JOHNSON. Why not?

HAROLD. I've left my box in the lodgers' room and they've been in there since this morning.

MR JOHNSON (*sits*). I've come home early because of the light. Can't see if you're missing any. Paint. Clouds, you know, came over early.

HAROLD. Cumulus. Before that, cirro-cumulus. Wind: north-

217

west. Speed: I'd estimate fifteen knots. Why should he want to kill you, Dad?

MR JOHNSON. A son has to kill his father, son. It's what life is all about.

HAROLD. I don't want to kill you.

MR JOHNSON. You've sublimated it all in gliding. That, of course, and the R.A.F. A man who serves the Queen can't possibly desire to ravish his mother.

HAROLD. I don't wish to ravish Mrs Johnson, Dad.

MR JOHNSON. That's what I mean: remove the primary cause and the secondary doesn't matter.

HAROLD. I see.

MR JOHNSON. As for me: I feel my death warrant's already signed.

HAROLD. I've got a travel warrant, but the times of the train aren't at all convenient. I even thought of flying. But I've never been up in a plane.

MR JOHNSON. Why they posted you in Scotland I'll never understand.

HAROLD. Johnson's a Scottish name.

MR JOHNSON. Can't you ask them to move you south?

HAROLD. There's not enough stations south: they only take people there from A to I; J to Q in Scotland.

MR JOHNSON. Where do R to Z go?

HAROLD. Overseas: the dominions; the empire.

MR JOHNSON. I read in the paper we've only got twenty-four supersonic fighters available at any one moment to defend us against the might of Russia.

HAROLD. It's the Queen we're defending, Dad. That's why it's 'Royal'.

MR JOHNSON. If it's only one person, we don't need as many as I thought. Where's your mother?

HAROLD. Resting.

MR JOHNSON. Means the bedroom must be unlocked. I think I'll go up. If I don't see you again, good flying.

HAROLD. Thank you, Dad.

(MR JOHNSON *goes.*

LILY *enters after a moment.*)

LILY. Harold.

HAROLD. Hello, Lily.

LILY. I've been looking for something to eat. But I can't find anything in the kitchen.

HAROLD. Mother's taken it with her. (*Feels in his pocket.*) I've got a bar of chocolate here. I've been lying on it. I fell asleep.

(LILY *takes it.*)

I'll have to be going soon. Unless I overstay my leave. I've nowhere to put this where it won't get knocked. I can't get into the lodgers' bedroom.

LILY. You can leave it in the cupboard.

HAROLD. There's not room when you're in there.

LILY. I'll put it back in the box when Mr and Mrs Farrer come out.

HAROLD. I don't like taking risks. All my professional training is against taking risks. Certainty and preparation are the two watchwords of the Queen's Royal Air Force. Ardua ad Astra: it's harder not to be constipated than to reach the stars.

LILY. You could leave the air force if you really wanted.

HAROLD. Mummy doesn't love me and Daddy pretends I don't exist. He thinks Gordon is going to kill him.

LILY. He is.

HAROLD. When?

LILY. Tonight.

HAROLD. How?

LILY. He didn't say.

HAROLD. Will that chocolate be enough?

LILY. I haven't eaten anything for days. I can hardly feel it.

HAROLD. Was Gordon in your cupboard?

LILY. Yes.

HAROLD. I knocked on the door.

LILY. Oh.

HAROLD (*holds up his glider*). I was going to fly my glider.

LILY. Remember the last time.

HAROLD. Yes.

> (*Pause.*
>
> FARRER *comes in, shirt loose, trousers; stretching.*)

FARRER. Tea going, is it?

LILY. My mother's got the kettle.

FARRER. Where?

HAROLD. In bed.

FARRER. Isn't there another?

HAROLD. No one has to use it.

FARRER. Do you mean there's no tea going? I'm parched.

LILY. There are some apples in the kitchen.

FARRER. I wouldn't mind apples.

LILY. My mother's spit on them.

HAROLD. She's counted them as well.

LILY. It's only breakfast and supper for lodgers.

FARRER. Could I boil some water in a pan?

HAROLD. She's got the tea-caddy.

FARRER. No tea.

HAROLD. Could I put my glider back?

FARRER. My wife is dressing. If you could give her fifteen seconds.

HAROLD. It was just the box. I knocked on the door.

FARRER. We thought it was your brother.

LILY. Gordon went to work this morning.

FARRER (*gazes at clock*). As late as that?

HAROLD. You've been up there all day.

LILY. That's somebody knocking.

HAROLD. Can't be anybody we know.

FARRER. How do you know that?

LILY. No one who knows us ever comes. (*She goes.*)

    (*A moment later* MRS JOHNSON *comes in, in an underslip and slippers, a scarf around her hair, the ends of which are fastened in curlers.*)

MRS JOHNSON. There's somebody knocking.

HAROLD. Lily's answering, Mother.

MRS JOHNSON. Did you have a good sleep, Mr Farrer?

FARRER. Very restful.

MRS JOHNSON. Your wife?

FARRER. She's rested very well as well.

MRS JOHNSON. Did you rest, Harold?

HAROLD. I lay down here.

MRS JOHNSON. You ought to rest, love. (*Pushes back his hair.*) It's rest that makes the world go round. That's his glider.

FARRER. He showed me.

LILY (*entering*). There's a man at the door asking for Mrs Farrer.

MRS JOHNSON. Liar!

LILY. Mr Farrer as well. Though it's Mrs Farrer he wants especially.

FARRER. Would you tell him that there's no one of that description living here.

MRS JOHNSON (*to* LILY). *You* can't go. You always lie. You go upstairs to your poor wife, Mr Farrer. I'll soon put his mind at rest.

FARRER. It's someone I'm particularly anxious to avoid.

MRS JOHNSON. You can rest assured, Mr Farrer. This is a private house, and everything in this house is private. (*To* LILY) Show him in.

(FARRER *goes, followed by* LILY.)

You can take that glider up as well. I don't think the gentleman'll want to see it.

HAROLD. All right, Mother.

MRS JOHNSON. Your father's in my room. Tell him I shall want him out in fifteen minutes. That room is closed between four and ten each evening.

(HAROLD *goes with his glider.*

LILY *re-enters.*

She's followed by PETERS, *a small, perky man in a raincoat. He's chewing gum and wears a trilby.*)

LILY. This is the man who was at the door.

MRS JOHNSON. Go back to your cupboard, Lily.

LILY. Yes, Mother. (*Glancing at* PETERS, *she goes.*)

(PETERS *examines* MRS JOHNSON *in her underslip with evident consternation.*)

MRS JOHNSON. Is there anything I can do for you. After you've taken your hat off.

PETERS. Oh, yes. (*Takes it off.*)

MRS JOHNSON. And taken that gum out.

PETERS. Oh. (*Takes it out.*)

MRS JOHNSON. I should take your raincoat off. It's extremely warm in here.

PETERS. Right. (*Bewildered,* PETERS *looks round for somewhere to deposit gum: in fireplace. Takes off coat.*) It's like this. My name's Peters, Ma'am. I'm a private detective. I'm trying to trace a girl called Judith Waterton.

MRS JOHNSON. My name is Mrs Johnson. My husband's name is Mr Johnson. We've lived here for over thirty-five years. There are three bedrooms, a bathroom and a W.C. upstairs, and a living-room and kitchen, plus a cupboard under the stairs, down here. Apart from a coalhouse that's all we have. Over the last forty years I've conceived five children, the eldest of whom died at eighteen months, the

remaining four of whom have survived to the present day
and may be seen from time to time at this address.

PETERS (*after a while*). Have you come across or become
acquainted with a girl called Judith Waterton or Farrer?
Or a man going under the name of Farrer, purporting to
be her husband?

MRS JOHNSON. This is a private residence. My husband's
antecedents can be traced back by even the most casual
enquirer to Doctor Samuel Johnson of Lichfield, the first
compiler of an English dictionary: similarly, my own
background is that of the landed aristocracy, namely the
de Johns, whose ancestors were notorious for the wide-
spread introduction of the water-closet.

PETERS. All I'm enquiring about is a girl called Judith
Waterton. I've got a photograph of her if you want to
look.

MRS JOHNSON. I don't wish to look at the photographs of
young girls. If you're trying to make indecent proposals I
better warn you that my husband is upstairs in bed.

PETERS. All I'm enquiring about, madam, on behalf of a pair
of distraught and grieving parents, is the whereabouts of a
girl of only seventeen years of age – their only daughter –
who has been taken from her house and – as far as we're
aware – illegally married to a man who – on this we are
quite certain – already possesses a wife in California in the
United States of North America.

MRS JOHNSON. I was taken from my home at the age of
sixteen and seduced beneath a tree in the grounds of my
father's house. The child conceived by that outrageous act
was my eldest son, Arthur, who died at the age of eighteen
months.

PETERS. I'm sorry to hear about your personal misfortunes,
madam, but I'd appreciate it if you'd tell me whether this
man or this girl have been to the house.

MRS JOHNSON. This is my personal history – not my personal misfortunes. I'm making no comment on the significance of this experience, merely on the fact that it happened and no private detective came looking for me. And that was in the days when social proprieties were observed to a far greater degree than they are at present.

PETERS. The parents have offered a large reward for any information leading to the recovery of their daughter.

MRS JOHNSON. How much?

PETERS. One hundred and fifty pounds if the information leads to her discovery.

MRS JOHNSON. How much of that do you take yourself?

PETERS. I have my own arrangement for the work I'm doing. This is an incentive to people not directly involved.

MRS JOHNSON. Why did you come to my door?

PETERS. I took a gamble, Ma'am. I know the girl came to this town yesterday afternoon. None of the hotels – there are only three of them – have seen her. I've looked up the advertisements in the local paper and of seven in last week's offering accommodation only two, as far as I'm concerned, fit the situation: that is, somewhere cheap and inconspicuous. Your address was one of them.

MRS JOHNSON. Whose was the other?

PETERS. The other was still vacant, Ma'am. I've taken the room myself.

(*Door opens.* EDNA *comes in.*)

MRS JOHNSON. This gentleman is looking for a Mr and Mrs Farrer, Edna.

PETERS (*bowing*). Peters, Ma'am.

MRS JOHNSON. The former having eloped with the latter, the latter's parents are offering a reward of one hundred and fifty pounds.

EDNA. One hundred and fifty pounds.

MRS JOHNSON. This is my daughter Edna. If you think she fits the description you can have her.

PETERS. This is a photograph, madam, of the girl herself.

EDNA. She's very beautiful.

PETERS. And this is the man we're trying to trace.

EDNA. He's very handsome.

MRS JOHNSON. Mr Johnson looked nothing like that when he had the temerity to elope with me.

PETERS. This man makes a living, madam, from eloping with the daughters of wealthy families. His own financial resources are non-existent.

MRS JOHNSON. With looks like that he doesn't need any other resources, does he?

(MR JOHNSON *enters: underpants and shirt.*)

MR JOHNSON. Who's been knocking at the door at this hour?

EDNA. This is Mr Peters, Father, who's looking for a Mr and Mrs Farrer.

PETERS. The girl in question, sir, is under age and has been married without the consent of her parents.

EDNA. They're offering for her, Father, one hundred and fifty pounds.

MR JOHNSON. What's she look like?

(PETERS *shows him.*)

PETERS. Could you tell me if anyone answered your advertisement in the local paper?

MR JOHNSON. ⎱No.
MRS JOHNSON. ⎰Yes.

EDNA. That's to say, my mother's niece and her husband are staying temporarily in one of the rooms upstairs.

PETERS. Perhaps I could see them, if it's not inconvenient, and satisfy my curiosity.

MR JOHNSON. My wife's niece is suffering from severe stomach pains as the result of an abortion and her husband,

225

who's in bed beside her, is recovering from gun-shot wounds which he inflicted on himself during a bout of severe depression. They both came here for quietness: to recuperate.

PETERS. Your room, in other words, advertised last week in the local paper, is no longer available.

MR JOHNSON. That's quite correct.

PETERS. In that case, I shall have no more cause to trouble you at present ... (*Picks up his raincoat.*) Good evening. (*To* EDNA) Good evening, madam. (*To* MRS JOHNSON) (*Picks up his hat.*) Good evening, sir. (*To* MR JOHNSON)

MRS JOHNSON. Good evening, young man. Edna, would you see Mr Peters to the door?

(PETERS *goes, followed by* EDNA.)

We might have got two hundred.

MR JOHNSON. People are not for sale. That has been the guiding principle of my life. That's why we live in the circumstances we do, divorced from the great wealth of your family, dependent entirely on what we earn ourselves.

MRS JOHNSON. We're not selling people: only information.

MR JOHNSON. Do you normally entertain visitors in your underwear?

MRS JOHNSON. Do you?

MR JOHNSON. I didn't know he was here.

MRS JOHNSON. Neither did I.

MR JOHNSON. It's the effect on ourselves we have to consider.

(*Neither of them stir. Then:*)

I've had a tiring day.

MRS JOHNSON. I've had an easy day.

MR JOHNSON. Is your kettle available for boiling?

MRS JOHNSON. No.

MR JOHNSON. I shall have to use Edna's.

MRS JOHNSON. It's locked away.

MR JOHNSON. In that case I can do without.

(EDNA *comes back in.*)

EDNA. He's gone.

(HAROLD *comes in.*)

HAROLD. I've put my glider away.

MRS JOHNSON. Did Mr Farrer allow you to get the box?

HAROLD. Mr Farrer climbed out of the bedroom window and down a drainpipe.

MR JOHNSON. Where is he now?

HAROLD. I've no idea.

EDNA. Hello, Harold.

HAROLD. Hello, Edna.

EDNA. Are you home on leave?

HAROLD. I've to be leaving in an hour.

EDNA. How long is it?

HAROLD. Three years.

MR JOHNSON. He came home because he had news that Gordon was going to kill his father.

EDNA. Who?

MR JOHNSON. Mr Johnson.

EDNA. Oh. For I minute I thought you meant someone else.

MR JOHNSON. Keep it in the family.

MRS JOHNSON. Naturally: we wouldn't want it involving anyone else.

MR JOHNSON. Where did Mr Farrer go?

HAROLD. He ran across the field.

MRS JOHNSON. What did Mrs Farrer say?

HAROLD. She didn't say anything. I knelt under the bed, then, when I lifted my head, I showed her my glider.

MRS JOHNSON. She's waiting for Gordon. You see. He's late.

EDNA. He doesn't finish till five o'clock.

MRS JOHNSON. He always comes home early if he's something special.

EDNA. I think we should sell Mr and Mrs Farrer to the cops.

227

MR JOHNSON. He isn't a cop.

EDNA. He's a private detective.

MRS JOHNSON. A hundred and fifty pounds: we could make sure of that.

EDNA (*at the window*). I think he's still waiting at the end of the road. We wouldn't be doing Judith any harm. What's she getting from Mr Farrer that she can't already get from Gordon?

MR JOHNSON. I wouldn't mind giving her a bit myself.

MRS JOHNSON. You dirty, filthy, disgusting beast.

MR JOHNSON. There's not all that physical difference between one man and another.

MRS JOHNSON. There's such a thing as quality.

MR JOHNSON. He's a Johnson.

MRS JOHNSON. And a de John. It's the mixture of the blood that counts.

EDNA. If he's waiting until we've changed our minds it means he knows they're here already.

MR JOHNSON. You've heard my opinion for what it's worth.

MRS JOHNSON. You want to seduce her.

MR JOHNSON. She's been seduced already.

MRS JOHNSON. You want to seduce her again. Seducing young girls is all you're good at.

MR JOHNSON. It's better than selling her, isn't it? Seducing's natural, though being married to you nobody would believe it.

MRS JOHNSON. I shall go upstairs in a moment and lock the door and you'll have *nowhere* to sleep tonight.

MR JOHNSON. There's always Mrs Farrer.

MRS JOHNSON. Mrs Farrer I shall take unto myself. Edna: send that sluttish, idle, good-for-nothing daughter. I want her to take a message.

MR JOHNSON. What message?

MRS JOHNSON. Never you mind.

(EDNA *goes.*)

MR JOHNSON. I'm going to bed. If Gordon wants me he'll know where to find me.

MRS JOHNSON. Touch that bed and you'll never live the night.

MR JOHNSON. I'll never live it in any case. Good night, Harold. You'll be gone, I reckon, by the morning.

HAROLD. Yes, Father.

MR JOHNSON. So will I. (*Goes.*)

MRS JOHNSON. Your father's a disgusting beast. He seduced me when I was only sixteen. Are you listening?

HAROLD. Yes, Mother.

(LILY *enters.*)

MRS JOHNSON. He produced this three ha'porth of nothing. Are you listening?

LILY. Yes, Mother.

MRS JOHNSON. Liar!

LILY. Gordon's just arrived.

MRS JOHNSON. Where is he?

LILY. He's gone to bed.

MRS JOHNSON. Which bed?

LILY. I don't know.

MRS JOHNSON. Liar!

LILY. He said not to disturb him, Mummy.

MRS JOHNSON. Liar. Everything she says is lies. Are you listening?

LILY. Yes, Mummy.

MRS JOHNSON. Liar!

(MRS JOHNSON *has been searching a drawer; she takes out paper, pen.*)

I want you to take this message (*writing*) to the man standing at the end of the road. Wait till he's read it and say to him, '*Is it understood?*' Have you got that?

LILY. Is it understood, Mummy?

MRS JOHNSON. Not *Mummy*.

LILY. Is it understood?

MRS JOHNSON. If he says 'Yes' come back at once.

LILY. What if he says no?

MRS JOHNSON. Kick him.

(LILY *takes the folded sheet of paper: goes.*)

Aren't you leaving, Harold?

HAROLD. I don't like leaving my father when he's about to be killed.

MRS JOHNSON. The golden boy's arrived. He'll be lying up there with his golden girl: thighs interlocked, his gigantic balls slung round her. He had enormous balls even as a child. As for his penis, it was bigger than your father's when he was only five. Is that the time? When Lily comes back send her up to me ... I'm just going up to deal with your father. If he thinks he can seduce *her*, he might just as well spend the same amount of time seducing me.

BLACKOUT

ACT THREE

Night.

The window opens. The figure of a man enters: PETERS.

He looks round; lowers window; hides behind settee.

After a moment the opposite window opens. A figure climbs through with some difficulty, cursing; gets caught in curtains; disentangles itself, goes to room door, hesitates; comes back to window; closes it.

MRS JOHNSON (*heard calling*). Lily? Is that you?

  (*Figure hides.*

  Pause.)

LILY (*calling, off*). No, Mam.

MRS JOHNSON (*calling, off*). Liar!

  (*Pause.*)

LILY (*calling, off*). I'm in my cupboard.

MRS JOHNSON (*calling, off*). Stay there. No moving about.

  (*Door closes off.*

  Pause.)

LILY (*calling, off*). Mam?

  (*Pause.*)

  Mam?

  (*Door opens off.*)

MRS JOHNSON (*calling*). What is it?

LILY (*calling*). I want to go!

MRS JOHNSON (*calling*). Wait till the morning.

LILY (*calling*). I can't wait, Mam.

MRS JOHNSON (*calling*). Liar!

  (*Door slams off.*

  Pause.

Figure rises slowly; goes to door; pauses; hurries back to chair and hides.

The door opens; a figure in trousers and vest enters; creeps stealthily over to the fireplace; feels round the hearth; finally lifts up poker; turns, goes back to the door.

A cry of 'Ah!' from the figure hiding in recognition; a cry from PETERS; *the two of them leap on the third figure and a fierce fight ensues; banging, thumping, groaning; raising of poker several times.*

Finally third figure staggers to the light and switches it on.)

GORDON. You!

FARRER. You!

    (GORDON, *in trousers and vest, and neckerchief, stands at the light switch, the poker still in his hand.*

    FARRER *stands over* PETERS *who lies in the middle of the floor, his head covered in blood.)*

GORDON. Who's that?

FARRER. You've killed him.

GORDON. I thought it was my father.

FARRER. I knew it was you.

GORDON. Your wife said you'd run away.

FARRER. I was called away on business.

GORDON. Who is it?

FARRER. A business rival I've been trying to avoid for some considerable time.

GORDON (*looks at him*). He's dead. (*Immediately feels in his pocket.*) He's a detective.

FARRER. No official capacity whatsoever.

GORDON. Here's a note. 'Come to the house at nine o'clock tomorrow morning and what you seek will be delivered into your hands. Signed Elizabeth de John-Johnson (Mrs).' That's my mother.

FARRER. It's only three o'clock.

GORDON. A photograph of you; one of your wife. 'Judith Waterton'. Is that her name?

FARRER. Her maiden name.

GORDON. Maiden no longer: I've seen to that.

FARRER. You bounder.

GORDON. You're a bounder. You're a professional seducer: it says so here. (*Back of photograph.*)

FARRER. What're you doing with that? (*Poker.*)

GORDON. I'm going to kill my father.

MRS JOHNSON (*calling*). Is that you, Lily?

LILY (*pause, then, calling*). No, Mam.

MRS JOHNSON (*heard*). *Liar!*

GORDON (*calls*). It's me, Mother.

MRS JOHNSON (*pause. Then, calls*). All right, my darling. Sweet dreams, Gordon.

GORDON (*calls*). Sweet dreams, Mam.

    (*Door closes off.*)

FARRER. You've killed him instead.

GORDON. Self-defence.

FARRER. What're you going to do with him?

GORDON. What're *you* going to do with him?

FARRER. It's not my concern.

GORDON. It's your photograph he's got.

FARRER. Are you sure he's dead?

GORDON. His head's bashed in.

FARRER. You better get rid of him.

GORDON. It's you he's after. I'll say you hit him: show 'em the poker. Wipe my prints off: plain as day.

    (PETERS *groans.*)

FARRER. He's still alive!

    (GORDON *raises his poker again.*)

(*Snatches* GORDON's *arm.*) If he's still alive I can't be had up for murder.

(PETERS *groans again; slowly raises himself, stiff.*)

PETERS. Where am I?

GORDON. You were breaking in. My cousin's husband here hit you on the head.

PETERS (*groans; holds his head*). Where am I?

GORDON. This is the residence of Mr and Mrs Johnson.

PETERS. Who?

FARRER. Do you recognize me?

PETERS. Never seen you.

FARRER. What about her? (*Shows him the photograph.*)

PETERS. Never.

FARRER. What about this letter?

PETERS. Never seen it.

FARRER. What's your name?

PETERS. I've no idea.

GORDON. If I hit him with this he'll never recover.

FARRER. I'm not being had up for murder. Seducing's one thing: disposing of somebody's body's quite another.

PETERS. Where's all this blood from? (*Looks at his hand, lowered from his head.*)

GORDON. You broke into a private residence and were confronted by my cousin-in-law who was obliged to hit you on the head.

PETERS. Why was I breaking in?

GORDON. You said you had a private grudge against my father, Mr Johnson, that you'd come to kill him – that you had killed him, as a matter of fact – and were attempting to escape. Whereupon my cousin-in-law had to hit you on the head.

PETERS. What with?

GORDON (*holds up poker*). The same instrument with which you killed my father.

PETERS. Where did I kill him?

GORDON. Upstairs in bed.

FARRER. I don't want any part of this.

GORDON. I've been waiting for years for an opportunity like this.

PETERS. What's my wife going to say?

FARRER. Who is your wife?

PETERS. I don't know.

GORDON. You're psychotic. Documents in your pocket suggest you have a long history of unstable behaviour. Police authorities throughout the country have been asked to keep an eye open for you.

PETERS. What I can't understand is what am I doing in this house. I don't know anybody here. I've never been here in my life before.

FARRER. I saw you here this evening.

PETERS. Here?

GORDON. You called on my mother. We have a note in our possession, written in her hand, pleading with you to leave my father alone.

PETERS. This is terrible. Why should I ever kill a man?

GORDON. You're insane. My father was a peaceable man going about his lawful business.

PETERS. Are you sure he's dead?

GORDON. His head is beaten to pulp. If you give me a few minutes to tidy the room, before you come upstairs, I'll show you.

PETERS. My God. What a terrible thing to happen. What do you say his name is?

GORDON. Johnson.

PETERS. Johnson. My God. It's like a nightmare. I can't remember a single thing.

(MR JOHNSON *enters in his underpants and vest.*)

MR JOHNSON. What's going on?

PETERS. Who're you?

MR JOHNSON. I'm Mr Johnson: the owner of this house.

That is to say, the lawful tenant. It's Corporation property and as a result I have never been given the opportunity to purchase it.

PETERS. This man has just said I've killed you.

MR JOHNSON. I recognize you now. You're Mr Peters.

GORDON. Is this the man who threatened to murder you, Father?

MR JOHNSON. You're the man who threatened to murder me.

PETERS. I'm going mad. I *am* mad. I must be dreaming.

GORDON. Is it not true he attacked you violently with a poker not a moment ago and, before you had an opportunity to defend yourself, split your head wide open?

PETERS. There's not a mark on him! I'm the one who's been beaten on the head!

GORDON. This is an aberration. What you're seeing now is a fantasy, induced by shock. My father is not standing here before you: he's lying in a pool of blood upstairs.

PETERS. I *am* mad!

MR JOHNSON. I'm not dead. I'm sure of that. I'm here.

GORDON. You're dead, you crazy fool. I'll see to that.
(*Raises poker to beat him down.*
JUDY, *entering, screams. She's dressed in a flimsy nightdress.*)

JUDY. Aaaaaaah!
(GORDON *lowers the poker.*)
Gordon!

FARRER. Judith!

JUDY. Patrick!

GORDON. I'll be back up in a moment, darling.

PETERS. This is impossible. I *must* be dreaming! I *am* dreaming! I'm going to wake up in a matter of seconds ... one ... two ... (*Clutches his head.*)
(LILY *enters in a long nightgown.*)

LILY. Is anything the matter?

236

GORDON. This man has just murdered our father, Lily.

LILY. That's Mr Peters.

MR JOHNSON. That's what *I* said.

GORDON. He broke into the house and Mr Farrer apprehended him. With this.

LILY. Shall I get a flannel?

MRS JOHNSON (*entering in nightdress*). What's going on in here? Have you been disturbing my guests again?

GORDON. This man has just murdered your husband, Mother.

PETERS. This man is Mr Johnson. He said so. Aren't you, Mr Johnson?

MR JOHNSON. That is my name.

PETERS. When I count to ten – I'm going to wake up ... three ... four ... What comes after four? ... My memory's gone again!

MR JOHNSON. He's suffering from amnesia: that's what's the matter with him.

MRS JOHNSON. He offered us one hundred and fifty pounds for information leading to the discovery of Mrs Farrer. Her real name is Judith Waterton, her age seventeen, married to Mr Patrick Farrer without her parents' consent and while the said Mr Farrer is still legally married to his former wife.

JUDY. Patrick!

FARRER. Sweets, there is an explanation for all this.

GORDON. Get back to bed.

PETERS. Four ... four ... What comes after four?

MRS JOHNSON. He *is* insane. The man's a dangerous criminal.

FARRER. I told you he was. That was the tenor of my complaint against him, Mrs Johnson.

JUDITH. Do you mean none of this is true?

FARRER. None, my darling.

GORDON. Get up to bed.

JUDY. Now?

FARRER. Really, it's quite all right by me.

GORDON. When I've killed my father I'm coming up.

JUDY. Gordon! (*Goes.*)

MRS JOHNSON. Lily, get into your cupboard. I want you to hear no more of this.

LILY. I haven't done anything, Mother.

MRS JOHNSON. You let this dangerous criminal into the house. What else have you been doing with him?

LILY. Nothing, Mother.

MRS JOHNSON. He's even killed your father.

MR JOHNSON. I'm not dead.

MRS JOHNSON. Liar! That's where she gets her lying from.

PETERS. Four ... four. What comes after four?

FARRER. There must be some simple solution to this.

GORDON. There is: kill him (*gesturing at* MR JOHNSON); send for the police; put the poker in his hand (*pointing to* PETERS). All four of us are witness.

LILY. I don't want to see my father dead.

MRS JOHNSON. Are you going to stop your own brother, Lily?

LILY. No, Mother.

MRS JOHNSON. In that case we can go ahead.

(LILY *goes.*)

MR JOHNSON. I don't want to be dead. I want to go on living.

MRS JOHNSON. You've lived long enough.

MR JOHNSON. I've only lived as long as you.

MRS JOHNSON. That's been my tragedy. (*To* PETERS) Mr Johnson seduced me when I was only sixteen. During the course of which he averted his eyes: that's the kind of man he is.

MR JOHNSON. It was the custom in those days; as opposed to nowadays when you can look as much as you like. One never interfered with a woman's private parts, except in the course of illness, and then, of course, not always then.

238

MRS JOHNSON. We shall assume those words were never spoken.

PETERS. Is this man dead or isn't he? I spread-eagled his head on the pillow. Blood, brains, bone – everywhere. I can see it vividly – I shall never forget it as long as I live.

MR JOHNSON. I shall go upstairs in that case, and wait for your decision. (*Goes.*)

FARRER. I think the best thing is if all of us forget it.

MRS JOHNSON. There are one hundred and fifty pounds connected with this. I shall notify my solicitor.

GORDON. You haven't got a solicitor.

MRS JOHNSON. I shall find a solicitor. And when I've found him I shall notify him.

PETERS. Four! Four ... what comes after four?

MRS JOHNSON. I was going to hand over the erring couple to this gentleman at nine o'clock in the morning, after you, Gordon, my precious, had had your second night of bliss.

FARRER. Anything he's offered you I can better. It's always the same with these society women: take them from their homes, give mummy and daddy three weeks to stew, then write them a note offering to return said daughter, unharmed, for consideration of a certain sum of money.

GORDON. I'll go up: kill my father. My mother can arrange the sum.

MRS JOHNSON. What shall we do with Mr Peters?

GORDON. Give me five minutes, then ring the police.

LILY (*entering*). There's someone at the back door, Mummy.

FARRER. The police. They've arrived already.

PETERS. What comes after four? Four! Four! For God's sake. Four!

LILY. He's not in uniform. He says he has an appointment here to meet Mr Peters.

PETERS. Me! Me! That's me. It must be the police. I don't

want to be fastened up inside. Five! Five! What comes after five?

MRS JOHNSON. It'll be Judith's father. That's who it'll be. The crafty Mr Peters has arranged it. Let him in, Lily.

FARRER. I better scarper.

MRS JOHNSON. He won't know you. It's Judith he's after.

GORDON. Put this (*neckerchief*) round you and tell him, accidentally, you've cut your throat.

(*Gives him his neckerchief.* FARRER *puts it on.*)

PETERS. What about me? What about me?

MRS JOHNSON. You hide under the table, Mr Peters. We won't let this nasty doctor near you.

PETERS. Doctor? What doctor?

MRS JOHNSON. The doctor who's come to treat you.

GORDON. Who's come to give you all sorts of nasty things.

PETERS (*hides*). Oh, God.

MRS JOHNSON. Leave me to do the bargaining. Where money's concerned *I* am the one to speak.

(*Door opens.* LILY *enters.*)

LILY. Mr Waterton, Mother.

(WATERTON *enters: a genial, well-dressed figure, 60s.*)

WATERTON. Are you Mrs Johnson?

MRS JOHNSON. Mrs de John-Johnson. My family were the first commercial exploiters of the water-closet. Their name is splashed across the pages of British history.

WATERTON (*to* FARRER). Haven't I seen you somewhere before?

MRS JOHNSON. This is my niece's husband: a very close relative and a friend to all of us in an hour of need.

WATERTON. What's the matter with his face?

MRS JOHNSON. I'll come to that, if I may, in a moment.

WATERTON. I had a phone message from a Mr Peters to meet him here in connection with my daughter.

MRS JOHNSON. Has your daughter got very fair hair?

WATERTON. She has.

MRS JOHNSON. Is her first name Judith?

WATERTON. It is.

MRS JOHNSON. And is her maiden name Waterton?

WATERTON. That's quite correct.

GORDON. I'm just going upstairs for the very last time. (*Goes.*)

WATERTON. Is my daughter in this house or not?

MRS JOHNSON. This is private property, Mr Waterton. What goes on in this house is my concern. What goes on in here is strictly private.

WATERTON. All I want to see is my daughter.

MRS JOHNSON. How much can you afford?

WATERTON. How much?

MRS JOHNSON. Considerable expenses have been incurred, Mr Waterton. Whatever it is your daughter has, the men involved with her at present are very desperate to obtain it.

WATERTON. She's only been missing three days. I was employing a detective recommended by a friend, but since he started on the case, apart from a message to come here, I haven't heard a word. He told me to bring two hundred and fifty pounds in cash. He thought cash would be a great inducement. It was the sum of money he'd offered a certain person to return my daughter to me.

MRS JOHNSON. The lying blackguard. He told me a hundred and fifty.

WATERTON. What was that, madam?

MRS JOHNSON. I said perhaps eight hundred and fifty.

PETERS (*heard*). Nine! Nine! What comes after nine?

MRS JOHNSON. Plus, of course, the original, which makes it a round thousand.

WATERTON. Where my daughter's safety is concerned, I'm prepared to make almost any sacrifice. I can write you a cheque for the remainder, if I could just set eyes on my daughter.

MRS JOHNSON. Of course.

PETERS. Ten! Ten! I'm wide awake! (*Rises.*)

(MRS JOHNSON *seizes kettle; hits him on the head.*

PETERS *disappears beneath the table.*

Meanwhile WATERTON *is getting out his money, pen and cheque-book.*)

MRS JOHNSON. If you write the cheque, and place the cash on the table, my nephew-in-law will make the necessary arrangements.

FARRER (*lowering neckerchief*). Right. I'll go ahead.

(*Goes quickly.*)

MRS JOHNSON. After all, we'd like to retrieve your daughter from the hands of this unscrupulous man intact.

WATERTON. Will there be any delay?

MRS JOHNSON. As soon as the money is paid, the process will be put into operation.

WATERTON. There's the cash. (*Sets notes on table.*) The balance ... (*Writes.*)

MRS JOHNSON. Mrs de John-Johnson.

WATERTON. Ah, yes.

MRS JOHNSON. What a lovely hand. 'Waterton.' Generosity. Patience. It's all there. 'Seven.' Responsibility. 'Fifty.' You're a family man. I'm a family woman, myself. 'Seven hundred and fifty.' My eldest son, surviving, is a member of the Royal Air Force, who have a special charter, unlike the army, to defend the person of the Queen Herself: from an overhead position.

(HAROLD *enters, with R.A.F. top but only underpants, and* EDNA *in nightie.*)

HAROLD. Mother: I want to get married.

MRS JOHNSON. Who to?

HAROLD. Edna.

MRS JOHNSON. She's your sister.

HAROLD. Then that makes it all the better, Mam!

MRS JOHNSON. I thought you were going back to report for duty, Harold.

HAROLD. I'm going to leave home for good. I'm going to leave the R.A.F. I'm going to get married.

EDNA. I tried to explain.

MRS JOHNSON. You don't have to leave home to fuck your sister.

HAROLD. Oh, Mother. (*Embraces her.*)
    (GORDON *enters.*)

GORDON. I've made enquiries about a certain party, Mother. Father is in there and is seducing her to death.

MRS JOHNSON. I'll kill him! (*Goes.*)

HAROLD. I'm going to be married to Edna, Gordon.

GORDON. Congratulations.
    (HAROLD, *his arm round* EDNA, *goes.*)

WATERTON. Is my daughter in this house or not?

GORDON. She'll be brought down very shortly, Mr Waterton.

WATERTON. There's no harm come to her, I hope?

GORDON. She's in better shape now than when she left you.
    (FARRER *enters.*)
    Did you break down the door?

FARRER (*lowers neckerchief: huskily*). Your mother's trying.

WATERTON. I'd give a very great deal to get my hands on the man responsible, I can tell you that.

GORDON. How much?

WATERTON. It isn't the money. The money is simply for the return of my daughter. The man's a different matter entirely. It's just that I'd like to be given five minutes with him inside a room.

PETERS (*heard*). Five! Five! What comes after five?

WATERTON. Say?

GORDON. What would you do to him, if you had him in a room for five minutes, Mr Waterton?

WATERTON. First of all I'd gouge his eyes out. Then I'd mutilate his body. Then I'd beat his skull against the wall. Then I'd break his fingers. Then I'd break his toes. Then, if he was still conscious, I'd take his teeth out. No woman would ever look at him again.

GORDON. If you'll excuse me, I'll go upstairs. (*To* FARRER) I shan't be long. (*To* WATERTON) Five minutes. (*Goes.*)

WATERTON. I didn't get your name.

FARRER. Johnson.

WATERTON. I understand you were a nephew.

FARRER. By marriage. I took my wife's name as a matter of fact.

WATERTON. That's very unusual.

FARRER. I wanted to reverse the usual procedure.

WATERTON. Procedure?

FARRER. Whereby a woman invariably takes her husband's name. I thought it a significant gesture if I took my wife's.

WATERTON. Where is your wife?

FARRER. She's looking after Mr Johnson.

WATERTON. She seems a very generous and resourceful woman: finding time to look after so many people. I imagine you haven't been married very long.

FARRER. Not very.

WATERTON. You have children?

FARRER. Not yet.

WATERTON. Children are a great consolation: until something happens like this. I'm only an average man. If you passed me by in the street you wouldn't give me another glance. Yet I'm a Britisher through and through; not much to look at, but when we're roused we're roused: by injustice, by seeing another feller do another feller down. Hitler discovered that to his cost.

PETERS (*heard*). Six! Six! What comes after six?

WATERTON. Say?

FARRER. Nothing.

WATERTON. Been in the army, have you?

FARRER. For a short while I was ...

WATERTON. It's only in wartime that anyone shows their fibre. Damn me: we knocked hell out of half the world and if it comes to the point, we can do it again!

MRS JOHNSON (*returning with* GORDON). That madman, Mr Waterton, has got your daughter in his room. He refuses to open the door and let me in.

WATERTON. You mean this man is here?

MRS JOHNSON. That's right.

WATERTON. I'll kill him.

FARRER. I shouldn't do that.

GORDON. I should do that. Did you say you'd gouge his eyes out? Death by mutilation might be the very thing we need.

WATERTON. Show me the way.

(*They go.*)

FARRER. If you'd allowed me to talk to him I could have persuaded Judith down. (*As* MRS JOHNSON *secretes money in her bosom.*) I trust I shall have a share of that.

MRS JOHNSON. Trust is not something that comes easily to a woman. Particularly to one with my experience: seduction and lechery have been my lot, poverty, ineptitude and recrimination. (*Crash and shouts, overhead.* WATERTON: 'Let me in there, sir.' GORDON: 'Go on! Go on! Get in there, Mr Waterton!'*) He'll have him kill his father and then we'll all be happy. And perhaps, if we're *very* fortunate, Mr Waterton might marry me.

FARRER. He's married already.

MRS JOHNSON. And well-to-do?

FARRER. He's very well-to-do.

MRS JOHNSON. When I was sixteen I scarcely thought I would spend the remainder of my life married to a house-painter employed by a local council, who was murdered in a bedroom by a respectable man who was well-to-do and married.

WATERTON (*entering, flushed; followed by* GORDON). I can make no headway, madam. The door is firmly fastened. I don't understand what this man is doing in this house at all.

MRS JOHNSON. He brought your daughter here as an innocent boarder. He rented a room. Little did we know he was holding her for ransom. Little did we know that, having incriminated us, he would demand we collect the ransom for him.

WATERTON. Where's Peters? Where is the man responsible for this?

MRS JOHNSON. Mr Peters is the dangerous criminal lunatic who organised this entire affair, paid your daughter's seducer to seduce her and hoped, at the end of the day, to reap the benefit himself. While endeavouring to detain him – during which incident my nephew-in-law here was severely injured – he locked your daughter and her seducer in her room, demanded that we raise the ransom – on forfeit of our good names and reputation – and escaped down a drainpipe at the back of the house. Should one word of what he attempted to do be leaked to the police he will leak the remainder to the national press, thereby blackening your daughter's name and making her prospects of an eligible marriage in the future very bleak if not impossible altogether – a fate of which I have some intimate and tragic experience myself.

WATERTON. What are we to do? We can't sit here like this.

GORDON. We could break down the door, kill the seducer and inform the police. No one, subsequently, would believe a word Mr Peters said.

WATERTON. I have never killed a man before.

GORDON. It will be Mr Peters' responsibility entirely.

WATERTON. I'm not a man given to violent reaction.

GORDON. I'll see if I can find a hammer. (*Goes.*)

WATERTON. I am sorry to have brought this nightmare into your home. An more appreciative than I can express of the gallantry of your nephew-in-law.

MRS JOHNSON. Are you happily married, Mr Waterton?

WATERTON. I am.

MRS JOHNSON. Is your wife in very good health?

WATERTON. She is.

MRS JOHNSON. It sounds a very improbable situation.

WATERTON. We have been married, Mrs de John-Johnson, for thirty-seven years.

MRS JOHNSON. And not a day too long.

WATERTON. My wife and I are very close. Though what an incident like this will do in my present state, I can't imagine.

MRS JOHNSON. There will always be a home for you here. And not only a home, but a hearth and a bed.

WATERTON. Mrs de John-Johnson: you're very kind.

GORDON (*reappearing*). I have the hammer. We'll go up now.

WATERTON (*hesitates; looks at hammer, looks at them. Takes hammer*). Right.

(*They go.*)

MRS JOHNSON. Shouldn't you go up with him, Patrick?

FARRER. It only takes one to swing a hammer. There are two up there already.

PETERS. Eight! Eight! What comes after eight?

MRS JOHNSON. Please be silent, Mr Peters, or I shall inform the police.

PETERS. Has the doctor gone?

MRS JOHNSON. He's coming back again. He's making a search of the house, therefore it is incumbent upon you to remain quite hidden.

PETERS. How did I ever get into this! (*Hides again.*)

(*Hammer blow and splintering wood upstairs.*)

FARRER. Was that his head?

MRS JOHNSON. It sounded like the door.

FARRER. It might have been wood.

MRS JOHNSON. In that case, of course, it might have been.

(*They listen: silence.*

After a moment, footsteps.

Door opens. WATERTON *comes in, jacket over arm, shirt sleeves rolled, tie loosened, hammer in hand.*)

Is everything all right?

(WATERTON *sits, dazed.*

GORDON *enters.*)

Has anything happened? Is the seducer dead, or is he alive?

GORDON. The bedroom, I'm afraid, is empty.

WATERTON. I leapt inside. There was no one in the room at all.

GORDON. The window was open.

MRS JOHNSON. You must organize a search. That wicked man must not escape.

WATERTON. I can go no further. I have paid a thousand pounds; I have beaten down a door; I have endeavoured to kill a man inside.

MRS JOHNSON. They can't have travelled far. This estate has no bus service after nine o'clock.

GORDON. Ten.

MRS JOHNSON. It's nearly eleven.

WATERTON. In that case, then, we'd better try.

MRS JOHNSON. I shall remain here and coordinate our

resources. I shall call in the might, Mr Waterton, of the Royal Air Force. Patrick, Gordon, escort Mr Waterton to the street outside.

(*They go,* WATERTON *pulling on his jacket.*)

PETERS. Has the doctor gone?

MRS JOHNSON. He has gone, but he may come back at any moment. I am going upstairs. (*Glancing at herself in mirror, touching hair.*) I shan't be a minute. (*Goes.*)

(*After a moment* PETERS *hesitates: is about to come out; hears sound; goes back in again.*

Door opens. JUDITH *comes in, nightgown covered by a dressing gown;*

followed by MR JOHNSON, *underpants and vest covered by battered raincoat.*)

MR JOHNSON. There, you see. The safest place for a prisoner to hide is where no one will ever look for him: inside his prison.

JUDITH. It was very good of you to rescue me from that maniacal rapist.

MR JOHNSON. The reward exceeded my greatest expectations. I am a resurrected man: I feel quite new.

PETERS. Is anyone there?

MR JOHNSON. Who's that?

PETERS. I am a dangerous lunatic and am endeavouring to escape. The police are after me. Don't give me away.

MR JOHNSON. Are you still here?

PETERS. A ghost!

MR JOHNSON. I am not a ghost. I'm resurrected!

PETERS. Oh, God! (*Hides once more beneath the table.*)

MRS JOHNSON (*entering in flowered dressing gown and ribbon in her hair*). You!

MR JOHNSON. You!

MRS JOHNSON. They're looking for you in the street outside. What have you done to this wonderful child?

MR JOHNSON. I seduced her, Mrs Johnson, like everyone else.

JUDITH. Mr Johnson has been very kind.

MRS JOHNSON. We'll see how kind he can be when the might of the Queen's Royal Air Force comes downstairs.

MR JOHNSON. Harold would never hurt his father.

MRS JOHNSON. Harold, very shortly, is going to be married.

MR JOHNSON. Who to?

MRS JOHNSON. *Edna.*

MR JOHNSON. As long as he keeps it in the family.

MRS JOHNSON (*to* JUDITH). Then we shall see what Harold can do!

PETERS. Is it safe to come out?

MRS JOHNSON. The police may return at any moment.

PETERS. I thought it was a doctor.

MRS JOHNSON. It is a doctor: he has a policeman's credentials, however.

PETERS. Oh, God. How did I ever get into this?

(*Door opens:* WATERTON *comes in.*)

WATERTON. Judith!

JUDITH. Daddy!

(*They embrace.* WATERTON *is followed in by* GORDON *and* FARRER.)

Patrick!

FARRER. Judy!

JUDITH. Gordon!

GORDON. Judith!

WATERTON. What is all this? Who is this man?

JUDITH. This is Mr Johnson, Father. The gentleman who rescued me from a violent man, who endeavoured to break down the door and attack me with a hammer.

WATERTON. Wait till I get my hands on him.

PETERS (*emerging*). Is it time to come out? Is it safe? Or do I have to wait here any longer?

WATERTON. Peters!

PETERS. Who are you?

WATERTON. I'll give you who I am. Are you pretending not to recognize me?

PETERS. I'm a dangerous criminal lunatic and must not be provoked.

WATERTON. Wait till I get my hands on you.

PETERS. Help! Help me! Oh, God! (*Runs out of the door.*)
(WATERTON *exits after him.*)

MR JOHNSON. I'm resurrected; I have powers within me I never suspected.

MRS JOHNSON. You see what depravities I've had to put up with.

FARRER. Shall we go upstairs, or will your father be returning?

JUDITH. I think we shall have time to put one or two of our things together.

GORDON. What about me?

JUDITH. If you would like to assist as well.

GORDON. Right!
(*They go.*)

MRS JOHNSON. Well, this is a turn-out, I must confess.

MR JOHNSON. It may be all right. She has ample resources, I believe, that child.

MRS JOHNSON. Us. I mean us! He'll demand his money back.

MR JOHNSON. Well, then, if there's nothing else I can do down here, I'll go and see if I can help upstairs. (*Goes.*)

MRS JOHNSON. I shall make a plan. I shall invite him back and get my money. I refuse to be cheated in anything.
(HAROLD *enters, already in uniform, with* EDNA.)

HAROLD. I'm ready, Mum. I'm ready now to kill my father.

MRS JOHNSON. It's too late to kill your father.

HAROLD. In that case, Mother, I'm ready to leave.

MRS JOHNSON. Where are you going?

HAROLD. I'm going to buy myself out at the end of the month.

MRS JOHNSON. What on earth will you use for money?

HAROLD. I've eight thousand pounds.

MRS JOHNSON. Eight thousand!

HAROLD. I've been in eighteen years. I've never had anything to spend it on. 'Cept gliders.

MRS JOHNSON. I hope, Harold, you're coming back home to live.

HAROLD. I am.

EDNA. He is.

MRS JOHNSON. I hope you'll both be happy. (*Weeping.*) Happier than I am, at any rate.

EDNA. Of course we will be, Mother. He's like a stranger, is Harold. But once he comes back home we'll very soon get used to him.

MRS JOHNSON. All that money. You might buy one or two comforts. For your room, I mean.

HAROLD. And for yours, too, Mummy.

MRS JOHNSON. Oh, I don't deserve it.

HAROLD. Yes, you do, Mam. You're the very best mother in the world to me. (*Kisses her.*)

    (MRS JOHNSON *turns away*.)

MRS JOHNSON. Go on. Go on. Enjoy your happiness. You're only young once: I hope it'll last.

HAROLD. Thank you, Mother. (*To* EDNA) I shan't be long. (*Kisses her; embraces her.*) I'll be back to claim you by the end of the month.

    (*They go.*)

MRS JOHNSON. Oh. What it is to have a family. What it is to be a woman: what it is to be a mother. What it is to have no redress. (*Weeps.*)

LIGHTS FADE

Lights come up.
> *Morning, several days later.*
> *Ringing of doorbell; knocking.*

MRS JOHNSON (*heard*). Gordon … ! Pat … Pat! Patrick, dear.
> (MRS JOHNSON *enters, dressed for a grand occasion: long,
> flowered dress, flowers, fur.*)
> Lily!

LILY (*entering*). I'm here, Mother.

MRS JOHNSON. Liar! Why don't you answer that door?

LILY. You told me not to answer it until I was dressed.

MRS JOHNSON. Are you dressed?

LILY. Yes, Mother.

MRS JOHNSON. Liar! You look exactly the same to me.
> (*Further knocking.*)

LILY. Shall I answer it, Mother?

MRS JOHNSON. How can you answer it if you're not dressed,
you stupid, illiterate, spineless, thriftless, brainless, simply
horrible venomous child.
> (*Further knocking.*)
Answer it! Answer it! How can you answer it if you
stand there waiting all the time.
> (LILY *darts one way, then another; then goes.*)
> (*Calling at room door.*) Gordon …! Patrick …! Mr and
Mrs Waterton are here!
> (MR JOHNSON *enters: dark suit; flower in buttonhole, hair
> immaculate, face gleaming, shaved.*)
Oh, it's you. I might have expected you to be down here
first.

MR JOHNSON. You're first.

MRS JOHNSON. I am always first. First, with me, Mr Johnson, doesn't count. Second with me is what's important.

GORDON (*entering*). Hello, Mater. All ready.

MRS JOHNSON. Darling Gordon. You won't let us down.

(GORDON *is dressed also in a suit: immaculate, hair greased.* FARRER *has followed him in: jodhpurs, silk scarf, sports jacket.*)

Nor Patrick ... How handsome you all look. My men!

(*Kisses them heartily, drawing back, however, at* MR JOHNSON.)

MR JOHNSON. Where's Edna?

GORDON. She's out buying her trousseau.

MR JOHNSON. Is she getting married again?

GORDON. She wanted something special for Harold.

MRS JOHNSON. Impetuosity has always marked that child. She was born, Patrick, two months too soon: she's never altered ... Mr Johnson, just look at your tie.

(*She turns from straightening it as* LILY *enters.*)

LILY. Mrs Waterton, Mummy.

(*A smallish figure enters, clad with some refinement and evidently grand.*)

MRS WATERTON. Mrs Johnson?

MRS JOHNSON. That's quite correct ... May I say, on behalf of my family, how pleased we are to have you as a guest inside this house.

GORDON. Isn't your daughter with you?

MRS WATERTON. She's only temporarily delayed.

MRS JOHNSON. And Mr Waterton?

MRS WATERTON. He too will be along quite shortly. I came ahead because I wanted to show the Johnson family my own individual gratitude ... for having saved our child.

MRS JOHNSON. We're always on the lookout, Mrs Waterton, to do a good turn. Aren't we, boys?

GORDON. Yes, Mother.

FARRER. Yes, Aunty.

MR JOHNSON. Yes, Mother.

MRS JOHNSON. This is my son, Gordon, who played such a prominent part in your beautiful daughter's rescue.

MRS WATERTON. I'm very pleased to meet you, Gordon.

GORDON. I'm very pleased to meet you, Mrs Waterton. (*Shakes her hand.*)

MRS JOHNSON. And this is my nephew, Patrick, who played an equally conspicuous part in your charming daughter's recovery.

(FARRER *clicks his heels together, bows, kisses her hand.*)

MRS WATERTON. What a gallant man.

FARRER. I hope you will forgive my attire, Mrs Waterton. I've been out and about my equine pursuits from an early hour this morning.

MRS WATERTON. It suits you, I must say, very well.

FARRER. Thank you, Ma'am. You're very kind.

MRS JOHNSON. And this is Mr Johnson who, while not playing a particularly conspicuous part in your daughter's recovery, at least was able to offer her consolation when the full weight of her predicament finally fell upon her.

MR JOHNSON. I'm very honoured to meet you, Mrs Waterton.

MRS WATERTON (*looks round*). This is a delightful place.

MRS JOHNSON. Our little nest, Mrs Waterton. Not a great deal to look at, but, beneath its somewhat austere if not impoverished appearance, beats a very large and human heart.

MRS WATERTON (*taking seat offered her by* MR JOHNSON). Thank you.

MRS JOHNSON. Would you like a cup of tea?

MRS WATERTON. You're very kind.

MRS JOHNSON. I'll go into the kitchen and make the arrangements ... Lily!

(*She goes, followed by* LILY, *who hasn't taken her eyes off* MRS WATERTON *and scarcely does so now.*)

FARRER. A cigarette, Mrs Waterton?

MRS WATERTON. I'm afraid I don't smoke.

GORDON. A cushion, perhaps.

MRS WATERTON. Thank you. There was one thing about which I meant to enquire. How was it that Judith came to this house, and what happened to her abductor?

GORDON. He escaped, Mrs Waterton. And while endeavouring to restrain him, the wretched individual very nearly broke my cousin's neck.

FARRER. That's quite correct. (*Clicks heels and bows.*)

GORDON. At one instance he seized hold of this. (*Grasps poker, raises it.*) And brought it down – or would have done – on my father's head. (*About to do so now.*)

FARRER. If I hadn't restrained him, Mrs Waterton.

GORDON. My cousin sustained injuries from which he has only recently recovered.

MRS WATERTON. I can hardly believe it ... that people nowadays could go to such extremes to put other people's interests before their own.

GORDON. When we saw your daughter, Mrs Waterton, we each of us said we'd do anything for her: am I or am I not correct in that?

FARRER. That is quite correct, Mrs Waterton.

MR JOHNSON. That tea's taking a long time. If you'll excuse me, madam, I'll go and see what's delayed our hot refreshment. (*Goes.*)

GORDON. Perhaps you would care to see our establishment, Mrs Waterton ... The room from which your daughter was rescued from a fate far worse than death.

MRS WATERTON. If we have a couple of minutes before the tea arrives, I might see the room itself ... I've heard such a great deal about it from Judith.

GORDON. I'm sure it's a room, Mrs Waterton, she'll remember all her life ... And, if you pardon my being so bold – since you haven't inspected it yourself – one which you, Mrs Waterton, may also be pleased to recollect with gratitude in the after years of a long and I'm very sure a happy and supremely restful life.

MRS WATERTON. That's very kind.

GORDON. I'll lead the way in front ... And Patrick can come behind.

(*They go.*

After a moment the door opens: MRS JOHNSON *enters, pursuing* LILY *and followed by* MR JOHNSON.)

MRS JOHNSON. How do you mean, distrustful, hateful, abominable child, that that woman isn't Mrs Waterton?

LILY. It isn't.

MRS JOHNSON. Liar!

MR JOHNSON. Have you made the tea?

MRS JOHNSON. Never mind the tea ... are you sure they've gone upstairs?

MR JOHNSON (*pauses, listens. Then:*) That's right.

MRS JOHNSON. How do you know it's not Mrs Waterton? Have you ever seen Mrs Waterton in all her life?

LILY. No. (*Weeping.*)

MRS JOHNSON. If you've never met Mrs Waterton how do you know it's not Mrs Waterton? (*Shakes her vigorously.*) Hateful, abominable, untruthful, treacherous girl.

LILY. I know it's not.

MRS JOHNSON. Liar!

MR JOHNSON. If she knows it's not, Mrs Johnson, let her explain.

MRS JOHNSON. She can't explain. She can't even put two words together that aren't a lie. How she was ever conceived by two people with pedigrees like ours I've no idea. There must be some awful strain in the Johnson family that's responsible for this: latent in *you* and manifest in *this*. (*Shakes her once again*.) Hateful, lying, reproachful child.

LILY. It's not Mrs Waterton because it's Mr Peters.

MRS JOHNSON. Mr Peters!

MR JOHNSON. The detective?

MRS JOHNSON. How do you know it's Mr Peters?

LILY. Because I recognized him, that's why.

MRS JOHNSON. Liar!

MR JOHNSON. She saw him out there as well as here.

MRS JOHNSON. How do you know that that lady is not a lady? Idiot. Buffoon. Gormless imbecile. Isn't she dressed like *me*! She's even got a fur like me ... And if she isn't a woman ... (*looks up*) what's she doing upstairs with Gordon?

MR JOHNSON. And with Patrick.

(*She and* MR JOHNSON *gaze upwards for a while*.)

LILY. I recognized her beneath her make-up ... I recognized him, I mean.

MR JOHNSON. It shouldn't be difficult to tell ... Any minute now, the truth will out.

MRS JOHNSON. If she isn't Mrs Waterton what's he after?

MR JOHNSON. Revenge.

MRS JOHNSON. I'll give him revenge. Attempting to seduce my son ... the abominable, terrible, deceitful creature.

MR JOHNSON. Maybe he's come here to get his share of the money.

LILY. There's someone at the front door, Mam.

MRS JOHNSON. Not another. (*Goes to window*.) Judith ... And possibly Mrs Waterton. Lily, you better say we're out.

LILY. I can't tell a lie, Mam.

MRS JOHNSON. Liar!

MR JOHNSON. I'll tell them.

MRS JOHNSON. No, you won't.

MR JOHNSON. Lily ...

MRS JOHNSON. Show them in.

MR JOHNSON. What on earth can you say to them, Mrs Johnson?

MRS JOHNSON. I shall tell them the truth, Mr Johnson ... If you would go upstairs and keep Mr Peters – quiet ... Here. You better take this. (*Lifts cushion; hands him kettle.*) If he shows the least unwillingness to cooperate – give him this.

> (*He goes.*
> A moment later, after MRS JOHNSON *has composed herself,*
> MRS WATERTON *and* JUDY *are shown in by* LILY.)

LILY. Mrs Waterton ... and Miss Waterton, Mother.

MRS JOHNSON. Hello, Mrs Waterton ... It is so kind of you to pay us a visit.

> (MRS WATERTON *is a middle-class lady of some pretensions: elegantly dressed, and a little alarmed if anything by the interior.*
> JUDY *is dressed too, evidently, to impress.*)

(*To* JUDY) My dear.

JUDY. Mummy, this is darling Mrs Johnson.

MRS WATERTON. I'm pleased to meet you, Mrs Johnson ... I've heard so much about you, and your family.

MRS JOHNSON. Oh, we're just an ordinary family, Mrs Waterton ... No better, I can assure you, and certainly no worse than most ... May I take your coat ... Lily ... take Judith's coat ... Would you like a seat?

> (*The two visitors are divested of their coats.*
> LILY *takes them out.*)

JUDY. Where are Gordon ... and Patrick ... and Mr Johnson, Mrs Johnson?

MRS JOHNSON. They're engaged at the present on some personal business. They'll be along quite shortly. Once they know you're here I'm afraid there'll be no constraining them, Mrs Waterton.

MRS WATERTON. That's very nice.

MRS JOHNSON. Would you like some tea, Mrs Waterton?

MRS WATERTON. That's very kind ... Oh!

(*Sitting, she comes across something painful beneath her cushion.*)

MRS JOHNSON. I was wondering where I'd put it.

(MRS WATERTON *takes out a tea-caddy from beneath her cushion.*)

Lily!

(LILY, *evidently waiting behind the door, enters immediately.*) Make some tea.

LILY. Yes, Mother.

(*Smiles warmly at* MRS WATERTON, *and more warmly still at* JUDY: *goes, taking the tea-caddy* MRS JOHNSON *has handed to her.*)

MRS JOHNSON. My daughter. She's extremely loyal. Not unlike yours. In some respects.

MRS WATERTON. ... Yes.

MRS JOHNSON. Will Mr Waterton be coming today?

MRS WATERTON. I'm afraid, Mrs Johnson, he's been very much delayed by work. However, he insisted – as did Judith – that I come here all the same. He is very much appreciative of the assistance you and your family gave, and assured me too of the welcome I should have.

MRS JOHNSON. Oh, anything we can do for Judith we're only too pleased to do for her mother ... (*To* JUDY) I'm sure you're anxious to see Gordon ... and Patrick, of course ... and Samuel ... (*To* MRS WATERTON) That's Mr Johnson. We have no formalities here.

PETERS (*entering, hat, hair awry, clothes dishevelled*). My God ... I've been attacked!

MRS JOHNSON (*rising*). Mrs Peters ... how nice to see you.

This is my sister-in-law. I'm afraid she's something of an eccentric. Aren't you, dear. Her favourite mannerism is to startle people by the dishevelment of her dress. This is Mrs Waterton and her daughter, Judith.

JUDY. Hello, Mrs Peters.

PETERS. Oh, hello ... Judith.

MRS JOHNSON. Mrs Waterton ...

PETERS. Mrs Waterton.

MRS JOHNSON. They're here to show their gratitude for the safe return of *Judith* from the hands of a professional seducer ... a man of appalling physical strength whom, by the payment of a very large sum, we persuaded to leave this building, *and* this dear child and return her to her parents.

MRS WATERTON. How large was the sum, as a matter of fact?

PETERS. Two thousand pounds.

MRS WATERTON. Two thousand pounds!

MRS JOHNSON. Two thousand pounds it *would* have been but we managed to beat him down to ...

PETERS. One thousand, nine hundred: that's as low as it would go.

MRS WATERTON. My husband told me it came to one thousand pounds. Even then I thought it excessive and considered reporting the matter to the local police. Finally he persuaded me that it was in Judith's interest to avoid publicity ... that is why, Mrs Johnson, and Mrs Peters, I am here.

MRS JOHNSON. I see.

MRS WATERTON. To beg you, as a matter of some urgency,. to keep what has happened here a secret ... not to tell it, in other words, to a single soul.

PETERS. My lips are sealed, madam ... providing that there is some restitution. A large part of the sum aforementioned came directly out of my personal private bank account and none of it, as far as I am aware, has ever been repaid. I am a lonely widow, with no one to provide for me: all I had in the world was sacrificed for the welfare of this wonderful child.

(*Pause.*)

MRS JOHNSON. I am sure Mrs Waterton will agree we all have our personal problems.

MRS WATERTON. If that is what my daughter's happiness, her future as well as her present happiness has cost, then I am glad to pay it. I'm sure my husband must have told you: her welfare is the one thing that lies closest to our hearts.

JUDY. Mummy.

MRS WATERTON. Could you pass my bag, my dear? ... To whom shall I make it out?

(PETERS *and* MRS JOHNSON *are about to speak together; then* PETERS *looks down at his costume, following* MRS JOHNSON's *glance.*)

PETERS. Mrs Emily St John Peters.

MRS JOHNSON. Mrs Elizabeth de John-Johnson.

MR JOHNSON (*entering, dishevelled*). Did someone call my name?

MRS JOHNSON. This is my husband. May I have the pleasure of introducing Mrs Waterton, Samuel. Mr Johnson: Mrs Waterton.

MR JOHNSON. Charmed ... I thought this was Mrs ...

MRS JOHNSON. Peters.

MR JOHNSON. Peters ... and this is Mrs Waterton ... Judith ... how are you, my darling, darling child.

JUDY. Samuel, it's so nice to see you.

MRS JOHNSON. Mrs Waterton has so generously offered to make up the balance of our debts.

PETERS. My debts.

MRS JOHNSON. Our debts.

MRS WATERTON. Money is a disagreeable business. ...
There. (*Signs cheque.*) One thousand, nine hundred pounds,
exactly ... and I've added one hundred, in lieu, Mrs
Peters, of interest that may have accrued in the time.

PETERS. That's very kind. (*Makes to take it.*)

(MRS JOHNSON, *however, picks it up and tucks it in her
bosom.*

LILY *enters with tray of tea.*)

MRS JOHNSON. Now there's a very pleasant sight ... And
my daughter, Edna. My darling child!

(EDNA *has followed* LILY *in.*)

EDNA. I've been buying my trousseau, Mother.

MRS JOHNSON. Edna is about to get married, Mrs Waterton.

JUDY. Hello, Edna.

EDNA. Hello, Judith ... I'm very pleased to meet you, Mrs
Waterton.

MRS JOHNSON. And this is Mrs Peters, your aunt, whom you
scarcely know, Edna – but who came over as soon as she
heard the news.

MRS WATERTON. And who is the lucky young man, Miss
Johnson?

MRS JOHNSON. Harold. He's been in the R.A.F. a considerable time – the Queen's Royal Air Force – with a direct
charge to protect Her Majesty Herself ... from a vertical
position.

JUDY. I'm so glad for you, Edna.

EDNA. Thank you, Judith.

(LILY *is serving out the tea.*)

MR JOHNSON. In the great aeons of time by which we're
surrounded the anguish of the Johnson family will be seen
to be very small beer indeed.

(GORDON *enters, dishevelled.*)

GORDON. Mother! Mrs Waterton has got away!

MRS JOHNSON. Mrs Waterton, my child, is here ... and enjoying, I'm glad to say, a cup of tea.

GORDON. Judith.

JUDY. Gordon!

FARRER (*entering, dishevelled*). Judy!

JUDY. Patrick!

(*They embrace in turn.*)

Mummy! This is Patrick ... and this is Gordon ... both of whom ...

MRS JOHNSON. Helped to rescue you, my dear.

GORDON. Then who is ...

MRS JOHNSON. Aunt Peters in one of her usual disguises ... she always intrigues the boys by turning up in some unexpected attire ... for example, on one occasion, she actually turned up disguised as a *detective*! However, since she is, after all, now, *one of the family*, we have to show – all round – a little understanding.

GORDON. I'm very pleased to meet you, Mrs Waterton.

FARRER. Excuse my equine attire, Mrs Waterton: I've just returned from a morning's ride.

GORDON. The horse, unfortunately, got away.

MRS WATERTON. And where do you do your riding, Mr ... Patrick?

FARRER. All over the estate, Mrs Waterton ... As a matter of fact, if you'd like us to escort you upstairs, I could show you some of the ground I usually cover ... the views up there are comprehensive.

GORDON. Perhaps, in the circumstances, I ought to accompany you, Mrs Waterton. I'm very familiar with the territory myself.

MRS WATERTON. That's very kind.

FARRER. I'll show the way, Gordon.

GORDON. And I'll take up the rear.

MRS WATERTON. Are you sure I haven't seen you somewhere before? Your face is extremely familiar.

FARRER. You may. You may. It's seen quite frequently, of course, in the national press.

MRS WATERTON. And what is your business, Mr ... Patrick.

FARRER. It's of an extremely secret nature. Not to be divulged, I'm afraid, Mrs Waterton. Except, of course, on pain of death.

(*They go.*)

JUDY. I suppose I should go up as well.

MRS JOHNSON. I should give your mother a chance to familiarize herself with the locale, Judith. It may come as a shock just how extensive is the terrain which Patrick and Gordon usually cover.

MR JOHNSON. I don't believe you ever saw my room, Judith.

MRS JOHNSON. Our room.

MR JOHNSON. Mrs de John-Johnson's room and mine. It has many more facilities than the one which you were previously familiar with, I'm sure.

JUDY (*to* MRS JOHNSON). I should so love to see the rest of the house. If that's all right with you.

MRS JOHNSON. You may. (*Hands key to* MR JOHNSON.) Remember: anything that takes place is *directly above my head.*

(*They go.*)

Edna, I should put your wedding attire in a safe place where your husband-to-be is not likely to see it.

EDNA. Yes, Mother. (*Goes.*)

MRS JOHNSON. Lily, wash up.

(LILY *has already collected the tea things; takes tray out.*

MRS JOHNSON *gets out paper; writes.*)

PETERS. This house, madam, is a house of ill-repute. No

sooner was *I* in the room upstairs than your son and the other gentleman – whom, I can assure you, madam, I *recognize* – divested themselves of all their clothes and leapt on me from the front as well as the rear.

MRS JOHNSON. I instructed my husband to call the police while you were upstairs. He informed them a man dressed as a woman had entered the house and was making indecent suggestions. They said they'd be here in a matter of minutes.

PETERS. I'll have a lot to tell them. You can be sure of that.

MRS JOHNSON. Mrs Waterton, whom you unlawfully impersonated in order to gain entrance to this house, can testify to your being attired as a woman, as well as to demanding money for your part in this affair ... the greater share, I believe you said.

PETERS. How much are you prepared to give me?

MRS JOHNSON. One hundred and fifty pounds.

PETERS. Out of two thousand: you must be joking.

MRS JOHNSON. It's what you offered us to turn in Mr Farrer.

PETERS. That was at the beginning of the game, before I knew how much was in it.

MRS JOHNSON. Two hundred.

PETERS. Three.

MRS JOHNSON. Two-fifty.

PETERS. I've got expenses. I've been on this case six days.

MRS JOHNSON. Five pounds a day. Two hundred and eighty.

PETERS. It's robbery. You've made two thousand out of this.

MRS JOHNSON. We, the de John-Johnsons, have made two thousand. I, personally, have made nothing.

PETERS. I want half; otherwise I'll tell the police myself.

MRS JOHNSON. Very well.

(PETERS *begins to take off his clothes.*

MRS JOHNSON *begins to do the same.*)

I shall say that you attempted to assault me.

PETERS. What?

MRS JOHNSON. Seduction is not something I'm unacquainted with. I shall say you forced me into that chair and endeavoured to perform a variety of acts upon my person of which the constabulary itself may never have heard.

PETERS. I was half crucified the last time! When I rang up Waterton he refused to pay me. He said he would sue me if he saw me again.

MRS JOHNSON. Three hundred, not a penny more. (*Hands him money.*) On top of which I've made one or two deductions.

PETERS. What for?

MRS JOHNSON. Entertainments. Tea. For quite some time you've enjoyed the benefits of that fire. It doesn't burn, I can assure you, by itself. Then again, we've resolved to make no complaint about your present attire. Some of us, I can assure you, were brought up in environments where behaviour of that sort was not the custom.

PETERS. Two-fifty. It's what it was before.

MRS JOHNSON. Lily, show Mr Peters to the door.

(LILY *comes in; holds door.*)

PETERS. I've lost my hat.

LILY. I've got it here, Mr Peters. (*Hands it to him.*)

(PETERS *looks at her;*
looks at MRS JOHNSON;
looks back at LILY;
looks back finally at MRS JOHNSON;
puts hat on.)

PETERS. Right. (*Goes.*)

(LILY *follows him; door closes.*
MRS JOHNSON *sits. Then:*)

MRS JOHNSON. Lily?

LILY (*off*). Yes, Mam?

MRS JOHNSON. Are you washing up?

LILY (*pause. Then:*) Yes, Mam.

MRS JOHNSON. Oh ... That's very sweet.
> (*Sighs. Leans back.*
> HAROLD *enters, in civvies.*)

Harold! What are you doing back so early?

HAROLD. I bought myself out sooner than I thought, Mam.

MRS JOHNSON. Not with your eight thousand, love?

HAROLD. I gave it to the Royal Air Force Benevolent Fund,
Mummy. They let me out almost straight away.
> (*Pause.*
> MRS JOHNSON *sinks back.*)

MRS JOHNSON. Your bride awaits you, Harold.

HAROLD. That's why I did it, Mum. I couldn't wait. (*Leans
down; embraces her.*) You won't regret it, Mam.

MRS JOHNSON. Let's hope your sister doesn't.

HAROLD. I'll be upstairs if you want me. (*Rushes out.*)
> (MRS WATERTON *enters, flushed.*)

MRS JOHNSON. Did you enjoy the vista, then?

MRS WATERTON. I seem to have lost my bag ...

MRS JOHNSON. It's bound to seem different, of course, at
first.

MRS WATERTON. Apparently there are one or two other
aspects they would like to show me.

MRS JOHNSON. It's always been the same ... A woman's lot
is never to be envied.

MRS WATERTON. Well, if anyone wants me, I'll be upstairs.
> (*Goes.*)
> (*A moment later* MR JOHNSON *enters.*)

MR JOHNSON. You here, Mrs Johnson, are you?

MRS JOHNSON. I'm here, Mr Johnson, yes.

MR JOHNSON. Has Mr Peters gone?

MRS JOHNSON. He has.

MR JOHNSON. Gordon is seducing the eyeballs out of

Judith. The son supersedes the father. It's the old, old story that history tells.

MRS JOHNSON. Still, Mr Johnson, we've got one another ... A fine, young family above our heads.

(MR JOHNSON *sits by her; she eases up to him; places her arm in his.*)

MR JOHNSON. In the great aeons of time by which we are surrounded the anguish of Doctor Johnson – not to mention the de Johns, the de Courceys, and very much else – will seem to have been very small beer indeed.

MRS JOHNSON. That's right.

MR JOHNSON. I suppose quite soon I might be dead.

MRS JOHNSON. At least, unlike many families – displaced by time and circumstance – the great families whose names echo down the centuries of our island's glorious past – we have found our true vocation. That is our achievement, Sam.

MR JOHNSON. Yes.

MRS JOHNSON. It's what we leave behind us ... a united family ... its two great progenitors – initiators, each of a different kind – holding above us our mutual heritage – the great canopy of civilization: one the inventor of a book, the other of a means by which we might dispose of it.

MR JOHNSON. Ah, yes.

MRS JOHNSON. With that behind us, what have we to fear of what lies ahead.

LIGHT FADES